THREATS OF SKY AND SEA

BY

JENNIFER ELLISION

For my family; you're 'unbelievable' in the best way.

Monstrous men will turn and flee,
When faced with threats of sky and sea.

One

I am already frozen when the scream reaches me.

The air bites my ears and numbs my hands. Seeking warmth, I burrow into the coat I'm wearing. The forest is still around me, the dead wood asleep. The distant river plays a lullaby.

I thought I was alone.

It's a gray morning, but Da sent me out for firewood and I'd intended to gather enough for the hearth to burn through dinnertime at the tavern. My axe kept me company, the steady thud of its beat against the tree a part of the forest's quiet symphony. But the scream broke the rhythm. It threw me off, and the axe missed its mark.

The air is quiet again. I strain my ears. I hear nothing.

Had I imagined it? I pick the axe up and glance at the firewood I've already bundled. Not enough to get through the night. There's still work to be done. I don't have time to worry about voices hanging in the ether when I still have a chicken to pluck and ale to water down.

The cry comes again and ices my blood. It begs investigation, but my skin prickles with unease. I can't ignore it, even if instinct urges me to. Abandoning my axe, I trudge forward, toward the source of the sound.

Probably it's only another villager from Abeline. Just last moon waning, I'd found Jowyck's boys deep in the belly of the forest, certain they were lost forever. Every so often, that happens. Someone wanders in and finds the woods a labyrinth.

It baffles me. They need only to listen for the river. If they follow its sounds, it'll lead them to it. Follow its course and they'll find their way back to civilization quick enough.

I pause, steadying myself on a tree frosted with morning dew. The frost tells me snow will be coming soon, and finally, I am sure that what I heard was the cry of a stranger. No one in Abeline would be so foolhardy as to brave the wood when winter threatens. Not even Jowyck's boys.

Fallen leaves crunch under my feet, but I hear shouts and they trample the small sound. My breath mists the air. The screamer is silent, but I am close.

There. I creep closer. Behind a dense gathering of naked trees, I see two figures. Their black cloaks would have been more at home against the dark pitch of a night sky. Here, where everything is bleached of color, my attention is drawn straight to them.

The figures are bent as they crouch over something I can't make out. The shorter one whips his leg forward, startling me backward.

The object cries out.

Gooseflesh eats at the back of my neck. The scream is an echo of the one I heard earlier. The strangers are beating someone, and they've reduced him to a lump on the ground.

Indignation is swift within me. Abeline is a peaceful village. We pay our taxes so the Egrian king's men don't come calling. We keep to ourselves and Elementals hide their gifts.

Above all, we do not invite trouble. How dare these strangers bring it here?

I grope about the forest floor, searching for something I can use as a weapon. A sharp rock, a thick stick— anything will do. I wish I'd brought my axe with me. A branch meets my palm, and I pull it to me.

A cough disrupts the watchers. The figure on the ground pushes itself to its knees. I move—slowly so as not to draw their notice—and flatten myself to a white-washed trunk. The cloaks don't obscure as much of their forms as I draw near. The one being beaten is a male.

"Please," the man—no, he's about my age—the *boy* pleads. The timbre of his voice breaks. His long legs are folded in on themselves as he huddles on the ground in a tortured bow. My heart twists for him. "My lady, I can't—"

"You can and you will." The answer is maple-sweet. I peer around the tree, and the woman throws back her hood to reveal golden curls bound in a twist. I can't see her face, but she's short and her hands are dainty. "Your meager attempts haven't been enough thus far, Adept Tregle."

Attempts at what? My brow crinkles. What was the boy meant to do for her? The woman's voice has an expectant note in it, and the boy sags.

"Come on," the squat figure taunts. Immediately, I'm filled with distaste. "What's wrong? Scared? Gonna piss yourself?" He snorts loudly. His demeanor makes me scowl, and he turns. A snout of a nose protrudes from his face and a pot-belly from his gut. He looks more pig than man.

I withdraw behind the shelter of my tree and adjust my grip on my branch. What's my plan here? To draw trouble back to the inn? I should go back and prepare dinner. Perhaps a few rooms on the off-chance that we wind up with guests tonight.

But I can't leave the boy here. His cry will haunt me for years if I do. I swallow. If I take Piggy and the lady by surprise, I *might* be able to fell them both and free the boy. It's chancy, but I must risk it.

"Don't goad him so." The woman holds up a hand to stop the other man. "Adept Tregle certainly knows better than to fail us again."

The boy—Tregle?—staggers to his feet, and leaves rustle as he stumbles.

Their attention is on him. Now is my moment, but I hesitate, branch raised like a sword. Why isn't he trying to escape?

His cloak matches theirs, I realize belatedly. They're together? Then why are they beating him?

His light brown skin is drained of blood, but when he raises his hand, a feeble flame bursts to life.

My breath catches in my throat. He's a Torcher.

What of the other two though? My body is afire with the urge to flee, but I resist. I have to know how many Elementals are inflicting themselves upon Abeline.

I take a chance and lean out from my tree, hoping they don't spot me but needing a clearer view. The fire in the boy's hand has flickered out. His mouth firms, forcing blood into his lips. I feel like I can't breathe, yet my chest rises and falls unerringly.

Tregle's hand waves toward his stout companion, and pellets of fire hail down around them. My suspicion that Piggy is another Elemental is confirmed when he dances through the flaming rain to send a stream of fire spiraling toward Tregle.

It scorches through the air in a roar, a lion of flame. The heat doesn't reach me, but I'm flushed with anxiety. They're not just Torchers. They're *reckless* Torchers. The woman does nothing to stop their careless performance. What do they think they're playing at, practicing where anyone can see them?

Surely they know the tales. Of Elementals—mothers and fathers, young women and men—spirited away in the night and borne off to Egria's capital to be trained for conscription in the king's army. Why would they risk that?

The sound of clapping envelops me, and the woman strides forward. "Much better, Tregle," she says approvingly. "We'll flush out the truant without so much as a hiccup if you keep that up. Try it again, with feeling this time."

My nails dig into the tree bark, fighting back a much stronger urge to sprint away at those words.

A truant Elemental. In *my* village.

These people aren't Elementals on the run, hoping for the luxury of both their freedom and their lives. If they're on the hunt for a truant, it can mean only one thing: they're the king's dogs. The ones he sends sniffing out after innocent people who would rather live a quiet life.

And if they're after someone in Abeline, it's likely someone I've known my entire life.

As Piggy enumerates Tregle's shortcomings, I inch back the way I came, no longer concerned over Tregle's fate. I wince with each whisper of the underbrush. The last thing I want is to alert them to my presence. I'm afraid to move, but I need to get back so I can warn the villagers of tracker Elementals. I can spread the word during supper in the tavern tonight. With a little luck, by tomorrow, word will have reached whoever it is that's hiding their abilities and they'll be able to flee.

It's an imperfect solution, but if it was me in their shoes, I'd think it better than the alternative: the choice between conscription...or execution.

I'm nearly free of the clearing when a *crack* splits the air. My heel. I bite back a curse. I'd let myself get all tangled up in my thoughts and failed to pay attention to where I stepped. I made the mistake of treading on a brittle branch.

I freeze, my heart shriveling in my chest. *Makers bless, please don't let them have heard that.* I pray that the trees around me provide enough cover. I don't dare move.

"Quiet." The woman's voice lashes out like a whip.

It's hard to keep my lungs steady, I discover, when my heart is dancing a jig on top of them.

Obliviously, Piggy continues to berate Tregle until the woman screams at him. "I said, quiet!"

The wind rushes past me in a sudden gust, sending branches straining toward her. It smacks into me and seeps through the fur lining of Da's coat. My stomach bottoms out. *Please.* My wish is a desperate plea. *Please not a Rider.* By the ether, the Torchers are bad enough. I don't need to bring the wrath of an Air Elemental down on my head, too.

Appropriately chastised, Piggy's gruff voice drifts to me. "Apologies, my lady."

There's silence for a moment. I hold my breath.

"My lady?" Tregle. "What are we listening for?"

"*We* are not listening for anything. I doubt you'd be able to hear anything over the screech of your innards as they begged you to seek shelter."

My innards and Tregle's would get along rather swimmingly right now. I close my eyes, cursing silently. If I'd bothered to think twice about it, I would have brought Da with me to investigate the screams. He's always berating me about that sort of thing—acting before I think my actions through. My feet grind into the dirt, wishing I could dissolve into it and hide.

It seems that hours pass in that moment. Days. Weeks, even. Summer is surely around the corner. I barely allow myself to breathe, concentrating on the quiet of the forest, the wind thrashing the bare branches, the occasional birdcall. I try not to think about the sound of my blood pounding inside my ears or the huffs of breath from the Elementals who are too near to where I stand, vulnerably out in the open.

Warm air wafts over my cheek, and I cringe, heart sinking. My nose catches the scent of mint leaves. Cool fingers follow, tracing my cheek. There's no point in keeping my eyes closed. It won't keep the Elementals at bay.

Icy blue irises blink back at me when I open my eyes. "Oh my dear, dear girl." The blonde woman is inches from my face. She steps back, stroking her palm thoughtfully. "What a place to find yourself alone. What a time to go prying into other people's affairs."

Before I can respond, the woman's hand switches tacks, slamming me into a tree. My spine grinds against it painfully. "I didn't mean—" I try for an excuse, and her fingers move to my throat.

My air supply evaporates. I choke.

The Rider is deceptively strong for someone of her small stature, I think wildly. I scramble for her arm, hoping to knock myself free, but no matter how much I contort myself, it's useless. She holds on, tightening her grip on my neck.

"What did you hear? One has to wonder."

All I can focus on are her clenched teeth as she grits out the question. I need *air*. I'll say whatever she wants if she returns my breath. My mouth opens to answer her, but all that issues from it is a strangled cry. My legs thrash out, aiming haphazardly for a kneecap. The impact as I make contact ricochets through me, though it does me no good. The only reaction I draw from the blonde is a surprised blink.

She presses harder, eliciting a wheezy hiss from me. The edges of my vision grow purple. "Well?"

That's the last of my air. My flailing grows feeble. My sight dances with spots. The burning in my lungs intensifies as my arms and eyelids drop.

I'm going to die.

"How tiresome." My would-be murderer sighs. Her hand falls from my throat.

Color rushes back into my world. I gulp down deep breaths of the frigid air. It cuts into my lungs. I barely have time to thank the Makers for sparing me before the woman's fingers snake into my short locks and yank me up by the hair.

"Please don't keep me in suspense any longer," she drawls. "What did you see? What did you *hear?*"

"When I…can breathe properly…I'll tell you," I gasp out.

A shove at my shoulder sends me barreling toward the branch-laden ground, my hands flying out to catch myself and scraping along the forest debris. I lost the branch I'd planned to defend myself with at some point. My hands scrabble at the ground, frantically seeking one to replace it. I'll have to fight my way out. I'm certain she means to kill me.

I stop when she steps onto my ankle, applying a slight but dangerous pressure. "If you want to *continue* breathing properly, you'll tell me now."

I glare up at her. I have my spirit back with my breath, and if she's going to kill me anyway, I don't want to die giving the king's Elementals what they want. "Who are you to go demanding answers from me on my da's own lands?"

We're not, strictly speaking, *on* Da's land. The woods belong to the realm. To the king. But our tavern is the closest dwelling and the surrounding wilderness certainly *feels* like it belongs to us.

Tregle and Piggy stand off to the side, mere shadows of observation to the woman's blinding rampage. She crouches beside me, her elegant black cloak sending branches clattering into one another. A red stone sparkles on her hood. I eye her warily, not sure what her next move will be.

She bears down on my ankle. The pressure is uncomfortable, but manageable. Determined not to let pain show on my face, I shift, trying to relieve it.

"I am the one who will either take your life or grant you a stay of execution," the woman whispers. She's so close I can see the faint scar at the corner of her eye. "It makes no difference to me which it is, but my liege does prefer things not to be messy. If messy is a route you wish to take, we can certainly explore the option."

Inspiration flashes through me. I could swear I sense an offer to let me leave beneath those words.

Throwing aside my attempts at pride, I sit up, trying for an earnest expression. I've already had a taste of what the woman can do. If she doesn't want me to know what they're up to, then I'm happy to feign ignorance. "I didn't hear anything," I say quickly. "I was standing too far away."

"Are you quite certain?"

"Absolutely," I lie.

"Suppose someone was to speak to you on the subject." She pushes down on my ankle. I wince against the pain. If she bears down any further, I'll be limping home. "What might you tell them?"

Her meaning is plain. The price for my life is my silence.

"I'd tell them I've never seen an Elemental and I couldn't imagine what one might be doing in Abeline." My response comes swiftly. There are times for defiance, but now is not one of them.

"Remember what you know of me," the woman cautions. She rubs her thumb against her fingers, and the wind responds to her summons. "If I wish it, I can bring your words to me."

Is that true? I wonder. Riders are wrapped in mystery and enshrouded in myth. Their talent is the rarest of the four Elemental gifts and little is known about exactly *how* they manipulate the world around them. And Da talks about the Elemental myths less than anyone, so my knowledge on the subject could *maybe* fill a page. More likely, a few paragraphs.

I've been silent too long, and she frowns. "I assure you I am not someone you wish to cross."

"I know," I lie again. I know nothing about this woman and hope I never learn. But it's as though I've uttered a secret password; she finally steps off of my blessed ankle. I snatch it away and give it a quick rub to put proper feeling back into it.

"Lady," Tregle speaks up, hesitant. My eyes narrow at him. To think I'd been about to rescue him. He can go rot for all I care. "Hadn't we better be getting on our way?"

"Right you are, Tregle. How nice to see you showing some initiative." Her eyes take on a teasing glint for a fraction of a moment, but then lock back onto mine, fierce. "Go. Now." She dismisses me.

I don't need any further encouragement. In my haste to get away, I scramble backward on my hands and knees. I'm still afraid to turn my back on them, but I rise to my feet and take off for home at a sprint before she can change her mind about releasing me.

Her voice follows me as I run. "Bear in mind what we've spoken of," she calls. "I don't do well with disappointment."

One thing I could have told her that would have been the truth: she's not someone I'll soon forget.

Two

It's a relief to stumble back over the familiar forest floor, to put distance between the Elementals and me. My muscles relax with every step I take toward the tavern. As Elementals go, Piggy would have been bad enough, but that woman... There had been an almost manic gleam in her eye. She'd *enjoyed* scaring me to within an inch of my life. I shudder.

The rushing sound of the river is as welcome to me as the sound of the closing bell after a particularly grueling shift in the tavern. The swinging sign over the doorway that depicts an arched bridge and a woman in a headdress, even more so.

Most days, I privately think that the woman's pinched expression looks more like she hasn't used the privy in a while than anything else, but today it seems a sweet greeting as I come upon the derelict Bridge and Duchess. I've never been so glad to see it.

It's hardly the height to which all inns aspire, but it's home. Three stories tall, but a slim building, it looks as though a sudden rainstorm might send it toppling to the ground. It's proved the assumption wrong time after time. I hope it continues to fault it.

I push my way inside, the door giving a mighty wail of protest. Da's already behind the bar. His bald head reflects the silvery sunlight that filters in through the windows as he pulls tankards for the night's use and stacks them on top of the bar.

"About time!" he calls.

I shrug out of the coat I borrowed from him and hang it on the coat rack just inside the door. It's still morning. It seems like I've been in the woods for days. I try to quell my trembling from a combination of cold and death threats.

"I hope you're plenty ready to work," Da continues, oblivious to my shivers. The tinkle of pewter as the drinkware clanks together plays a background to his words. "Jowyck's wife sent word that he's been ill with the drink for two days now, so they won't be serving any of their brew tonight. We should have quite the crowd. I've fixed up a rabbit stew to warm everyone's bones. Think we'll get snow soon?"

"I'd bet on it."

"Don't go promising our coins away," he says.

I ease myself onto a stool before the counter. This is good. This is a normal conversation. I can forget that the Elementals ever happened.

"It was only a joke, Da. I'd never gamble our profits." We barely keep the tavern running as it is.

"A simple 'yes' would have sufficed then. But that's

good news, the snow. *Might* be that people will be wanting to avoid the cold by staying here. We'll get 'em good and soused and, with luck, have a few rooms let tonight. But we won't be able to keep them here if we can't keep the place warm, so I hope you've got that firewood."

The firewood. *Damn.* I remember where I left it: set beside my axe. The entire reason for my presence in the Makers-forsaken wood in the first place.

"N-no." I bite down on my chattering teeth and try to keep my feelings from squirming their way into my voice. "Got distracted. Sorry, Da."

"Distracted?" Da's head pops up and gives me a hard look, brows wrinkling.

I don't fidget. It would be a dead giveaway. I tell Da just about everything, but I don't need to worry him with this. Now that he's over the bar, I can see the tufts of gray hair still left near his ears and the matching mustache that rests above his lip. He says his hair used to be a reddish-brown like mine, but time weeded the color away from him. I've wondered before if he had his hair shorn as mine is or if he was the vain sort, wearing it long and tying it back.

"You've been gone nigh on two hours, Breena Rose. What in Egria's green pastures distracted you for that long?"

I met a few Elementals and had a little romp about the woods, Da. Didn't I tell you that was the plan? The sarcasm is on the tip of my tongue, but I let it slip back, remembering the promise the Rider made.

"Helped someone get back to the village," I say instead.

"Ah." The confusion on Da's face clears. "Bet that cost you a fair bit of patience," he says, winking at me.

I force a laugh and roll my eyes. "You've no idea." *None.*

"Not everyone finds their way to the river as easily as you, my girl." He disappears below the bar again. "Best be off though. We really do need the wood for a fire tonight."

"Right." I slip the coat back on and don my fear with it. The coat is still cold to the touch. I don't want to return to the forest where the Elementals might be waiting, but there's nothing for it. We need the firewood and we need it soon.

Later that night, I'm grateful for the rare crowd that floods into The Bridge and Duchess. The work helps take my mind off of things. I've barely had time to pause to wipe the sweat that forms on my brow between filling tankards.

Some men might balk at the idea of their daughters working a bar, but thankfully Da's not one of them. I ladle stew into a bowl for a hungry patron. I like contributing to our livelihood, and the pace of serving in the tavern isn't bad either.

"Thom," the customer in front of me says to his comrade. Bits of chicken hang in his beard, and he wipes his sleeve over his mouth. He's slopped a fair bit of stew onto his shirt collar as well but isn't too fussed about cleaning *that* up. "Would you believe it if I told you I was a Shaker?"

My ladle stills. I've moved down the counter and I'm three patrons away from him, but his whisper drifts to me. Is this man the truant that the Air Rider's hunting party was after? An Earth Elemental? I eye him, heart speeding up when I realize that he's only one of many unfamiliar faces here tonight. They're part of a band of travelers heading north to Clavins. Maybe the truant *isn't* someone I've known my entire life.

Guilt swamps over me at the relief that thought brings. I should still warn him.

But I can't.

"Shut it, Jerald," Thom says, darting a look around. Moving closer, I drop my eyes. I don't need them thinking I'm eavesdropping. Thom's voice lowers to a hoarse whisper. "You haven't had a Reveal, have you?"

"Nooo," Jerald draws out with a sly grin. "It's only your Ma *swore* she felt the earth move when she was with me last night."

Thom shoves him, groaning. "Right. And I'm the Duke of Secan." He takes another swig of his ale.

I should have guessed it was only a joke. I roll my eyes and move on. I'm still no closer to knowing who the truant is.

Not that I can help them anyway.

I swipe my graying rag at an unidentifiable bit of food someone's left behind and push the thought aside. "What'll you have?" I ask of the scruffy man who's elbowed another aside for a stool at the counter.

It's, by and large, a pointless question. The Bridge and Duchess only has one kind of ale in its barrels, but the larger the customer's pockets, the less it gets watered down.

"Your finest ale." He hiccups, but thumps a silver coin down.

He'll be wanting the ale with less water then. I grab a clean glass and retrieve the requested beverage.

I fill four tankards while I'm at the spout and slide from behind the counter to wait on the tables. They've been neglected since there's been a run on the bar. Hustling the drinks off to the different seats that they belong to, I keep an eye on the sloshing liquid near the brim of the cups. It's a point of pride for me that I rarely spill a drop now. When I first started serving in the tavern, I was twelve. Still in my child's skirts and tripping about in the pretty slippers I'd begged for on Market Day. Back then, it had been a miracle if I made it to a table with one glass I carried still full.

The fire in the hearth jumps a bit higher, and I eye it nervously.

None of that, I silently warn myself. I can't go overthinking everything. Nature doesn't always do what you expect. That doesn't mean that Elementals are involved.

Rushing about has taken my mind off of things a *bit*, true enough, but I haven't managed to put the incident out of my mind completely.

I'm not even sure which type of Elemental the mysterious truant *is*. It could be any of the four elements. A chill runs through me. It could be anyone.

The tavern's full of people I've never seen before, travelers passing through who heard the raucous gathering of Abeline villagers inside and sought to fill their stomachs with warm food and drink. I set a tankard in front of a woman perched on a brute's lap in the corner. There's a mole above her upper lip, and she adjusts her spectacular cleavage. I don't know her either. My troubled imagination turns on me as the woman trails a suggestive finger over the man's collarbone.

If it's her maybe the woman will turn out to be a Shaker, and the moment the man spurns her advances, the ground will quake beneath our feet. *Or*—my mind spins me a story as I collect their discarded bowls and scurry back toward the kitchen—perhaps the brute's a Thrower and he'll send water spiraling toward the flames, leaving us blanketed in darkness while he makes a getaway with the night's profits.

I keep a sharp eye out after that thought occurs to me. Elemental or not, we can't afford to let any coin slip away.

The customers are slinging back drinks faster than I can carry them. I pause to collect another empty mug. I've been called "barmaid," "brat," and "wench" more times than I can count tonight.

Despite the fact that we'll likely earn a decent profit for a change, I long for the tavern to be quiet, filled with only the crowd of regulars. At least *they* call me "Bree." But they're few and far between tonight—though I think I spot Jowyck, the rival village brewer, ducking into a back corner. I'd know those wiry gray curls anywhere. Wonder if his wife knows he's "recovered" enough to come have a drink.

Da disappeared into the kitchen earlier tonight, claiming to be checking on the stew. Our customer's stomachs are filled, but still—I maneuver around a puddle on the floor—an extra pair of hands delivering drinks would be appreciated. I take a moment and pause, slipping behind the counter to rotate my ankle. My feet are beginning to ache.

They'd ache that much more if the Rider had made good on her threat to break them.

I don't have the time or the patience to wallow in my worries right now. With effort, I throw the thought away and take a moment for myself to cool off, customers be damned. It's like a waterfall is running down my back from all the sweat.

A regular sneaks in. Break's over. I know just what to get Bitsi; she likes the weak ale. I grab a mug.

"Crowded in here." Da's voice comes from just behind me.

Despite myself, I jump.

He startled me. It's growing so loud that I barely heard his quiet voice over the din of clanking drinks and booming laughter. Lucky it's only him. I'd have my *own* hide if some petty little pocket-filcher snuck behind the counter and got away with our earnings.

"You didn't expect anything else, surely," I say, a little rattled. "Don't you know the Bridge and Duchess is the only place to be tonight?"

Next to the taps, Da balances a stool on two legs. His expression is contorted in concentration, narrow nose wrinkled. I can't help but be amused, but still...

"Fine time for you to play a game with the furniture."

The legs clatter back to the ground. "I'm not playing *games,*" he says, affronted. "I'm testing the sturdiness of our seats." He pauses and sweeps an examining eye over me. I don't let my worries show on my face. "I've been busy in the kitchen. Are you all right, Breena?"

"Fine," I say irritably. My face is too telling. I push a sweaty strand of hair from my face and lean to the side to ease the strain in my back. "Oh no, please, don't get up." I put syrup in my voice as Da continues to sit. "I wouldn't want to trouble you. You might lose what little hair you have left."

Da waves an airy hand. "I trust you to handle things. Carry on."

"Yes, your lordship." It's muttered beneath my

breath.

Da catches it and shoots me a grin. "I suppose I can help a little peasant like you out."

Well, thank the Makers for their small blessings then.

He hops from his seat, chucks me under the chin, and winks. I laugh, shoving his hands away. Grabbing two mugs, Da fills them to the brim and shouts theatrically. "Oy! Who'll trade me a coin or two for these? Someone please relieve me of my heavy burden."

The patrons greet him with shouts and cheers.

I shake my head as I whisk trays from vacated seats at the counter. Da always could playact better than anyone else I know, stepping into whatever role he deems appropriate with ease. He'll never change. I'd never want him to.

With two sets of hands, the night speeds by. Da takes one side of the bar, and I take the other. But when he reaches for the pulley of the tavern's bell, I sag with relief. There's not a single part of my body that isn't aching. I scratch at my head. I swear even my hair hurts.

"Settle up!" Da's voice rings out after the bell. Coins jangle amidst several grumbles. "Stop your wailing. It's practically the new day," Da tells one prune of man who's trying to wheedle his way into "just one more."

When the dimly lit tavern is finally clear of anyone who doesn't belong there, Da grabs the sack of the night's profits for us to count out, while I let myself fall, stomach-first, onto a bench. My breeches will be pulled even more than they already are from the splinters in the wood, but I can't bring myself to care.

"I'm dying," I groan. "The Makers are calling me home. I can see the light of the Great Beyond." I turn on my side to look at Da through one eye. "Tell the cat I loved her."

"We haven't got a cat."

"There's that stray that's been lurking about. She's taken a shine to me."

"Ah. Well then. Tell her yourself when you see her in the morn."

"No sympathy for those at death's door. I see how it is." I peer at the modest pile of copper, silver, and a hint of gold. The hustle in my step tonight may have been worth it. "How'd we do?"

"You get to eat another day."

I stretch, sitting up. "That's a comfort. Do I get to enjoy a roof over my head with my meal?"

I meant to keep my tone light, joking, but something must bely the stress of my day because Da looks up sharply from the pile and eyes me.

"Things aren't all that bad for us, Breena Rose."

He's lying. I look away in annoyance. I hate it when he does that—when he coddles me—mostly because it's so rare an occurrence. Da and I are business partners. I know the state of things: the Bridge and Duchess breaks even most nights, but only just. A night we turn an actual profit should be cause for celebration.

I look back at Da's carefully benign expression. He'll never admit to any of that. He wants only to protect me from the truth of things. I drop the subject. "Any rooms let tonight?"

"Not a one. The travelers preferred to camp in the cold and save their coin for drink." Da stands and rolls his neck. "It's off to bed with me. If you'll do the sweep up, I'll do the morning scrub down."

I agree, and he musses my hair before heading upstairs.

Surveying the night's damage, I don't think it's too much to hope that the sweep up won't take long. The windows are all intact. That's definitely positive. There's a broken chair in the corner, but I'm fairly sure it's the same one we've been putting back together at least once a week for the past month. Da always settles it just so, balanced so that it looks all right in its spot of shadow. But whenever someone heavier than a lady's peacock plume takes their seat there, down it goes again. It may be time to chuck it for firewood.

Heaving a sigh, I take up the broom to push the glass, scraps of half-chewed food, and probably a few rat droppings into a pile. I keep telling Da we can spare a few bits of coin for some traps, but he insists the vermin add to The Bridge and Duchess's "roguish charm."

The ache in my back makes me slower than usual; I'm unwilling to push my body for more speed after the day I've had. Unfortunately, the tedious work leaves plenty of time for me to ruminate on its events.

How *exactly* did the king's little hunting squad know to look in Abeline for the truant? I wonder. Is it some sort of magic, like the fire scrying that priestesses do in the old myths? Simple investigation? Did they hear a rumor and follow it up? Or—I hesitate, the broom's bristles hovering over the floor—is it the Rider's doing? Does she just sift through the air for whispers of an Elemental? If that's the case, she could know anything she wished.

And she's clearly the leader of the three. Piggy just enjoys the cruelty of the job; he wears it like a medal of honor. Tregle's plainly afraid of the other two. So afraid that he wouldn't even try to help me. Coward.

My dealings with them are over now. The thought is a small comfort as I empty a pile of dirt and bread crusts into the waste bucket. The most I can do is hope that, whoever this truant is, they're clever enough not to flaunt their abilities. I can't spread the word of the hunting party and risk my neck—or Da's, if he were to get caught with me—for someone that the trio mightn't even find.

Contrary to what I thought, sweeping up the room takes longer than I expected. Hours later, well past the time when the moon rose to its highest in the sky, I'm still downstairs. I grab a candle, douse the fire, sweep up the ashes, and as I stow my broom in the cupboard, finally finished, the door rattles.

Couldn't be the wind, could it? I take a hesitant step toward the door. I hadn't noticed it howling, but that snowstorm may well be moving in. It's a bit late for someone to come wandering for a drink, so I doubt anyone's waiting outside.

It's got to be the wind.

A shadowed figure appears in the window, knocking insistently, and my hand flies to my heart.

"Shh!" I exclaim, realizing belatedly that he—or it could just as easily be a she, I suppose—can't hear me through walls that separate us. My voice is too low. "Ready to wake us all up for a pint of ale," I mutter, moving forward. Candlestick in hand, I call loudly. "Tavern's closed! We open again at dusk tomorrow."

"What a disappointment."

I recognize that voice. An icicle runs a malevolent caress up my spine.

"We were so hoping to make ourselves at home."

Three

Why? I resist the urge to scream in frustration. I haven't said a word, not to anyone, so why has the nightmare trio followed me home?

"We're closed," I repeat. This time, my voice quavers. I hope they don't notice. I want to sound confident and firm, someone not to be trifled with. It's hard to give that impression to someone who's done their best to choke the life out of me, but I'm determined to try.

"Let's not play games." The Rider's voice seeps into the room. It's soft and shouldn't carry through the heavy wooden door, but it winds its way through the thick slats and grazes my ears. I flinch away instinctively. "I trust you understand that we are able make our way inside with or without your assistance. Should you wish to avoid a considerable scene, I'd suggest you unbolt the door."

I raise my arm and scoff at myself in the same heartbeat. *What do you think you're going to do? Wave at them?* I bring my hands together to clutch at the candlestick as if in prayer instead. They need something to do.

Maybe they only want lodging. Elementals have to sleep, same as anyone, right?

I dismiss the thought. The coincidence that they've sought me out again for simple lodgings would be too easy. They're here for something else, though only the Makers know what.

But the woman's right. They'll be coming in one way or another, so I might as well pretend they're entering on my terms. Before I can change my mind, I flip the latch and slide the bolt aside. I open the door with the haste of a lover awaiting her beau and a dread that I sincerely hope is misplaced.

The moonlight illuminates the three on my front stoop, and the soft glow does nothing to lessen the impact of seeing them again. It's a vision I hoped would only visit me in nightmares. I pinch the soft skin of my underarm and it stings. I'm most assuredly awake.

The shadows under Piggy's eyes are darker now, making him seem all the more menacing. Tregle's eyes are a little sharper, the color in his cheeks a bit fuller. He looks recovered from his beating earlier today.

The Rider's hair is threads of silver and gold, unspooled. Her blue eyes are vibrant and her age difficult to determine. Older than me, that's for certain, but by how much, I can't say. Twenty years? More?

"I don't believe we've been properly introduced," she says, stepping inside. Feeling instantly crowded, I step back. The backs of my knees bump against a table bench.

"It's terribly rude of me. I am Lady Katerine du Eirya, Countess of Saungri."

She's looking at me expectantly, but I can't do anything but stare back, flummoxed.

"Ugh. Country folk," she mutters. "And *you* are?" The question is pointed. I guess this is information that I should have volunteered.

"Bree. Breena," I correct myself. Somehow, I sense that the short form of my name won't do here. "Breena Perdit. Um, barmaid."

"Charming." Katerine's lips draw tight in a facsimile of a smile. "Now, straight to the point: are you an Adept, Breena Perdit?"

I'm thrown by the question. I don't know what an Adept is, so I highly doubt that I am one. I look at her in confusion. "No?" I ask.

A clatter from the bar makes me turn, and I frown at the sight of the brawny Torcher pawing through the tankards Da and I collected from our customers only hours ago. "Oy! Piggy! Knock that off!" I say, without thinking.

A startled laugh bursts out of Tregle. It surprises me as well. If he finds my short-name for the other Torcher entertaining, maybe he's not as closely aligned with them as I thought. But a glare from Katerine abruptly silences him.

"I suppose I didn't introduce my companions. The oaf at your bar is Baunnid." At his name, Baunnid sneers an acknowledgement. "This is Tregle." Katerine flips a careless hand toward him. "Now, again, to the point: are you an Adept, Breena Perdit?"

"I've no idea what you're talking about," I say truthfully.

Katerine seems far more reasonable now than when she was standing on my ankle. Really, the countess shouldn't make an imposing figure. She stands a thumbs-length shorter than me, yet manages to look down her nose. She reminds me of the poisonous snakes I sometimes see at the river banks: tiny, seemingly innocuous creatures, but lethal. There's power in their small size.

Forcing myself to relax, to pretend that she's just another village woman, I ask, "What's an Adept?"

Katerine sighs, and irritation rushes over me. *So sorry that explanations are such a chore for you, my lady.*

"Someone who can control air," Katerine says, indicating herself. "Fire." A grin from Baunnid and a small shrug from Tregle. "Water or earth." She says the last two as though they barely warrant a mention.

I understand what she means now, but I've always known "Adepts" by a different name. "You mean an Elemental?"

She grimaces as though I've uttered a filthy swear. "I despise that word. It's just so *base*. But essentially, yes. Our sources and searching have led us here, and we can only surmise that an Adept is inside your darling little…hovel."

Ordinarily, I'd take offense at the slight to my home,

but I'm so caught up with the beginning of her sentence that most of the tension leaves me. I slump with the relief of it. This is a mistake, that's all. Their "sources" are wrong ,and as soon as they realize that, they'll leave.

"Nope, no Adepts here," I say cheerfully, stretching my arms behind my back. There's a pop as my elbow cracks. "I'm only sixteen. Don't even have the proper seventeen years it takes to be one. And we haven't got any rooms let tonight, so if your sources brought you here for a guest, the last lad left about three days ago."

"Interesting." She scrutinizes me for a reaction. "Is there no one else? If I recall, you mentioned that we were on your father's lands?"

"Da?" I falter. I can't think of any real reason that Da couldn't be an Elemental except... "I'd know if my own *Da* was an Elemental, wouldn't I?" I dismiss her question confidently.

"Not necessarily," Tregle speaks up. His shoulders straighten. "I didn't know I was one. This lot just showed up and told me so." He jams a finger toward Baunnid. "You can imagine my joy."

I suppress an unwilling smile at his attempt with humor. I do not want to be this Torcher's friend.

"Do call your dear father down for us," Katerine simpers at me. "I must meet the owner of this charming establishment." This gets sneered at the walls of the Bridge and Duchess like they've done her a personal offense. For a moment, I wish that the deer's head mounted above the hearth would return to life long enough to charge at her.

I hitch my breeches up at the waist and scratch my thigh absently. "Sure."

The sooner I fetch Da, the sooner the Elementals will be out of Abeline, on the road back to where they came from. They can report to the Egrian king that his hunting instruments need some seeing to. His sources are faulty.

Weariness sets in as I climb the stairs. Now that I've got little reason to fear consequences from the Elementals—sorry, *Adepts*—in our tavern, I'm just in a hurry to get through the process that'll show them Da's not the truant they're looking for. I take the stairs two at a time, my mind already moving ahead to what it will feel like to sink onto my soft pallet, pull my thick quilts up to my chin, and drift away into temporary oblivion for the rest of the night.

I pass the second floor where any guests would sleep and keep climbing. My arm steadies me on the railing as I ascend the steep steps to the third floor where our rooms are. I fetch the brass key from inside my bodice and undo the lock on the landing.

"Da." I rap sharply on his door. Light taps won't do anything to rouse him; Da sleeps like the dead sometimes. A brief shuffling issues from inside the room before he's blinking into the unexpected light of my candle.

"The inn had better be burning down," he says, rubbing wakefulness into his brown eyes.

That's not completely out of the question. I think

fleetingly of the two Torchers I've left downstairs with a Rider who could fan the flames. Striving for nonchalance, I say, "Maybe it is, maybe it isn't. I need you downstairs for a moment."

He grumbles but pulls his quilt from his pallet without further protests, winding it around his body like a caterpillar in a cocoon to follow me.

"Got a squad of Elementals here that say they're on the trail of a truant," I explain as we descend. "Figured you could put in an appearance and we'll both get back to bed quick enough once they realize whoever they're looking for isn't here."

He stops dead on the second floor landing.

I hold my candle higher. Maybe it's just the flickering light, but I would swear I've never seen that look on his face before. He's clutching his quilt tighter. His fists are clenched around the edge.

"What—" he croaks and clears his throat. "What exactly did you tell them?"

A tremor of anxiety runs through me, sending my weariness fleeing. Why does he look worried? "That it's ridiculous," I say slowly. "It is, isn't it?"

Comprehension dawns over Da's features. Dread hooks into my stomach with clawed talons. He doesn't respond but sets his quilt down on the landing and thumps down the stairs, shoulders squared. He's walking with a grim resignation. Like a man on his way to his own execution. A chill steals over me.

"Da?" I fly down the steps behind him, heart

pounding, wings suddenly at my feet. He's already taking the last few steps into the tavern when I catch up with him.

I take a worried look at the Elementals. Tregle looks to be practically asleep on his feet and Baunnid slides a tankard back and forth across the counter between his hands with a bored look on his face.

Katerine turns when we bang into the room. A slow predatory smile slides across her face, revealing gleaming white teeth that could rip skin from bone. "Hello, Ardie," she purrs.

That's Da's name.

I look back and forth between the two of them as fear tears into me anew. It suddenly feels as if the ground beneath me has vanished and my stomach is plummeting as I fall.

Da nods once, stiffly, and raises his chin.

"Hello, Kat."

Four

After greeting each other, Da and Katerine simply stare, competing to see who will break the silence first. I count the time by my pounding heartbeats, by the restless fidgeting I can't seem to stop, by the number of times they blink at each other.

They know each other. *How?* We've lived in Abeline my whole life. Before I was born, Da apprenticed with an innkeeper in a village somewhere just south of here. So where would he know the king's Rider from?

I have to ask. The words stick in my throat. It takes several swallows for me to clear a route for them. "How—how do you know my da?"

Baunnid crosses the room to force my head down in an odd approximation of a bow. "I've had 'bout enough out of you. Hold your tongue. You owe her ladyship your respect." He spits the word in a self-satisfied manner, crossing his arms across his chest.

Oaf. I grit my teeth but keep my head down.

"Oh, not so," Katerine finally speaks up. "We're near equals, this young lady and I. Peers! Isn't that right,

Ardie?"

"Peers?" She must be confused. I'm a barmaid. "We've got no ties to the nobility."

A muscle in Da's jaw works. He refuses to comment.

"But this is fascinating!" She turns her attention to me. The look on Da's face, in his eyes as they move from me to Katerine and back again, seizes at my insides and twists them until I want to bolt out the door to spill my last meal onto the brittle grass outside. "I didn't know that Corrine was with child when you left."

Corrine. It's hardly ever spoken in our home, but I know my mother's name. Da's face fills with grief whenever he mentions the mother who died birthing me.

"*Left?* From where?" Despite Baunnid's instructions, my tongue refuses to be held. My head jerks up. "Da—"

The blow to my ears takes me by surprise. "I'll not tell you again!" Spots dance in my vision as Baunnid rubs at his fist, looking disgruntled. I suppose I have my hard head to thank for that. Anger tugs at me, but I reel it in hard. My teeth grind together.

"I'm only trying to have a conversation with my father," I say. I'm proud of how even my voice stays. Da takes a step forward at Baunnid's sudden violence, arms outstretched.

Katerine tuts, looking amused. "Really, Baunnid. I hardly think that was necessary." His shrug is unapologetic.

I lean back against a wall, rubbing my ear and glaring at Baunnid. I'd *love* to catch him with my chopping axe in hand. See how he likes a good thumping when it's his turn.

Two warring winds are tearing at each other—despite the closed door and the fire in the hearth. That *has* to be my imagination. My father and Katerine have resumed their silent war, but Da can't be a Rider, too. I'd *know*.

Wouldn't I?

My nose prickles, and I sneeze. Katerine's emotionless eyes remain trained on Da, but they miss nothing. "By the ether, Ardin. Your daughter's cold. Fetch her a coat."

"I feel grand." I don't want a coat. I want answers. This woman, a countess, knows my father. And knows him well to call him Ardie. "Ride—er, your ladyship, may I ask again how you came to know my da?"

She smirks, and my stomach sinks. Somehow I know that I won't like what she's about to say. "You really don't know, do you?" She turns to Da. "Well? Would you like to tell your daughter who she really is? Who *you* really are?"

He straightens, meeting my eyes. "She knows exactly who I am. In all of the ways that matter."

A shaky breath rattles out of me. *Not exactly comforting, Da.*

"Enough, Ardie," Katerine says. Her next words are for me. "We were correct. The truant *is* here. But I could not have hoped for such a bounty as this."

If she's hoping I'll question her, she'll be disappointed. I won't be toyed with like this. Not when it's obvious that she's eager to spill Da's secrets.

"The king will be so glad to have you home, Your Grace."

Your Grace? Can't be. "Your Grace" means a title. It means nobility. It means...

"Have you not *heard* of the missing Duke of Secan?" She phrases it innocently, genuinely curious, but it pierces me like a barb.

Thing is, I *have* heard of the duke before. The Duke of Secan was one of the king's most loyal servants before he vanished. His legend is spread all over Egria. Most assume there was foul play by one of the king's enemies involved somehow. Others say he dissolved into the air he commanded. Rare is the whisper of someone voicing suspicions that the duke left of his own accord.

And rarer still is the whisper of someone claiming to have seen him.

I never imagined he still lived, nor would I have cared if he did. I would have *laughed* if someone suggested to me that my da was nobility.

But his face is impassive and I know that what Katerine says is true.

I'm paralyzed with shock as she motions Tregle and Baunnid closer. The shackles are snapped over my wrists before I can think to run. Da allows them to truss him up like a present for the king, face swept clean of any emotion.

If he's the Rider they say he is, why isn't he fighting back?

"You always could play a part well," Katerine says.

The words smack into me, an echo of what I'd thought only hours earlier. She really *does* know Da. He really *is* the duke. As they push me toward the door, it drives the point home, a nail boring into my chest.

We're marched outside like common criminals. The air is frosty. The stars blink out at me from their stations in a sky painted black with night. My breath huffs out in small clouds.

At Baunnid's prod, I stumble. Gravel rips into my knees, and I hiss against the pain.

"It's freezing," I say, struggling to get to my feet without the use of my hands. "I'll take that coat now."

Da's heavy overcoat sails through the air and crashes into me. Unable to don it, I clutch it close. The fur warms my hands but does nothing for the ice freezing through my heart.

"Come, Ardie," Katerine says. "It's time to go home."

"We have a home," I spit. The Bridge and Duchess is cloaked in shadows. I can still see the flickering flame of the hearth through the window.

Katerine turns, regarding the building as though she's forgotten it. "That *does* present a problem," she agrees. "One can hardly have two homes."

What does that mean? Foreboding strums through me. I feel it etch itself across my features. And she can tell. Satisfaction spreads Katerine's lips in a malevolent grin.

"Burn it," she says.

"What? *No!*" Burn the Bridge and Duchess? It's unthinkable. I catapult myself forward, running toward the open door of the tavern, but a strange arm hauls me back.

Sixteen years. I scrabble against Baunnid's hold. *Sixteen years* I've lived there. My entire life.

Da's stoic—a statue standing in my father's place. Why isn't he fighting back? He can't be willing to just let them destroy our home.

Tregle kneels beside the doorway. Is he hesitating? I stop struggling for a moment, trying to see. I can't tell—can't see his eyes. Maybe he's not the coward I thought. If he's going to fight them on something, Makers bless, please, *please* let it be this.

"You don't have to do this!"

He turns, but I still can't read anything in his eyes. My heart riots, torn between hope and despair. For a moment, I let myself believe that he'll refuse to act.

Katerine taps a foot. "We are short on time, Adept."

Just like that, the moment is broken. I feel it snap like a thread has been cut.

A flame soars from Tregle's hand to the dry roof, and I scream my rage, whipping my fists over Baunnid's large arm as it catches light. If it had snowed, maybe it would have spread slower, but the roof is nothing but tinder, consumed by flame. I twist. Strain. Try to claw my way free as Baunnid's low chuckle taunts my ears. My feet fly at his legs as the fire licks toward the sky.

Tregle steps back, observing his handiwork silently, and my struggles slow. This isn't a fight I can win. The fire is hungry. It's gobbling down the Bridge and Duchess as though it is starving. Tears prick at my eyes, and I pretend it's the smoke. I have to look away.

In the morning, the inn will be gone. Only ashes upon the ground there to testify that it ever stood. And the stars will be the only witnesses left.

Five

The peaceful oblivion of sleep does not come that night. Or the next. Two days later, as I trudge along beside Tregle, I decide I don't even need oblivion at this point. I'll settle for rest. A few stolen winks. A nap. Anything. I'll take it, whether it means dreams of dancing flames, whispers of lies, or sleeping with a rock digging into my back. I can barely lift my feet anymore.

We've been walking for two days straight, and I've long since stopped trying to take my mind off of things. Who gives one drop in the river that the stars look like tiny jewels in an endless expanse of black? Or a toss in the coffers that I might have once thought the wind rushing through the trees sounded like the Makers whispering to each other? Who cares if the grass shushes gently against my shoes in a playful caress? The soft sound does nothing to abate the stabbing pain in my feet, I'll never hear a breeze quite the same way again, and the stars have seen far too much of my pain lately.

I would kick at the ground like a child in the midst of a temper tantrum if I wasn't afraid of Katerine's reaction.

Sixteen years, I think again. The pain is only a dull knife this time. They undid sixteen years of my history in one night. Burnt it to the ground.

At least I can be grateful that the road we're traveling is bound south. Shivers overtake me periodically. It's not quite as cold as Abeline, but a chill still hovers in the air and I hadn't had time to dress for it. It should warm up the farther south we get.

I try not to think what else lies ahead on this road. The capital of Egria is south. I know that much about it, and I'm sure that's where we're headed. To the king Da abandoned years ago.

Raising shackled hands to cover my yawn, I look back to where Piggy and Katerine prod Da along. No one would ever know he's been awake as long as I have. He still holds himself alert and, occasionally, even smiles. It annoys Katerine. She glowers at him and jabs him in the back whenever he has the nerve to be so bold. But the dark circles under his eyes betray him. Sleep would be as welcome to him as it would to me.

The chains on my wrists rattle as I settle them back in front of me, and after days of silence, my voice is a hoarse croak. "Can't you make them stop? Just to rest?"

Tregle glances over at me. He's been my warden on the trek thus far. "Come on. You've seen them."

I can't deny that. But I've seen him, too, and he's done the most damage of any of them. He looks as tired as Da and I do though.

"At this rate, we'll be dead of exhaustion before you even get us to the king's door." Saying it out loud makes me wonder, and I stop in my tracks, looking up at him with wide eyes. "Or is that the plan?"

He snorts. "Even if it was, *I* wouldn't know about it." My eyebrows shoot to my hairline. The idea that this is a plan he's simply not involved in is not encouraging. He seems to realize that he's been less than comforting and hastily adds, "It's probably not though."

I stumble over a tree root and curse it for lying in my way. It should know that lifting my feet properly isn't a job I'm up to right now. "Don't Elementals have to sleep like everyone else?"

"'Course we do." Tregle yawns. "But I don't make the rules. That's Lady Katerine. Who, by the way, it wouldn't hurt you to make a friend of. At *least* start referring to her as 'Lady.' And stop calling Baunnid 'Piggy.'"

"Oh, come on." The grin sneaks up on me. "That's funny."

He shrugs, and I smother my smile. I'll not be making friends of any of them. "You're just not doing yourself any favors, that's all."

We walk a while longer in silence. The talking's helped. I'm more awake now, my eyelids drooping slightly less. But sooner or later, I'm going to collapse. The growing weight of my arms pulls me into a slump toward the ground. My feet feel heavy; they're moving through the grass like mud clutches at my feet with every step.

The dark that surrounds us really *is* soothing, I think. Like a thick quilt drawn over my head. Or the river at night, with the calm rushing sounds that have lulled me to sleep since I was a child. Or...the inside...of my eyelids—

"Lady Katerine?"

Tregle's voice makes me jerk my head up. I'd been seconds away from either sleepwalking or passing out on the ground. I wouldn't care to find out the consequences of either action.

A few feet back, Katerine looks at Tregle expectantly. I'm as curious as she is about what he's going to say. He glances at me. "I'm dead tired, my lady. I'll hardly be able to guard the prisoners properly if I go on much longer. Could we make camp here?"

Gratitude fills me, but I tell myself that I shouldn't be grateful. It's the least he can do after what he did.

He's picked a decent spot. It's open enough that we'll be able to see if anyone approaches us, ensuring that we're safe from bandits, but off the beaten path enough that no one is likely to stumble across us.

"Very well. Give us a small campfire then, gentlemen."

I need no further encouragement. My legs fold underneath me. I turn on my side in the dirt and burrow into Da's coat, the only thing I could bring with me from the Bridge and Duchess.

Katerine and Baunnid march Da past me to the end of the clearing. He tosses a wink at me, and I try to look impassive. The man's *lied* to me for the past sixteen years. I can't forgive him just because he's trying to keep my spirits up about it.

My eyelids grow heavier, so I resolve to save my brooding for another day.

"Hey, Tregle?" I yawn out.

He looks up from where he's crouched over a pile of dry leaves and branches. I struggle with myself but finally manage a "thanks" before closing my eyes.

And at long last, oblivion comes.

Six

I wake to cool rain splattering my cheeks. Lifting my head from the damp dirt, I stare up at the water plunging from the sky, bouncing down from the leaves above. I close my eyes, reveling in the feel of the cleansing drops on my face.

I'm sure I'll be sorry for the rain in a minute or two. The chill of winter clings stubbornly to the air, and walking in cold and sodden clothes will grow tiresome. Right now though, I'm glad for the water splashing down, drop by playful drop. It's the closest I've come to bathing in days.

Stretching my bound wrists over my head, I wince. My muscles are complaining loudly that they're stiffer than they're meant to be. Sleeping among rocks and tree branches hasn't done my sore body any favors. But I no longer want to cry from sheer exhaustion, so I accept the aches. I'm just happy I had the chance to rest.

Tregle's already awake, hunched over and pulling his hands inside his cloak. He looks more miserable than usual, bowing his head in an attempt to avoid the falling drops.

"That afraid of a little rain?" I ask.

"Hardly," he mutters. Baunnid stirs from his position several feet away, and we hush until he quiets down. Da's still asleep, too, peacefully resting with his fingers threaded across his chest.

Lady Katerine is missing from our camp. I jerk my head toward the others.

"Where do you suppose her ladyship ran off to?"

"No telling. She keeps her affairs private."

Silence covers us, and I shift uncomfortably. Tregle is not a friend—*friends* don't bind your wrists and burn your home down—but the quiet's pressing in on me.

"When do you suppose we'll be on our way this morning?" The question blurts its way out, rushing to fill the silent gap.

"When the Lady Katerine commands it," Tregle says, without inflection. He has the air of someone reciting lines by rote. He glances at me from the corner of his eye. "Didn't think you'd be so eager to get a move on."

"I'm not." Not at all. But the realization is slowly seeping into me that going home is not an option.

In fact, chances are good that I'll never return to Abeline. I'll never convince Da to set those rat traps. Or replace the broken chair he kept stacking in the corner. We won't be able to patch the roof or even to anticipate a crowd when Jowyck fails to open shop.

Broke as we'd been, I'd liked the life we lived, but that life is gone. Dismay curdles inside my chest. My throat tightens. I'd expected to spend my life in Abeline, to turn the Bridge and Duchess around. Now, I don't have a plan. I've no route to follow but one drawn for me by others. Tears sting my eyes, and I inhale sharply, rubbing at them to rid myself of the wretched things. One slips before I can catch it, and I let it slide its way to my chin. Raindrops are still coursing over my face, and it's unlikely anyone will be able to tell one from the other anyway.

Tregle looks over from where he's been digging his boot under the dirt. It's to his credit that he doesn't bother asking me useless questions like, "What's wrong?" Instead, he sighs and lets his hands slip from the folds of his cloak.

"It might not be so bad," he says. "If the king's in a good mood when we bring you and your father in, he might just welcome him back to his armies. I've heard they were good friends."

"Have you?" I ask. I'll let him distract me from my might-have-beens. Of course, I've heard of the Duke of Secan—I mean, Da—too, but I can't remember many of the stories. I never thought there was a reason for me to pay attention.

"Oh, sure," Tregle says easily, relieved that I'm no longer on the verge of a breakdown. "Your father's practically a legend. His disappearance is regarded as one of His Majesty's great personal tragedies—losing his best friend, you know? Of course, everyone always assumed that he was kidnapped by a hostile kingdom or something because of his services to the realm, but—"

"Services?" I break in. I can't remember this part of Da's "legend." I know by now that he's a Rider, but was he like Katerine, hunting truants down? "What do you mean 'services?'"

Tregle clams up, folding his lips in. He won't say anything else, no matter how much I press him. "Not my place," he insists.

Shaking my head in annoyance, I look away. The rain is falling harder now, and Baunnid jolts awake, swearing at the sight of it. Da stretches himself awake languidly. He looks endlessly amused.

A thought niggles at me, one I can't shake. I try to push it away, back into a cozy cave in my mind where I can leave it to shrivel up and never bother me again, but the idea's persistent and crawls up to my lips.

"Tregle." I whisper so Baunnid and Da can't overhear us. He looks over at me. "You said *if* the king is in a good mood." I allow the idea to ripple in the air, spreading out to encompass us both. Tregle's mouth is downturned. I'm certain he knows what I'm going to ask. "What if he's not?"

Silence is his only answer.

Seven

We slush through the cold rain for two weeks. The ground soon ceases looking like a forest floor and becomes reminiscent of a swamp.

I don't really mind the rain, but the mud bothers me. The feeling that the earth and water have united in an effort to swallow me whole preys on my patience.

And if water and earth are on my imaginary list of life-ruining elements, then fire and air top it.

I look at the Elementals who command them. Tregle's mouth hasn't left the form of a hard line in days. Katerine and Baunnid's moods, too, have swiveled. They'd been overly pleased with themselves, but for weeks now, they've been thunderclouds on the verge of bursting.

My stomach rumbles; I'm starving. We haven't stopped to eat since the night before, and we're well into the afternoon now. The sky's a hazy gray. If we'd still been in Abeline, I would have been right about the snow. The clouds are exactly right for a blizzard.

I don't bother suggesting to Tregle that we stop for food. Frankly, with the fare that we've been presented with as of late, I'd almost rather the pangs of hunger that gnaw against my insides.

For the past few meals, Da and I have been fed undercooked squirrel. My stomach turns over at the remembrance. The stringy meat still tasted of blood. One bite and I hadn't been able to help it: I'd spit it into the grass. Da had continued chewing thoughtfully. Maybe he preferred bloody squirrel to no meat at all, but I'd voiced a protest. At least the day before we'd had *cooked* meat. I'd earned myself a wallop from Baunnid for my trouble.

Tregle's snapping his fingers repeatedly, brow furrowed in concentration. His frown deepens, and he wipes his hand on his cloak. I can't understand why. The rain hasn't stopped, and the black fabric is soaked through. He starts snapping again, but stops when he sees me watching, whipping his arms to his sides.

It's such puzzling behavior that it takes me hours to work it out, and when I do, I nearly exclaim out loud. It makes perfect sense now why our captors are in such poor spirits. The rain must affect Torching. If their hands are wet and the air soaked through, any fire would be extinguished before it could start.

Which means... Hope flares in my chest and, rain be damned, refuses to be snuffed. Could Da and I get away?

They don't let us near each other often. If I'm right and we can subtract their elements from the equation, it'll come down to a physical contest. Tregle will be easy to take out. I almost feel a trickle of remorse as I think it. He's the best of the three of them. His legs are strong from their travels hunting truants, but I honestly can't picture him raising a hand to me without specific instruction. And Da can certainly handle Baunnid. He's thrown larger, more muscular men out of The Bridge and Duchess for starting fistfights. And even with his hands bound, he should be able to control the air a *bit*, giving us an advantage.

Air. Katerine. Even when we're asleep and she disappears, I'm sure she's never far. I have much less faith on the odds of three to two, especially if she's factored in.

My spirits sink back to where they started. Whether or not fire is removed as an entity, air still remains.

Back on the first night, when we stopped to make camp, they'd been determined to keep me and Da separate. Probably to prevent us from plotting an escape.

It has to be the rain that's changed things now. It's harder to threaten us with Torchers who can't torch. Now we all sleep in a congregated mass while the skies drip down on us.

I lay awake. The raindrops slow until there's a pause in the deluge of water, and I let myself admire the stars as they twinkle out at me, a friendly face among so much misery. They've witnessed the undoing of my world, but they're a comfort tonight.

A toe taps my foot, and I flinch away.

"I know you're awake, Breena Rose," Da says.

I roll on my side to face him. Tregle's taken to lightly binding my ankles instead of shackling my wrists when we stop to camp for the night. I'm thankful for the small mercy. I can't run, but it makes sleeping an evening's worth just a little easier. I stretch my arms to get the blood flowing again.

I don't answer Da. The crickets chirp. The underbrush rustles. A frog croaks. The rain's completely ceased, and the air hangs damp and heavy over us. He just stares at me, expression placid and patient. Waiting. Finally, I break my silence. He may not have qualms about keeping things from me, but I've never been good at keeping things from him.

"How could you not tell me who you used to be?"

Brown eyes slide away from mine as he shifts, looking up through the trees. "Warm night, isn't it?"

"Da."

My voice cracks a little. I don't care that he's a nobleman—well, not *much*—or that he'd once been friends with the king he proclaims corrupt loudly and often. I don't even care that he's a Rider. I care that he lied about it. For someone who's supposed to trust me, he has an odd way of showing it.

His sigh fills the air. "It's not something I'm proud of, Bree. I thought I'd left all of that behind me. I saw no sense in dredging up old memories when I thought they'd never find me." A bitter laugh trips out of his lips as he crosses his ankles. *His* arms are still bound tightly. "I mean to say," he continues. "His Grace, Duke Ardin of Secan, operating a tavern in the High North? No one ever would have believed it!"

"But…" *Why?* That's what I want to say. Why drag your pregnant wife across the land, forsaking Makers and country to run the taps for a tiny village? It doesn't make a lick of sense.

And what happened to my ma? Da'd always told me that she'd died birthing me, but after everything else turned out to be a lie, I'm not sure I believe that anymore.

I'm afraid of the answers, and I can't ask this stranger with my father's face any more questions. He lets my words vanish into the quiet.

Several yards away, Tregle sleeps slouched against a tree, and Baunnid lays collapsed in a pile of leaves, using them as a makeshift pallet.

Katerine disappears once she thinks we're all asleep. I'm surprised she entrusts our guard to Tregle and Baunnid. She doesn't strike me as the type to delegate well. Maybe she's just afraid to show a vulnerable side. After all, it's hard to look dangerous while adrift in a dreamworld.

Da breathes out his ruminations like smoke filtering from the flames of his thoughts. "I just don't understand how they found me."

I shrug, more to myself than anything. I don't know either. Anything that the Elementals said before they'd discovered me eavesdropping in Abeline's woods had been vague and unrevealing.

"Sources," I say aloud. "Lady Katerine said they had sources."

Da sits up as if a bolt of lightning's licked down from the sky to light upon him. "When did she say that?"

I realize I never told him about the woods. I quickly review the scene for him: how I followed their shouts; how I saw them "training" Tregle; how I was discovered, threatened, and told that Katerine could bring my words to her ear on a breeze—which is why I hadn't immediately told him about it.

Da pinches the bridge of his nose, words failing him. In the dim light of the moon, I can just see his deepened worry lines.

"You doomed us."

For a moment, I think I heard him wrong. Surely he's not trying to find a way to put the blame on *my* shoulders. But the weight of it settles there, nestling in as he continues.

"How could you keep that to yourself? How could you fall for such an asinine idea? You know, most *children* don't even believe those stories—that Riders can fly about on the clouds and hear anything they wish anywhere in the land. We have to at least know where to send the cursed breeze, Breena!"

"Well, you'd know, wouldn't you?!" I shoot back, my voice lancing through the darkness. "Having had so much experience with Elementals." How dare he accuse me? As though he has any space to talk, as though he gave me *any* proper warning about Elementals? He could have dispelled the myths if he'd told me who he was.

"And of course, you're a Makers-blessed expert when it comes to keeping secrets, Da," I spit out. "Ask yourself this: if you'd told me about this, any of this…would we be where we are now?"

At some point during the course of our exchange, I've managed to push myself to my feet. The anger propels me to raise my voice, and I'm shouting down at him on the ground. For all of our teasing, I've never spoken to my father like this—never. My nails carve moon-shaped slivers into my palms. I've never felt so angry, so helplessly betrayed before in my life.

A sleep-drenched voice answers me before Da can. Baunnid. "S'enough out of the pair of you." He drags himself over. "On your feet, *Your Grace.*"

Da's expression is stone. He lurches to his feet and shuffles away at Baunnid's prodding. The tidal wave of my anger ebbs, leaving me staring at his back in…not regret. Not exactly. But something close to it.

Da and I are all the other has.

I slump back to the ground. The thought lays a chill over me, and I barely suppress a whimper. All I want is for Da to comfort me, the way he did when I was little and I'd had a nightmare.

Enough of that, I scold myself. I won't do myself any favors by wallowing.

The self-encouragement has the opposite of the desired effect, sending me into a spiral of misery. Since when am I someone who needs to be coddled? I can take care of myself.

But I'm beginning to realize that maybe I can't. Da's world came and found us, and not even he can take care of me now.

Eight

"Do you mind?"

Days later, and Tregle's just trod on the back of my feet again. It's a nasty habit of his when he's trying to keep pace behind me. Can't rein his long limbs in, I suppose.

"Sorry." He slows for a second before speeding up. There's a certain alacrity to his step that wasn't there yesterday. He looks almost...happy. It's been weeks since I've seen the emotion on anyone's face but Lady Katerine's. Tregle actually looks eager to complete our journey.

I survey the horizon. The trees and rain gave way to sand days ago. I can't imagine anyone living out here; it's dry and hot and heat ripples the air. I'd had to abandon Da's coat several days ago when all traces of damp and cold fled.

At first, I'd kept wearing it, sweat soaking my hair and beading down into my eyes. The coat was the only bit of Abeline I'd managed to bring with me. Da'd had it since I was little, and I'd loved burrowing into its fur in front of a fire on long winter nights when it seemed there was no end to the wind's howl outside or the frost that nipped at my bones.

It's so strange that this place belongs to the same world as that one. I lick lips that beg me to quench my thirst.

My last morning with the coat, I'd woken and been unable to imagine picking it back up, towing it around like some rich merchant's baggage. I caught Da looking at me with sympathy while I contemplated it. My shoulders had stiffened, and I'd left the coat there like moss over a log. Like it had always belonged in the wilderness and never to Abeline, to Da, to me or my history.

Off to my right, Baunnid and Katerine are also livelier. Katerine tugs at Da's shackles in an attempt to move him along faster. He looks rather bemused by her, but he, too, stares ahead. Everyone knows what's coming except me, though I have an idea.

"We're close?" Tregle looks at me, and I tilt my chin to indicate Katerine. "I'm just guessing."

"I'd say a day. Less, maybe, if your father decides to lift his feet when he walks."

"You'd drag your feet, too, in his boots."

He nods an agreement. We walk in near-companionable silence, the only sounds the shifting of the sand and my panting. It's like even the moisture in the air is missing, but I'm the only one who seems to notice.

"Can I ask you something?"

Tregle draws even with me, and his mouth quirks up. "You just did." His golden-green eyes twinkle. After waiting a beat, he grants me permission for another question with a nod.

"You said that you didn't know you were an Elemental. So how…"

"How did *they* know?" he finishes and shrugs. "It was just after I'd turned eighteen—"

"I thought Reveals happened at seventeen."

He hums a disagreement. "No, that's just the *earliest* they can occur. And my abilities aren't as strong as some people's. When my Reveal came, I didn't realize what it was.

"I was apprenticed to a baker in Orlan," he says. I know the name. I recognize it from a few fishermen who'd passed through Abeline once. It's a large port city in the east. "It was my mother's idea—she thought that I'd meet a nice girl in the shops or something like that. She wanted grandchildren, you know? Only I wasn't very good at my job. I had a tendency to burn loaves of bread, wandering away when I should have been minding the coals. My master was an old friend of my father's, so he let it slide most of the time."

His voice cradles the memory, soft and tender. I can visualize a younger Tregle, covered in flour, long limbs falling all over themselves around delicate pastries, elbows clipping bowls as he went around corners.

"On my birthday, my master celebrated by allowing me the ingredients for a cake. It had been months since

I'd had sweets that weren't a bite stolen here and there. I was thrilled." He's amused with the recollection, a small smile playing about his lips. Abruptly, his voice sours. "I tended the fire more carefully than I ever had that day, staring through the grate of the oven. I remember when things went wrong."

"Wrong how?" I cringe at myself. I'm an insensitive clod. I hadn't meant to interrupt him.

"The flames weren't...acting right. They *jumped* onto the cake and reduced it to ash. I thought I was seeing things. I remember yanking the oven door open, and then they jumped out at me and then...nothing." He shakes his head. "I woke up at home. The bakery burned down. They thought I'd forgotten what I was doing and left it unattended. I already thought that I'd been hallucinating, and to be honest, their version sounded more like me. My mother wouldn't look me in the eye for a week, and my master... Let's just say I was still searching for a new apprenticeship when they found me."

There's a look in his eyes, like he's lost within his own memory, but disgusted and ashamed of it. Like it's a dirty thing.

"Anyway, Lady Katerine and Baunnid came for me. She wasn't thrilled with me. Like I said, my Torching isn't some great thing, but you know the law of the land. Any Elementals must do as the king asks. There was nothing left for me in Orlan. I had no reason to try to hide."

"How long have you been with them?"

He shrugs. "Nine or ten months maybe? I'm not exactly sure. I did a *very* brief tour with the king's army. And then I was put back into Lady Katerine's care to be 'properly trained,' and we were in the capital for a while before we were assigned a new truant."

It's so different from my story. Not that it's a happy one, not by any stretch, but in a way, Katerine gave Tregle a second chance when his future had looked bleak. Sort of the opposite of what would happen for me and Da.

Still, his story doesn't quite answer one question. "But how did they *find* you?"

He sighs and tucked his thumbs into the sleeves of his tunic. "Me, they found easy. Rumors get spread around incidents like mine and one made it to someone important's ears, so they set off for me. Others are harder, especially if they're in hiding, but there are some Adepts who can...sense the direction of things. How things might go or, in the case of something they're hunting for, where it might be. The king has a few those Adepts at his disposal."

"Can Katerine do that?"

He scoffs. "Not hardly."

I suppose it makes sense in as much as any of this does. Except that I still don't understand how they hadn't found Da before now.

Tregle slouches over. The memory's still visibly eating at him, so I slide the question into the recesses of my mind, hoping I'll live to see the day that I can ask it.

Nine

It feels like stealing, the way we finally slip into the city's boundaries without anyone noticing us. Like the black sky's leaked down to cover us from wandering eyes. Katerine leads us around bends and corners, through muddy alleys and concrete cooling after bearing the day's heat. She moves swiftly, like the feline Da short-named her for.

I hate that I have no choice but to follow, but every corner where I pause, Tregle nudges me on. Baunnid attempts to mimic Katerine's fluid movements but mostly bumbles behind her next to Da, who refuses to play at stealth. He follows them, sure enough, but does so with his spine erect and footsteps plodding through the mud with an ordinary squelch.

The city is quiet. It sprang up before us in the midst of a stretch of sand, but inexplicable trees dot the landscape. I can only assume Earth Shakers are responsible for their presence.

My feet stutter to a halt when Katerine stops. I run my fingers along the rough stone of the closest structure, using its scrape against my palm to pretend I'm somewhere else. Clotheslines flutter overhead as breezes trapped between buildings fight to free themselves. My eyes travel up the worn gray walls, wondering at the citizens who live so close to the Egrian king's stronghold. The open windows reveal simple shadows: a hint of a doorway, the mere suggestion of a dressing table. Do they sleep easily in their beds and pallets while their king schemes at his throne?

"Lady Breena," Tregle whispers.

"Bree," I correct him automatically, snapping out of my trance. It's the first time anyone's called me that, and the "lady" bit is discomfiting. I smile at him weakly. "Only Da calls me Breena."

Having regained my attention, Tregle lifts his chin to urge me forward. We stand behind Katerine at the edge of an alley. Being a Rider holds one advantage I hadn't considered for the countess. She manages to stay cool. Of her trio, she's the only one who still wears her cloak, though her hood's fallen back to let the city shadows coil in her blue eyes.

"*There*," Katerine breathes.

Hulking shadows dwarf the long, squat building before us. I can't tell what they are in the darkness. The shorter building, though, comes into sharper focus as Katerine leads us closer. Bricks upon gray bricks. Bars over the window openings. A man in an official uniform patrols outside, and a heavy door blocks the way in—no. The way *out*.

No wonder Katerine's so pleased with herself. This isn't just a building. It's a prison.

We've arrived. We stride forward, and I can't help balking. Tregle takes my elbow in his hand.

"Trust me," he says.

And despite myself, I sort of do. Tregle's been—not necessarily *kind* to me, exactly, but he's treated me like a fellow human being. It's more than I can say for Katerine or Baunnid.

"Running right now will only make things worse for you. We didn't see them because Lady Katerine prefers her mystery, but the king's men are many in number and all throughout the capital. They'd have you back in hand before you made it out of the city."

"They're going to kill us anyway." I hear the hitch of hysteria in my voice as Katerine and Baunnid confer with the guards. Impossibly, Da's found it within himself to whistle. "So what's the point?"

Tregle looks at me, contemplative. His golden-green eyes glint as he cocks his head to the side. "The king wants something from your father, so, you know, I doubt that. I doubt that very much."

How could he *know* that? I'm not persuaded, but the iron door swings in on its hinge and we're frog-marched down a dark, dank corridor to a small cell. I stumble as Baunnid rips me from Tregle's arm to shove me inside after Da. The door clangs shut behind me. The lock clicks, and I wince.

"Watch them," Katerine barks from the other side of

the bars. "I'm sure His Majesty is most eager to reunite with his dear old friend."

She spins on her heel, cloak billowing behind her as she retreats, Baunnid at her back like an overzealous puppy. Tregle grants me a sympathetic nod, but then he's gone, too.

The guards linger curiously after they leave, probably wanting a glimpse of the Duke of Secan and wondering what the king's dear old friend is doing in their cells. Probably wondering who I am that I'm mixed up in it. I refuse to meet their eyes, and Da keeps whistling that increasingly irritating song, so they drift away.

"Would you stop that?" I hiss when they're gone. The melody's imprinting itself on my mind, and sleep is going to be precious hard to find tonight as it is. I don't know what awaits us in the morning, but I want to be ready for it.

Da cuts off mid-whistle. "You don't recognize the tune?"

The heel of my hand goes to my head. "That's hardly the point. I just don't understand why you're not taking this seriously."

Da sobers. "I'm taking it very seriously, Breena Rose. Remember when I told you that if a Rider wanted to catch my words, she needed to know where to send the breeze? A certain countess now knows exactly where to go looking for them."

Oh. The whistling's to discourage any attempt to eavesdrop on us. Katerine can listen to our conversation from anywhere as easily as if she stood outside our cell. She's surely tired of the song by now, though. Makers know, I'd been ready to plug my ears and start chanting like a child if it meant the noise would stop. If she's not listening, maybe Da can let me in on his plan. He must have one. And if he can prepare me for tomorrow, tell me what to expect, I think maybe I can get some rest.

"What do you think—"

"I know you have questions," he cuts in. "But I can't answer them for you now. We have to choose our moments carefully." He surveys me and sighs, laying down and turning to a wall.

"Try to get some sleep." His voice echoes around me, and I settle onto the hard ground.

"Night, Da," I say tiredly. But somehow, I think sleep is unlikely.

Ten

The clanging of the cell door disrupts my restless sleep. I glance out the high window to gauge the time. The sky's lightened to purple, and the stars barely peek through. Dawn can't be far off.

A shadow stumbles into our cell, pushed from behind. He surges up immediately, shooting toward the entrance, near where I've claimed my spot, but the bars have already swung shut on him. He grips the iron between his fists. My eyes adjust to the darkness. Curly brown hair the same shade of a woodchuck's fur sits above pointed features. The boy has tanned skin that looks like someone's tried to leech the color from it.

"Come back here at once!" he shouts at the retreating guard. He rattles the bars emphatically, and his voice rings out with authority. "You can't keep me in here!"

"Don't suppose you'd keep it down? We're trying to get some rest." My voice is sleep-muddled.

His shoulders straighten beneath a cloak, and the stranger slowly turns to face me. Warily, he regards me through eyes that don't quite meet mine. He must have thought he was alone in the cell. He studies me for a moment, probably taking in my muddy cheeks, my filthy clothes, and my position on the floor—which, I realize belatedly, I'm still sitting on.

My knees scrape against it as I push myself up.

I'm too close to him. We're breaths apart, and I take a step back, uncomfortable. An odd sense of discomfort that has nothing to do with sleeping in a cell and everything to do with our close quarters prods me.

"What'd they get you for?" I try to sound careless as I occupy myself with brushing dirt and dust from my hands. The boy's too polished to be an ordinary market thief, and it's odd that he's been thrown in with us. Whatever he's done, it must be big.

His laugh is tinged with bitterness. He rubs his wrists where shackles would lay. "Political affiliations."

I wince in sympathy. He may well be in as much trouble as us then. If talk about him is right, the king has little tolerance for those who go against his beliefs. If you fill your voice with treason and the king gets his hands on you...well, you might not have a voice—or a head, for that matter—for long. I'm sincere when I wish him luck. He acknowledges it with a small tilt of his head.

But there's this strange sort of energy to this other prisoner. Maybe it's in the way that he's more disgruntled than anything else. It's like he's not really *concerned* with the fact that his neck is on the line. More annoyed by it. As though it's an inconvenience.

"Got a name?" I ask. I bite at a frayed nail. Maybe

he's a wealthy merchant's son. The fibers in his cloak are certainly finely wrought enough.

"A name?"

"Something to call you by. For example, *my* name is Breena Perdit." I extend a hand. "I've also been known as Barmaid, Bree, or when I've got my most shining personality on, Brat. Something like that. Got one of those?"

"Breena," he repeats thoughtfully, finger to his chin.

Something about the way he says my name is disconcerting. He rolls it on his tongue like a wine. *Nonsense.* He's only repeating it so he doesn't forget it. I've used the same technique with newcomers in the tavern. I repeat the name a few times and I'll remember it for at least a little while.

But when he doesn't say anything else in response to my question, I begin to entertain the thought that he's perhaps a bit mad. Maybe I should withdraw my hand.

"No," I say slowly, drawing the word out. "You can't have 'Breena.' That one's mine. Any other ideas?"

He comes back to himself and coughs into his sleeve. "Rick," he says gruffly. He seizes my hand, still dangling between us, and gives it a hasty shake.

I glance him over from the top of his well-groomed head down the length of his lanky form all the way to the tips of his barely scuffed shoes. Back in Abeline, we'd had a Rick who frequented the Bridge and Duchess. A bit of a ne'er-do-well, his hair always long and uncombed. He had a beer belly and was missing several teeth.

This boy is not a Rick. A Leopold, maybe. I'm sure he has a name that's as fancy as his cloak and isn't some shortened thing that his friends call him. If he doesn't want to give me his real name, I don't much care to hassle him for it. Maybe he just wants to pretend to be someone else before he's sentenced, or maybe he has another reason. Either way, it doesn't affect me.

"Don't you want to know my family name?"

"Why bother?" I ask, feeling weary. He must have an answer prepared. "You'll probably just tell me it's Smith or Jones or some other name that every other person in this kingdom lays claim to." This is my life now. People who deal in falsehoods and omissions.

"It's Williams, actually," Rick says, tilting his chin at a proud angle. He draws himself up to his full height. He doesn't tower over me like Tregle does, but I do have to crane my neck a bit.

I wave aside this information. "That would have been my third guess." I deflate as a wave of tiredness washes over me. "Look, there's still hours to dawn. I don't know about you, but I find sleep a much more pleasant place to be when I'm here."

He nods stiffly.

"No funny business," I warn him. "You stay on your side, we'll stay on ours. And," I add in a fit of inspiration, remembering Da—who's miraculously slept through all of this undisturbed. "My da here's a Rider. You'll not want to cross him." There's little enough comfort to be found in the knowledge of his power, but at least I can use it now.

Rick looks affronted. "Lady Bree—"

"Just Bree." That makes twice in the space of several hours that I'm making this correction.

"Do I look the sort to cause trouble?" he asks. For the first time, he looks me directly in the eye. I catch my breath as his eyes slam into me. They're the gray of the sky right before a blizzard.

"Well, they did just throw you into a cell," I say, voice soft. "But, no." I break our gaze, finishing my thought silently.

You look like the sort who brings it.

Eleven

My father never told me fairy stories of princes and princesses.

Which, when I think about it now, makes perfect sense.

Instead, he told me fables of shadows that whisk naughty little children away in the night. Of rivers and earth that come alive when strangers trespass upon their land. Tales of anger and punishment—these were my bedtime stories.

Da had seemed to think the stories important as he imparted them to me. Even as a child, I understood how serious he was about them. His eyes were grave when they held my wide ones, and he'd tuck my quilts up to my chin before beginning.

I hadn't been a *bad* child, but I had tended toward…mischief. Da's stories, when I'd first heard them at six years old, had scared me into a week's worth of unnatural *goodness.* I didn't respond to any barbs from the local bully on Market Day, didn't have to be asked twice to perform a chore, woke up early to sweep the hearth and give the glasses an extra polish.

I rested easy. The shadows would not come for me.

After noticing how unlike myself I was acting, Da changed tacks. He told me instead of a magical little village, tucked away under cool sunlight where shadows wouldn't think to pass. Gentle hands smoothed down my hair, and he dropped a kiss onto my forehead.

"The lands here know you, Breena Rose. They'll keep you safe from any shadows, even if you do have a naughty moment here or there."

He'd hesitated in my doorway, I remembered now. The flame of his candle trembled on its wick. "Besides," he added. "They're only stories."

Perhaps that was when the lying began. And it never truly stopped.

Light floods into the cell when I wake up, illuminating the squalor Da and I have spent the night in. A film of dust and dirt coats the floor. Liquid sluices down over the rocks that comprise the walls.

Maybe it's a good thing I hadn't grown up wanting to be a princess. I'd be far more apt to scream when a rat scurries past the bars of the cell if I had.

But I'm used to seeing rats. They're almost comforting. I stretch as I sit up, feeling a satisfying give when my elbows pop. Arching my back, I look at Rick, still asleep in his corner of the cell. Thankfully, the eyes that so disconcerted me last night remain closed. Long lashes rest upon his cheeks. I stand and glance back at Da. Also still asleep.

Rick shifts, and his cloak falls open over his hip. Is that a scabbard? I can't believe they'd have brought him in here with a weapon in it if it is. I lean in closer for a better look.

"If you're planning to kill me, please make it quick."

With a screech of surprise, I lurch backward, falling onto the ground. Rick sits up, stretching, and finally, Da does, too.

"I see we have company, Breena Rose," he says, blinking back and forth between me and Rick. "Do introduce me to our guest."

Oh, *now* he's every inch the proper duke. I snort. "Da, Rick. Rick, Da." Rick crosses the cell to give his hand a quick shake.

Da lengthens his body until he's reclined against the wall. "Call me Ardin. What brings you to our humble lodgings, Rick?"

"Political affiliations," Rick and I say in the same breath.

"I see." Da's eyes narrow in on Rick's other hand, squirreled away in his pocket where he's toying with something. I follow his gaze and catch the glint of a purple stone on one of his fingers. "My daughter and I suffer from a similar burden. Good luck to you."

Rick inclines his head slightly. "And to you, sir."

A loud clanging draws our attention. It sounds like someone's playing the bells—badly. We all shift to the bars as the source of the clanging moves into view. It's Katerine, dragging a stick lazily across the cell bars. Her stare lights upon us.

"You're awake. Pity. I was hoping to have the pleasure of waking you myself."

I'd wager she was. Katerine's idea of a proper wake-up is probably a kick to the stomach.

"Oh, but then you'd deprive us the pleasure of seeing your grand entrance, Kat," Da says, grinning beatifically.

"Why, Ardie, you sound like your old self."

"It must be the return to the old homestead."

Katerine's smile sours. "You have an audience with His Majesty in three hours. I'm to make you presentable."

"But what will be done about you?" I interject sweetly, batting my eyes.

Ouch. Da elbows me hard in the side. His look couldn't be plainer; I'm to leave the verbal barbs to him. Katerine's glare speaks of blood.

"And what about me?" Rick pipes up. He's practically as cheerful as Da.

The countess's glare shifts, becoming slightly docile. How curious. "I'm sure you're fine," she says flatly. She calls a guard to unlock the door, and four appear at her summons. One takes my arm firmly in hand and another takes Rick. The other two go to Da.

"Well, then," Katerine says brightly. "Busy day ahead of us. We'd best get started."

⁓�’⊚⊚’⁓

In the light of the day, I can see that the previous night's hulking shadows are actually the palace. It's a monstrosity of a thing. The gray parapets of the central castle sit atop high rocks overlooking a cliff. Crumbling towers of varying height surround it in a mismatched set. The structures leer down as I pass beneath them.

We sail into the halls of the castle, guards tipping their heads in respect. With Katerine as our escort, no one stops us to ask any details of our trip into the king's home.

She leads us through a labyrinth. We take so many turns and climb so many stairs that I wouldn't be able to find my way back to the exit without help. Purple banners line the walls, and stern portraits look down at me. Finally, we follow her up a spiral staircase where ivy wilts along the banister. Dark wooden doors greet us at the top.

Katerine jerks her head at the room. "In you go."

I move to obey before I realize that no one is following me. "Aren't you coming?" My question is for Da, but it's Katerine who answers.

"Ladies and gentlemen prepare for court in separate wings." She shakes her head at Da. "Honestly, you could have told the girl that much."

A queasy ball rolls around inside me. "Then *you'll* be readying yourself with me?"

"I do not require readying," Katerine snaps.

Pardon me, then.

"Besides, I think I had best stay by the side of my old friend. We wouldn't want him to lose his way again."

My mind stutters. It's bad enough to be trapped in this mess with Da, but to be trapped in it *without* him? I shake my head. The strands of hair that have grown out over the past several weeks flutter about my ears. "I—"

"I'll see you soon, Breena Rose," Da says. He sends a smile my way. "We'll be meeting His Majesty together in few hours, isn't that right, Kat?"

"Of course. Father and daughter must be together for such a momentous occasion."

"There. You see?"

I crack a knuckle in agitation. It's not as though I have a choice, but I can delay the moment when I'll have to face things alone just a little longer. My eyes wander past Da to where Rick stands with his guard.

"What about you?" I ask.

He looks surprised to be addressed. "Me?" He grins like he's suppressing a smirk. I'm so glad he finds the situation humorous. "I'll be fine as well. I believe I'm to meet with His Majesty about the same time. Correct, Lady Kat?"

"Lady Kat." It suits her. I resolve at once to begin using it. Especially when I see her expression upon hearing it. She looks like a worm's crawled beneath her nose and her nostrils are flaring to put some distance between them. "Indeed."

I nod and take a deep breath, waving away the guard's hand as he moves to push the door in. "Please. I'd like to do it myself."

He sends a questioning look to Lady Kat, who nods her acquiescence.

The metal handle is cold in my grasp. What waits for me behind these doors? I imagine hands reaching out for me from the darkness, a militant overseer barking out orders, my skin being scrubbed raw. On the count of five, then. One, two, three—

I push the doors open and don't let myself look back at Da as they close shut.

It's an old trick Da used on me growing up. He'd let me brace myself for a moment, but wouldn't allow me all the time he'd promised. I had a few seconds to get used to the idea, but not enough time to panic about it.

The memory's painful. Every instance Da had used the trick on me had been in the Bridge and Duchess. The time he'd drained an infected cut sprang to mind. My pallet and quilt had boiled with my fevered sweat, and I'd *howled* as the sterilized knife sliced the wound open. Da had hushed my cries and mopped my brow.

But my pallet burnt away with the tavern, and laying the memory to rest with it would hurt me less.

Inside the doors, two women sip from teacups. Gossiping on their settees, neither of them notices me, so

I take my time investigating my new surroundings, ignoring their prattle.

What a contrast to the prison cell. I'm in an extravagant sitting room. Shelves of books line the wall, interrupted only by a gold-framed painting and two windows. Heavy rose draperies cascade from golden curtain hooks sculpted in the shape of small suns. The room is warm and pretty and, given what I'd been bracing myself for, not at all what I expected.

My surveying over, I tune into the women's conversation.

"Have you any idea why we've been called here?" a wisp of a girl with black hair and brown eyes asks.

"None." This from the other woman, who bears no resemblance to the first, with corkscrew red curls piled on top of her head. She adjusts the skirts of her pale pink dress. "I know only that my lady was told they had a mess that required fixing and it necessitated her sparing one of her maids."

The other girl murmurs that the same had been asked of her mistress.

A frisson of irritation vibrates through me. A mess, am I? I clear my throat as obnoxiously as possible.

The girl with the dark hair is the first to hear me. "Oh!" She gasps loudly. "I'm so sorry, sir." They rise to their feet, hastily setting aside their teacups with a clatter and clasping their hands before them. "Have you come to tell us why His Majesty requires us?"

Earnestly curious eyes flick over me, and I burn with embarrassment. With my short hair and dirty figure, they think I'm a man. Maybe I *am* a mess that needs fixing.

"I'm Bree? Breena Perdit. Lady Kat sent me in here to get...groomed, I suppose. My da and me are supposed to be meeting the king in a little while."

Blushes spread over their features at their mistake.

"And *I*," the dark-haired girl says. She claps a hand to her mouth like she hadn't meant to speak.

"Sorry?"

The redhead bustles forward. "I apologize, Lady Breena." She executes a quick curtsy. "Gisela, your ladyship. Our Emis here has a love affair going on with language and sometimes speaks too quickly in the name of preserving it."

She examines me, measuring the task before them. "Emis?" The other girl moves to assist her, instructing me to lift my arms so they can get proper measurements.

"You can call me Bree," I offer as Emis tilts my chin. I feel like a buffoon with my arms stretched out as if they're wings. "No need for that 'lady' bit."

"Fine bone structure. Lovely eyes," she comments.

"Lady Breena, we are lady's maids," Gisela says. "We wait on *ladies*. You must understand that that makes you one."

Not if I can help it.

"First thing's first. We need to scrape off a layer of that dirt."

Behind a silk screen that I hadn't noticed before is a heavy porcelain tub. Emis sends Gisela running for servants to fill it, and they parade in, carrying buckets of steaming water and throwing curious looks my way. None of them ask me why I'm here, and I wonder how often this sort of thing happens. Maybe they're instructed not to acknowledge the guests, but I'm no guest. I'm a prisoner.

I long for a mirror. Vanity's never been my biggest flaw (my impudent tongue has that dubious honor), but this is different. I must be a sight if the rest of me is anything like my hands. Mud cakes them and my cuticles are red and frayed.

On second thought, if my hands are this bad, maybe it's better I don't have a mirror.

"Lady Breena, I do hope that you don't take offense at my asking," Emis says, peeling my sleeve from my arm. I flinch when my arm hair peels with it. "But when was the last chance you had to bathe?"

"Um…" I flap my arm to shake the dried mud loose and think back. We traveled for around three weeks. I'd dunked myself in the nearly frigid river behind the Bridge and Duchess with a bar of lye a few days before I stumbled upon Kat, Tregle, and Baunnid in the woods, so… "About a month?" I hazard a guess, sinking into the hot water with a hiss of surprise at the heat. It's nearly scalding. What skin is visible beneath my grime turns pink.

Emis's mouth drops in astonishment. She pats me awkwardly on the arm. "Well, let us just give thanks to the Makers that you're here with us now."

"As nice as you two are, I'm quite far from thanking the Makers for it." The words slip out, and I clamp down on my tongue with my teeth. Curse my runaway mind. I don't need to burden these women with my problems.

They wisely keep their silence, and for that, I *do* thank the Makers. I want to explain my circumstances about as little as I want to be in them.

After three rounds of scrubbing, the water's long-since cooled, but I'm reluctant to get out of the tub, where evidence of the past few weeks has been washed away. Gisela holds out a towel entreatingly, and I sigh, running my fingers through my hair to shake out any excess moisture. They despair over the length of it—or, rather, the lack of length. Apparently, it's the highest of fashion crimes for a woman to have such short hair.

Emis contemplates the merits of a wig aloud, but Gisela dismisses the notion.

"Lady Breena is probably unfamiliar with the weight of a wig," she says. "I am sure that we don't wish to burden her with something else when she is being presented at court for the first time."

Presented at court? Is *that* what they think is happening? I hold back a strangled burst of laughter. If they only knew. Perhaps I'll be presented at court, but not the way they think.

I step into the towel's warmth, and their hands

descend upon me, inspecting to be sure that they haven't missed any stubborn spots of dirt.

"Can't have you meeting His Majesty looking like you did," Gisela says.

"Which color do you think would suit her best?"

Gisela sighs. "I do wish we could put her in lavender. I think it would go nicely with her blue eyes and set off her hair splendidly. But you know how the king feels about that."

"He's got something against purple?" I ask doubtfully, remembering the banners I passed by. "Then why does he have it plastered about his halls?"

Emis rubs vigorously at my scalp with a smaller towel.

"That won't make it grow any longer, you know," I tell her.

"The king believes that shades of purple should be reserved for members of the royal family," Emis says. "It's not a *law*, per se, but he does…frown upon it."

"I'll bet he does more than frown."

The girls pause tellingly, mouths in grim lines.

"As I said," says Gisela. "I think it's best we choose another color for you."

"Gisela, do fetch the seamstress. They told us that we could use royal funds to see to our task. A modest gown surely falls within the realm of reason, and I'm sure she has one to spare."

"A gown?" I ask, dismayed. I haven't worn skirts since I was a child. They always got in the way.

"Couldn't I just...I don't know...have a clean pair of breeches?"

Gisela turns slowly. "Ladies of the court do not wear *breeches*." She says the word like it's rolled around in my washed-away dirt.

After she returns, they settle on a blue dress and stuff me into it like a doll. They put some black stuff on my eyes, and a simple comb is run over my hair.

"I'm beginning to rethink this hair style of yours, Lady Breena," Emis says playfully. "It suits you quite well." She holds up a looking glass so I can see their finished product.

A lady looks back at me. A stranger with sad eyes that I simply don't know.

Twelve

The ladies aren't permitted to go down to the throne room with me, but they clasp my hands before I leave and wish me luck. I still haven't told them why I'm here, but they seem to sense I'll need it.

"May the Makers be with you," Emis whispers into my ear. I squeeze their hands in gratitude before a guard leads me away.

The palace is a maze of halls, windows that look out into courtyards, staircases, and people who appear as if from nowhere. The guard with me is silent. No stern fingers on my forearms this time. Maybe he doesn't want to muss my dress, but I think it's more likely he knows I have no hope of escape. We reach a pair of plum-colored iron doors. Purple again. They're easily four times my height. The guard's elongated axe thumps down onto the floor as he locks his eyes forward. I guess we're to wait here then.

"Worked in the castle long?" I ask, simply for something to do.

No answer.

"Do we just…go in?"

Nothing.

"Right," I say slowly. "I'm just going to nip outside for some fresh air then, shall I?"

The long axe blocks my path.

It had been worth the attempt. I hold my hands up in surrender and consider the doors once more. What lies beyond them? Besides the king and his determination of my fate that I don't have any say in.

I'm uncomfortable in the dress I've been stuffed into. A shade of blue so pale it's almost silver, the fabric is itchy. It looks thin, but my skin is stifled and can't breathe.

Where's Da?

As if cued by my thoughts, a figure appears at the end of the hall. I'm relieved to see the height and gait of the figure match Da's. Despite the situation, I grin. The silhouette of a cape billows behind him. It's so odd to see Da in such a costume. It's like he's an actor in a festival play.

The figure draws closer, and I slump in disappointment. Not Da. Only Rick.

"So nice to see you, too," he murmurs as he stops even with me. He nods coolly at his guard, who abandons the grip he has on his arm with an apologetic shrug.

"Thought you were my da."

"I've aged before my time then."

My opinion of him dips. I hadn't pegged him as a vain peacock. Rolling my eyes, I look away. I don't think he's funny right now.

"Breena."

I turn slightly to meet his eyes.

"I'm sorry if I caused offense. Any excuse for a bit of levity to lighten this horrible atmosphere, you understand."

My annoyance is somewhat alleviated. "Right. So how was your trip to the groomers?"

"Excuse me. Groomers are for poodles. *I* was in the menagerie's spa area."

I stifle a laugh. "Of course."

He tips me a half-smile. "It was far from terrible. I expect worse in the coming moments to be quite honest with you."

"Me as well." My trepidation returns, and I rotate to face the doors. I half-expect them to burst open, to be dragged inside and told that Da and I are to be summarily executed. It's one of the *less* painful scenarios that my imagination is spinning about.

Rick nudges me and indicates the hall he entered from. Another tall figure clips down its floor. This time, it actually *is* Da.

Any residual doubts that he is who Katerine says he is vanish. He's utterly at ease in his waistcoat, embroidered with gold. Black leather boots, finely cobbled, adorn his feet. His posture is relaxed, his head scrubbed clean, and his mustache has disappeared. He raises an expectant eyebrow at the guard, who releases him with a cough, cowed into submission.

See, now *that* would be a useful skill. Why couldn't he have taught me that attitude?

I probably would have been rubbish at it anyway. I've never been able to pretend the way he has, to instinctively sense how to act with each person to get what I want. I'm a bad liar. I try to stick with the truth, even if it gets me into trouble.

"I believe our entire party is here," Da says. He reaches for the heavy door's handle, and no one stops him. He claps the knocker down once and then three times in quick succession before standing back.

As though being cranked wide like a drawbridge, the doors open to us. Da strides inside. I swallow a hard gulp of air and follow, with Rick and the guards at my back.

It's more than I feared. The elaborate throne room is filled with noblemen and women in all of their assorted finery. I catch the flash of sapphires and sparkle of diamonds on their wrists, fingers, and throats. Braids of gold chains dangle from a few women's ears. Perhaps that's a fashion here. I let myself be thankful that my ears aren't pierced. The glittery threads of metal remind me of the farmers in Abeline and the way they'd tagged their cows to mark them as their own.

I recognize Lady Kat at the front of the room, but Baunnid and Tregle are missing from the gathering and I wonder at it for a moment.

We walk down a long violet carpet to a dais where several thrones are erected. In the lowest one sits a girl about my age with long black hair spilling over her shoulders like ink. Her gaze is impassive, the yellow-green of it piercing. Is she the Egrian princess? No, that can't be right. I could swear the king only has one child, a son. The girl crosses her ankles subtly beneath her emerald skirts. She doesn't care what happens to us today. She looks bored, as though she'd prefer to be somewhere else. So would I. But my fate's going to be decided upon in this room, and I don't have that option. My heart knocks against my chest.

Beside the girl is an empty throne—the prince's. I assume he's away, waging some war in his loathsome father's name. And speaking of…

My eyes shift reluctantly to the figure rising from the dais. Hard gray eyes are set above a bristly red beard. Swathed in purple from head to toe, he descends from his throne.

"Ardie," the King of Egria says. "Welcome home."

Thirteen

Silence dominates the room. Utter stillness. There isn't even a rustle of fabric against skin. I'm not sure the king blinks as he hold Da's gaze. I'm reminded of the confrontation with Lady Kat in Abeline.

Da crooks his arm across his middle and bows low at the waist, keeping his eyes on the king. Rick coughs behind me. When I turn to him, frowning, he nods meaningfully at Da's bow. Oh. I bobble a humiliating curtsy to the king. Sweat beads on my back under the scratchy fabric of my dress.

"Your Majesty," Da says, voice low. He makes it droll, the punchline of a joke in the tavern.

I close my eyes briefly in denial. Really, Da? I couldn't stop him if I wanted to, but I wish he wouldn't test our luck.

In a scarlet red gown, Katerine pushes her way over to the herald, who watches the scene, arrested. She grinds her heel across his toes. He jolts, lips going white as he smothers a yelp.

"May I present His Grace, Duke Ardin of Duchy

Secan, Royal Adviser and Court Rider—"

"—*Former* Court Rider," Katerine interrupts.

"—and his daughter, Lady Breena Rose of Duchy Secan."

I want to shove the words back into his mouth. It's not a title I want. I know nothing of the duchy Secan, except that I don't belong to it. But my mind quickly processes Da's titles. Royal Adviser and Court Rider, eh? These must be the services Tregle alluded to. Da used to be the king's adviser. It doesn't surprise me as much as it should. I already know that they were friends once and that Da's a Rider. It's not such a great leap from that to Court Rider.

"And," the herald continues. "His Royal Highness, Prince Caden Garrett Langdon Edric Richard of the House of Capin." He pauses. "The Fourth," he adds lamely.

This one does surprise me. The only person who's come with us is... I turn, and Rick looks back at me mildly. "I do *prefer* Rick."

I'd figured him for a merchant's son. Not a prince.

"I don't blame you" slips out. Even the small flutter of my words reverberates around the still marble room. "That's a lot of names."

He laughs, and Makers help me, but the joy in it is such a welcome sound right now that I can't suppress the smile that blooms on my face.

"Wonderful," the king pronounces loudly over us. "I flatter myself to think that you already know who I am, and those introductions were tedious enough. I hope you all agree?"

A chorus of nervous laughter echoes throughout the room. My smile wilts and dies. A nervous-looking woman hides her twitches behind a fan.

The king's steely gaze is leveled at me. I meet it, though cringing inwardly. "What did they say your name was, my dear?"

"Breena," I whisper. It takes effort to get the word out.

"Lovely," he says. "Truly, a lovely name. I'd like to tell you a story, Breena, if I may."

I doubt I want to hear his story but doubt even more that a protest from me would matter.

"When I was a little prince, all of the realm's knights trained at the palace in the capital. We grew up together, all of us. It was a happy place, you know, Breena. The finest meats. Hot baths every night. Lavish parties. I'm sure you can imagi—then again, I suppose not."

I bristle at the intended insult.

Pacing before us, the king continues. "I developed a deep friendship with one young man. A young noble, heir to a duchy who, like myself, was particularly gifted in war studies. Rubbish with a sword though." Hands in the air, he chortles good-naturedly. "Sorry, Ardie. You know I could always best you in a duel."

Wind rattles at the windows. Da looks innocent, but I know it's him. It's a warning to the king: Da may not be good with a sword, but he has other weapons at his disposal. Weapons he no longer needs to hide.

The king tuts and twists a finger in his beard. "None of that now."

"I know all of this already," I burst out. Fury ignites Katerine's eyes. "Your Majesty," I add quickly.

"You're well-informed, young lady." His voice carries in the quiet hall. "But others are not. Perhaps you'll permit me to continue.

"The best of friends, we were. When I began to see that Egria could be so much more than what it was, that same noble from my boyhood—a duke by then—was there at my side. There were others, of course, but it was him whom I knew I could count on against our enemies. He was gifted, Breena. Loyal. A difficult combination to find.

"Unfortunately about sixteen years ago, he and his wife disappeared. Just—poof!" His fingers flick open. His smile is more bitter than a berry picked before it's ripe. "You cannot imagine how thrilled I am to reunite with my dear friend."

He halts before us. The rancid stench of red wine wafts from him and stains his lips. Up close, I can see the resemblance between him and...Rick? Prince Caden. Their eyes have the same shape and color. The king has given his son his nose, a slope of a thing that's just a little too pointy to be called feminine. He claps a hand on Da's shoulder and turns to me.

Regret fills his tone. "But it's treason, what he's done, Lady Breena. Would that we were peasant boys reuniting after years in different villages, but your father abandoned his liege. He was sent on a mission of goodwill to the island kingdom of Nereidium and asked to retrieve a treasure. Your father's wife went missing at court one morning when we broke our fasts. Neither was ever heard from again. What do you make of that?"

"Maybe my ma was sick of the corsets." Distaste for the man in front of me makes me bold. Da's mouth hitches up proudly before he smothers the grin.

The king sighs. He's nearly as convincing an actor as Da. Nearly. But the pretend emotions never touch the creases around his eyes.

"It's a difficult position I'm in. Difficult indeed. For all I know, you've been trading state secrets for the past sixteen years."

"I've been running an inn in the northern province for the past sixteen years." Da says it as a matter of fact. Word of where he's been must not have had a chance to spread yet for gasps and whispers surround me. The king hushes them with a raised hand.

"Tell me, Ardin. Why did you flee?"

This is a test. I'm certain of it from the way the king's jaw clicks. He grinds his teeth. I hold my breath, waiting for Da's reply. If he gives the right answer, maybe nothing bad will befall us. The wrong one and—

"It's as Breena said," Da finally says. "Lady Corrine tired of being strapped into a corset."

The king's jaw disengages as though swinging open from a hinge. "Kill the girl," he spits. "Duke Ardin will spend his life in the dungeons." He whirls and stalks back to his throne.

Kill the girl. The words wallop into me like a physical blow. I stagger back, seeking an exit while a wave of excited chatter and exclamations sweeps through the nobles. *But I'm not ready to die,* I think. As though it's up for discussion. The king's knights move toward us.

And life imprisonment for Da. The king will prolong his suffering. He's probably enjoyed getting us cleaned up only to tell us that it would be the last of any such moments. How long can even Da last in the squalor of the cells on little food? A few years?

A hatred such as I've never felt boils up within me. If I'm going to die anyway, I'll go having told the king what I think of his justice. Angrily, I open my mouth.

"Wait."

My jaw snaps shut. Two voices have spoken as one, but neither is mine.

Da's charade of aloofness is gone. "Please, Your Majesty. My daughter knew nothing of any of this."

I pull at the sleeve of his waistcoat. "What are you doing?" I hiss. "We're in this together."

"I won't see you die for my crimes."

"Yes, Father." This comes from the prince. His is the other voice I'd heard. "It's unjust to punish the offspring for the trespasses of the father. Particularly in such a case as this." His eyes hint at a hidden meaning. "Duke Ardin's daughter has committed no crime and is of noble blood. By rights, the duchy belongs to her now."

My fingers fly of their own volition to Prince Caden's sleeve as well. My arms hang between him and Da, and I feel like if I can keep them tethered to me, I can suspend this moment.

"And what are *you* doing?" The crescendo of voices from the crowd covers my panicked question.

"Helping you," he says quietly.

"Well, *stop it.* I'm staying with my da."

"You're not," he says, plucking my hand from his sleeve. He's speaking quickly, under his breath. "My father isn't bluffing. It's this or he'll have you executed. Let me help you, please. There's no reason you should die."

I can't fault that explanation, and I let my hand fall, struck momentarily wordless.

The king smiles, but it's tight around the eyes. They froth with rage over being publicly contradicted. "Oh, very well," he says. "My errant son makes a point. The Lady Breena will be brought into court society. Send Duke Ardin to the dungeons."

"No!" The cry tears out of me, and I lunge for Da. The prince is right—and I don't want to die. I know that easily enough. But being separated from Da is nearly as unthinkable.

The hands that raised me catch my shoulders and lock me in a fierce embrace. I press my face into Da's shoulder, trying to keep the world at bay for a minute longer.

"They'll try to tell you who you are, Breena Rose, but

don't you listen," he whispers into my ear. I shift and see the king's guards moving in over his shoulder. "It will all be different now, but you're my daughter and I swear—I *swear* to you I had good reason."

A cold circle presses into my palm as Da clasps shaking hands over mine. He doesn't say anything, but something tells me to keep the object hidden in the folds of my dress as the guards tear him from me.

They maneuver him roughly back down the violet carpet and through the plum doors. He shrugs their arms off of his shoulders, and they seize him at the wrists, a guard at his back with a threatening scythe.

When the doors thud shut behind him, all eyes swivel to me. I try desperately to get my breathing in check and swipe at the tears coursing over my cheeks. I stand in the center of the throne room.

And I'm alone.

Fourteen

I'm sure that words are said after that. I'm sure that threats are made and emotions betrayed. I'm sure that someone explains to me what my life will be like now.

I don't remember any of that.

I have a vague recollection of fingers on my wrist, as my feet followed a guide mechanically. Of shoes being slipped from my feet, sheets being tucked in at my side, and feathery down suffocating me like a cloud with murderous intent.

It must be a long time that I lay there, for when I next open my eyes, it's a new day and a worried face peers down at me. It's one of the ladies-in-waiting who attended me yesterday. Her name is lost in the haze of all that happened afterward. What is it? Ami? No. Emis, that's it.

"My lady?"

Jolting upright, I press the heel of my hand to my forehead and swing my legs over to the floor. Solid wood is beneath my feet. Good. That will ground me when reality quakes my world again.

Da's in prison.

The thought whisks through my mind, taking all traces of sleep with it. This morning is not like every other morning of my life. I won't walk out of this bedroom to find Da wiping down a counter or preparing a barrel of ale. Even when Katerine and her band of Adepts had held us captive, I'd known Da was there. Now, the only thing I have of his is the object he pressed into my palm.

My hand is empty. Where is it? I pat the mattress down, feeling the beginning stirrings of a frantic energy. The sensation is quelled when I encounter something cold and metal and clutch it in my hand. A relieved puff of air escapes me.

I'll have to examine whatever it is later. It doesn't seem wise to have Emis see it. I don't know where her loyalties lie. Until then, I'll need to keep it hidden. On me, where no one else will stumble across it.

"My lady?" Emis repeats, voice raised louder.

I snap to attention. "Don't," I beg her, my voice emerging hoarsely. I'm not sure if I mean don't call me lady, don't try to comfort me, or just don't *be* here right now.

Emis bites her lip, looking indecisive. "I must, Lady Breena."

I close my eyes, denying the sunlight that wades in, uninvited. "Why are you here?" I ask tiredly.

"His Majesty sent us to help you acclimate to palace life."

Palace life is unimportant. What does adjusting here matter when I intend to flee with Da as soon as the opportunity presents itself? "Can I see my father?"

"No, my lady. At least…not just yet." Emis turns and exchanges a significant look with Gisela. I hadn't noticed the other woman's quiet presence along the wall, but there she stands, hands neatly folded before her.

I don't understand the king's game. Why had he listened when Rick intervened on my behalf? For that matter, why had Rick—Prince Caden, I have to start thinking of him that way—intervened at all? And what does the king mean to achieve by keeping me imprisoned separately from Da? For I'm certain he's not keeping me at court simply out of a prodded sense of justice. All I have are questions.

Still, I have to admit that residing within the palace will afford me certain opportunities. Maybe I can get answers here, find some resources to assist in our escape. And the king *is* keeping us alive; that's something.

They can make me a "lady" if they want—or, at least, try to. I'll focus on getting answers first, getting to Da, and then getting out of here. Maybe out of Egria altogether.

Emis continues, seeming surprised that I haven't seized the quiet as a chance to interrogate her. "His Majesty called us your nobility ambassadors, Lady Breena, but please think of us as your ladies-in-waiting. We've discussed it and agreed. It's the work we're used to."

"I don't need ladies-in-waiting. Makers know I'm the saddest excuse for nobility you'll ever behold." I stand and look out the floor-to-ceiling windows. The sun is still dragging itself over the horizon. I can do the same—pull myself into a new dawn in these new lands.

"But I could certainly use some friends. And some help," I admit. I shove Da's parting gift beneath the covers where it can stay hidden until I'm finished dressing. I can't fathom figuring out the proper trappings of court life myself, so I motion Gisela and Emis closer, bracing myself. "Have at me, then."

To my dismay, riding is first on their agenda. In the back of my mind, I'd expected to be forced into another meeting with the king, but it seems he's had enough of me. For now, anyway.

The only animal I've ever ridden in my life was a mule during a festival day when I was little, and at least *then,* I'd been in a sensible pair of pants and been able to throw my legs on either side of the mount.

The ladies insist that I don my skirts again. Thankfully, today's are sewn from a material that breathes a bit easier than yesterday's. Honestly, do they *really* expect me to balance on the saddle with both my legs *and* my skirts weighing me down on one side?

I am glad to be out of doors though. There's

something to be said for it, especially here in the south where I don't worry that I'll suffer from frostbite if I'm out here too long. The warm sun on my face and a distinct lack of shackles on my wrists almost let me forget that I'm still a prisoner.

Emis and Gisela lead me to a large pasture on the castle grounds where a dappled gray gelding waits with a handler. The handler is quickly dismissed, and I can't suppress my relief. One less person to see me embarrass myself.

It's a struggle to heave myself up and over the saddle. When I finally manage it, instinct prompts me to toss my leg onto the other side.

"We'll start out with a nice canter, shall we?" Gisela says brightly after I'm properly situated. If I'm not mistaken, I detect a strain beneath her determinedly upbeat tone. Perhaps she's just realizing what an undertaking she's been saddled with in making me fit for a life at court.

I'm alarmed. "'Canter' sounds fast." I look up from where I'm cautiously patting my gelding's neck, mentally promising him that I'll find some way to get a carrot to him later if he doesn't drop me.

"A trot then," Emis says in compromise.

A *poor* compromise. As it turns out, a "trot" is a cleverly disguised brand of torture. I bounce up and down in the saddle, fighting to a keep a posture that will allow me to stay on the horse. My posterior bruises from the abuse.

Seeing my struggles, Gisela pulls her mount alongside mine and corrects my posture. "No, hold steady on the reins, my lady," she says. "Valor is a good steed, but he's like any other animal. He must know that *you* rule him and not otherwise."

The king employs a similar philosophy when it comes to his people. He views us as animals to be controlled. And penned in. There's no chance that I'll forget I'm a prisoner now. Even for a moment.

But I scrutinize the way the ladies move with their horses. It looks a far more harmonious ride, and I attempt to mimic their movements.

The pasture is lined with thick trees, shades of green so dark that they descend into blackness in patches. Looking at the woods, I can almost make myself believe that it belongs to a different world, one in which it's night and the sun's hidden itself until it can blaze again tomorrow. I wonder again at the oddity of the capital's location, at how these trees thrive here when I know that only sand stretches before the city.

Figures atop horses ride out from the trees. One stands out from the rest, his light brown curls flopping in rhythm with his ride. I shift uncomfortably in the saddle and raise a hand to shield my eyes. It's Rick, dressed for hunting in dark green breeches and a brown tunic. He has a bow slung across his torso and a quiver at his hip. He'll have answers to at least one of my questions.

"Rick!" I shout to get his attention and drop the reins to wave my arms wildly.

"Lady Breena!" Gisela scolds, sounding scandalized. She reaches over from her horse to smack my arm down. "That is *His Royal Highness* Prince Caden. You cannot bellow a moniker at him as such."

Right. The prince, not Rick. I don't know why this is so hard for me to adjust to. I hadn't believed his name was Rick from the beginning.

The prince looks toward us and says something to his companions. I can hear the low hum of his voice, but his words are indistinguishable. The men with him laugh as they head off to the stables while he rides toward us.

His trot is nowhere near as painful as mine. He manages to move with his steed, two parts of one being. I push away a wave of envy and pat Valor on the neck comfortingly.

"Let's try it that way next time, shall we?" I murmur. "There are lots of carrots for you in it."

He snorts, tossing his mane. I make a mental note to acquaint myself with the kitchen staff—I'll need them if I'm going to keep promising treats to the horses.

We halt so Prince Caden won't have to work to catch up with us.

"*Try* to pretend at etiquette please, Lady Breena," Gisela begs me.

It's nice that she understands me so early in our acquaintance.

The ladies incline their heads and back away as the prince pulls his horse up.

"Good day, ladies," he says. He's obviously been

active this morning. His skin glistens in the sunlight, slick with sweat. Perspiration lines the folds in his tunic.

"Your Highness," Gisela and Emis murmur as one. Gisela looks mildly panicked about the fact that she can't execute a curtsy atop a horse.

"And to you, Lady Breena," he says. He hitches his bow up on his shoulder.

"You as well, Your Highness." Gisela's relieved at my decorum, but "Your Highness" doesn't feel right. "Or...Rick?" I try. "Prince Caden." The frustration gets to me. "What *should* I call you?"

His shoulders shake with silent laughter, and he jerks his head for me to follow him. Valor takes a hard step in a divot as we move, and I seize up on the reins to steady myself. I feel another bruise forming. A hot bath isn't going to be unwelcome later.

"Most people choose to address me as 'Your Highness,' but as long as we're not in a formal dinner, I believe I can allow Caden."

Emis and Gisela have pulled back to put a respectful distance between themselves and Caden and I as we speak. They sit alertly, watching. I wonder if they can hear us.

"All right. So, Caden," I say, testing it out. It's much lighter on my tongue than "Your Highness." "Tell me, do you always spend the night in your father's holding prison?"

He stops. I feel like he's measuring me as I yank on the reins to get Valor to pause. "Don't mince words, do you? I just sleep better there," he says, completely straight-faced.

I scoff. As though I'd believe the prince found stone floors preferable to a plush bed. Is it a joke or does he actually think I'm stupid enough to believe that?

"In truth, my father was a bit...*vexed* with me." Caden settles on the word lightly, but I hear the understatement in it. "I'd failed to attend a few state dinners, and I've missed the Mark Service several weeks in a row."

There has to be more to it than he's letting on. I doubt that a prince would truly abandon his state responsibilities to do as he pleased. Especially *this* prince. He doesn't strike me as the sort to shirk his duties. But I'm hardly a beacon of responsibility myself. Who am I to judge him?

"I haven't been to a Mark Service in years," I confess.

He's relieved to change the subject and latches onto my statement. "Some objection to the faith?"

"No." My denial is a knee-jerk reaction. "It's not that I have any quarrel with the Makers." That isn't exactly true at the moment, but I forge on. "The nearest chapel was far outside our village, and the travel proved a hassle. Even for the high holidays. Usually, we were too snowed in to drag ourselves there."

"A hassle indeed. I could sum up the whole production of chapel that way. You see, then, why I took my leave of the capital."

"Without your father's permission?" That explains it.

The king wouldn't like his son doing anything other than what he's told, and if he'd *left*, I can see why he'd make a production of his punishment.

"Yes. I suddenly felt it a most pressing matter that I attend the eastern provinces. I'm told I missed quite the party on the day of my nineteenth birthday. Father was a bit put out." A mischievous smile slinks across his face before he changes the subject, with his nose wrinkled in distaste. "But you say you've no quarrel with the Makers? Wait until you attend your first palace service."

"I expect I will do soon enough. Your da seems determined to keep me busy."

"Of course he is." He's matter-of-fact about it. Turning, the sun highlights his profile and catches on the shiny silver of the arrowheads at his side. "I stood for you in front of his entire court. It wasn't how he would have had things."

This is my chance. "Why *did* you stand for me?" I ask. The farce of a hearing happened so quickly I'd had no time to ask, no time to stop him.

He pats his horse's neck, looking puzzled. "Why wouldn't I? Any crimes against the crown are your father's, not yours. It's no justice for you to die for them. Or even to rot away with him."

It's that simple for him. Honesty shines in his eyes. There's right and there's wrong, and the punishment the king had intended for me wasn't right in Caden's eyes.

I wonder what he thinks of my longer leash here in the palace. If I run now, gallop my horse into the trees and lose myself to the wilds or the desert beyond, will he let me go?

"Lady Breena." My half-imagined escape plans are abandoned as he calls my name. It's got that same disconcerting lilt to it as when he'd been "Rick." "Is there no one whom we might summon to be here with you? A mother?"

I shake my head. "It's always been just me and Da."

"It's as much the same in my family. Only my father and I."

"And your castle full of servants." I wince, regretting the barb—he's done nothing to deserve it—but he takes it graciously.

"True enough. But my father understands the burden I am under as his heir apparent."

"He doesn't strike me as the understanding sort." I remember his temper with Da, his rash sentencing, and I grapple with my own rage.

"And you'd be right there. My father is—" Caden sighs. "He's not a good man. Not a particularly kind ruler. But in many ways, he's been a good father to me."

"He threw you in the dungeons," I remind him. I feel it bears repeating.

"Yes, well, think of it as a peasant child being sent to a corner of the room to think over what he's done. Banishing me to my very comfortable suite would have been a poor punishment. That reminds me, how is yours, may I ask?"

I can only stare at him in response. Have I not made it

clear I'd prefer *not* to be in said suite?

"It's nice," I say stupidly.

"Is your agenda free later this afternoon? I'd be happy to show you the palace. Perhaps the capital city at large? It's not something you should miss."

He's watching the ladies, and his voice is carefully blasé. I'm suddenly certain that they *can* hear us. They're much closer than I remember them.

With regret, I reply, "Afraid not. Your da's given my ladies a full schedule for me."

He chuckles, shaking his head at his own foolishness. "Of course he has. I might have guessed. He didn't plan for you to be about the castle, and now he's left to solve the puzzle of what to do with you."

I falter as the statement hits me, accidentally pulling on Valor's reins. The gelding prances in place and huffs. Caden looks at me quizzically, gray eyes confused. "What is it?"

"Nothing." I try to muster a joking tone, but fall short. "It's just that I'm trying to figure out what to do with me as well."

Fifteen

And so go my days. They're filled with bustling through hallways, torturously bumping over pastures, and lessons in etiquette from my ladies. If they tell me one more time that I'm using the wrong fork for a part of a meal, I swear I'll show them exactly how multifunctional the utensil can be.

The green-eyed girl who'd sat in a throne during Da's sentencing passes me often in the meandering halls. Emis and Gisela can always be counted upon to execute a quick curtsy to acknowledge the girl, so I assume she's a member of the royal family, but I have heavier matters on my mind than one girl's social standing.

Nearly an entire week passes before I know it. I've barely had time to study the talisman that Da left with me and wonder over its meaning. I take it out only when my ladies deposit me in my rooms for the night, bone-tired and drained from the struggle of pushing myself into their ill-fitting mold for another day.

The dark steel shines faintly under the flickering light of the torch I've liberated from a hall sconce. The small disc has the imprint of a hand with crudely sketched representations of the four elements on each finger—a flame, a drop of water, a leaf, and a swirl that must stand for air. I pull it closer. I can't figure out what the symbol on the small hand's thumb is. It's too tiny and smudged with wear. I imagine it stuffed into the depths of Da's pocket for the last sixteen years as he worried the symbol into obscurity with his thumb.

I'd ask Tregle about it—I *think* I can trust him to at least be discreet—but the novice Torcher is nowhere to be found. Chances are slim that he'd have any idea what it means, but I don't have anyone else to ask.

Thankfully, I haven't seen Baunnid either, but Lady Kat seems to be everywhere he's not. I can scarcely turn a corner without finding her lurking in the shadows, a ruby at her neck, stroking a golden lock of her hair between her fingers as she studies me thoughtfully. She's kept her power from reaching for me, but I gulp down my fear when I pass her. I know well how violent she can be.

Despite running into him for that brief conversation astride our horses, Caden is a rarer presence, and I find myself lamenting that. His father's son or not, Caden's been kind to me, seemingly without a shred of the pretense that cloaks the king like a second skin. I pass the prince in the halls sometimes, usually as I trail beside my ladies or caught behind a bevy of skirt-swishing noblewomen on their way to a sewing circle.

I mumble "Your Highness" with a respectful incline of the head during such passings—we all do. My voice is just one in the chorus. Excepting those moments, I see him only at dinner alongside his father and the other royals.

I dine with them in a grand hall, with purple stained-glass windows that let a violet light filter in and slant over our faces. It takes a few meals before I adjust to the fact that everyone around me looks like a blueberry.

Though most nobles outside the royal family sit at the surrounding tables, I am at the head table with the king, Lady Kat, Caden, and a few select others. I suspect it's done simply to discomfit me. I spend the majority of these dinners in silence, letting the chatter of the nobility fill my ears and pretending that the silverware clinking against glass is just tankards clanking together. The illusion is spoiled when I look around and Da isn't there.

One evening, a visiting lord is seated beside me. I don't catch his name, but he must be close to the king. The gossip that envelops me has reached his ears, and after imbibing too much of the wine accompanying the meal, he asks me about growing up in a tavern.

There's a grin on my face before he completes the question. It's nice to be reminded of happier times amidst the worried clouds that hang about my head. No one else here acknowledges my past, but it is a barrier between me and the rest of them, even unspoken.

"It was hectic usually, my lord," I say. My toothy smile spreads unabashedly as I imagine darting from table to table, clutching a bunch of pints in my hands. "We competed with another brewer in the village for business, but the villagers always said that Da and I were the better of the two. They told us that we Perdits were—"

"That's quite enough." The king's goblet smacks down on the table. I jump and swivel to face him, shocked at the interruption. "Hold your tongue, Lady Breena. If I find you continue to misuse it, then by the ether, I will cut it out."

"As you should. I mean, really," Kat says from several places down. "Must we discuss your uncouth past at the dinner table?"

Uncouth? Furious, my fingers clutch around my fork—which is the wrong one, I am sure, for stabbing the back of Lady Kat's hand.

"Quite right." The king nods his agreement. The red bristles of his beard fold between his fingers as his hand comes up to settle on his chin. "And need I remind you, you are not a Perdit, Lady Breena."

It is physically difficult to restrain myself from snapping at them as Lady Kat meets my gaze and holds it, smirking. The metal handle of my fork pushes a groove into my palm so hard I'm certain it will darken into a bruise. I *am* a Perdit. The name is mine. They'll not take that, too. Secan is nothing to me.

And I'm *not* uncouth. If anyone is, it's them. They dirty the kingdom with their leadership by the simple fact of their *presence* in it.

I rip my eyes away and stare down at the bowl of lentil soup in front of me. Tiny ripples dance in the sea of spices.

I hadn't been aware that the subject of my upbringing was forbidden. The injustice burns through me. If I'm to be the subject of palace gossip, it seems ridiculous that I can't provide my own point of view.

"Is something wrong, Lady Breena?" Kat simpers. "Is the soup not up to your high standards?"

The soup is fine, I feel like saying. *Delightful, even. It's* you *who aren't up to my standards.* I hurriedly spoon the soup into my mouth before the words can fly loose from my tongue.

It's best I abandon this particular vein of thought. It's in my best interests for them to see me as obedient. Perhaps it'll be easier if I tell myself that I'm imagining all of this—every bit of the last few weeks. Just to get through the meal.

This is a dream, I tell myself firmly, trying it.

But no, that doesn't work either. "This is a dream" turns into "this is a delusion" before both are thrown overboard for "this is a nightmare."

And honestly, if that's the case, I'd quite like to wake up.

The king watches me from his seat at the head of the table, his head leaning comfortably on his hand. Caden sits at his right, and next to him, the green-eyed girl. Both of their faces are wiped of expression as they methodically work their way through the meal.

"Lady Breena, I believe you were asked a question," the king prompts. His eyes glint dangerously, waiting for me to misstep or openly defy him.

I take a sharp breath. I'll tell *him* what I think of his sodding soup—

Caden's rigid manner breaks as his eyes meet mine and he gives a barely perceptible shake of his head. Not now, he seems to be telling me. Choose your moment.

My mouth closes. I swallow hard.

"The soup is fine."

Sixteen

The stories go that our world was the second one made. Before the land that holds realms like Egria and Nereidium, there had been another, the one unto which the Makers, the Father and the Mother, had been born. But that world was filled with such corruption and death that they retreated into the sky, where they beheld with sorrow the world that they loved falling to ruins from war and hatred.

The Mother wept, and the Father lapped up her tears until his thirst was so quenched that he could do nothing more to ebb their flow. And so he joined her, intertwining her body with his until, between them, the glowing lakes and oceans emerged. And there, they saw, was a new land, pregnant with promise, cleansed of the evil from their former world.

Here was a chance, they thought, to start anew. For the beings that lived there to live *good* lives. They tied some of the people to the world itself so that they would avoid the temptation to pollute it with darkness, as had happened in the last lands.

Those chosen ones had been the first Elementals.

I don't know *all* of the finer points contained in the Creation Scrolls, but I understand one thing: the Makers failed. Our world is as corrupt as the last.

Perhaps that's just the nature of life, of sentience and free will breathed into a creature. They turn from good intentions. Not all of them, but they all make choices. Some decisions are the right ones; some are the wrong ones; and whatever they do, they lead their fellow man further down a path of good or evil. Creatures created from truth learn what it is to speak a lie and—even worse—that there's *gain* to be had in those falsehoods.

What I'd told Caden was true: worship services when I'd lived in Abeline had been a rarity. We didn't have a chapel in the village and such a trek to visit the priests and priestesses necessitated that Da and I learn to appreciate the Makers in the comfort of our own home.

It's not an option I'm given here; services in the palace are mandatory after my first week.

Midweek, Emis and Gisela escort me past the stables, past the pasture where I'd ridden a few days ago, to a rocky outcropping of jagged white stones that jut up from the earth, defiant, lining the edge of a cliff. There's a pretty path of flat stones leading up to the chapel doors, but I'm distracted by the sight beyond them.

The ocean. How can it be here? The lands around the king's stronghold are as confused as the castle itself. Just as the castle's design looks like it sprang from dozens of different minds, the earth in the capital changes from desert to forest to sea.

The waters draw me forward as if I'm pulled by the ebb and flow of the tide itself. My ladies fall behind me as I move toward it.

I've never seen such a large body of water before. The closest I've come is the river behind the Bridge and Duchess. But the sea below me smells of salt and secrets and stretches beyond the horizon to somewhere where the Egrian king is only a name whispered on the wind.

From the dizzying height of the cliff, I watch it buck like an untamed animal, seething and reaching up for the earth that towers above it. It crashes, roaring mightily and lashing its frothy waves against the cliffs.

It wants me.

I shudder, breaking free of the hold the hypnotic waves have on me. Bodies of water aren't capable of thought, and even if they *were,* what business would they have with me? I doubt the ocean wants a pint of Bridge and Duchess ale. Not that I have that to offer any longer anyway.

"Lady Breena?" Gisela's voice is hesitant and penetrates the fog of my thoughts. The tinkling of chimes reaches my ears, announcing that services are about to begin.

"Coming," I call. I fall back from the edge, the wind whipping the short strands of my hair. I hook a lock of it behind my ear absentmindedly as I follow my ladies.

The chapel is impressive. Situated precariously amongst the cliffs and pointed rocks, it makes a disconcerting statement. It looks like it sits at the end of the world. Built with heavy white-washed stone, a pale wooden door bars the entrance with the symbol of the Makers burned into it: two clasped hands with a single teardrop hovering above.

I hustle inside behind my ladies, out of the range of the sun's rays beginning to beat down upon us.

Services are supposed to take place midday. I remember that much (though dimly) from the few services Da and I made it to when I was a child. The children of the Makers' world are supposed to pause all other tasks in the middle of the day—in the middle of the week—and give thanks for the world we've been blessed with.

I can't stop the blasphemous thought that races through my mind: I have precious few blessings to be giving thanks for these days.

The chapel fills with people as the chimes grow louder and louder. Gisela points me to the front of the aisle, between the rows lined with fluffy pillows to kneel upon.

"We'll be seated in the back," she says. "Only nobility are permitted to sit so close to the priests and priestesses."

My heart squirms in my chest. The king and his family are seated up front beside Lady Kat and a slew of nobles I don't recognize. If I have any say in the matter, I'll be keeping far away from them.

"I'd much rather sit with you ladies," I say, doing my

best to sound firm about it.

Emis gives me a sad smile. "You cannot, my lady. You would only make things worse for yourself."

"That seems an impossibility," I mutter. How can things get worse at this point?

Emis gives my hand a quick squeeze. "You have the right to sit there, my lady. Don't let them make you doubt yourself."

"I'm not doubting anything," I say quickly. "It would simply please me to sit in the back." My proclamation emerges louder than I would have liked, and several heads twist in my direction.

Gisela starts to placate me. "Lady Breena—"

"Stop calling me that—I'm not a lady," I hiss. The words run together, leaving without my permission. My tongue curls against my teeth as I regret the outburst.

Splendid, Bree. You're going to do very well getting Da out of prison if you can't even last a week without testing the ropes that bind you.

I clear my throat and straighten my shoulders, ignoring the piteous looks my ladies are now giving me and the attention I'm drawing from the strangers festooned in silks and jewels. Giving up the argument as a lost cause, I sidle through the crowded aisle to the first available pillow I see and settle myself down.

At least the palace chapel has the comfort of the pillows to be said for it. The small chapel in the north had boasted nothing but hard wooden floors—a great discomfort to kneel upon for the hours of worship. If *this* was what Da had been used to in services before he'd lived in Abeline, no wonder he hadn't wanted to make the trip to worship. They barely warrant comparison.

"Lady Breena!" The voice rings out over the assembled conversation.

I cringe, ducking my head and wishing for the power to be invisible. There must be an element with the ability to hide me, and I wish with all of my might for the power to wield it now.

My eyes travel to the front row where the king's expectant gaze meets mine. This is the man to whom all in the kingdom are expected to bear an implicit loyalty. If it wasn't such a terrible thought, I could laugh at how starkly it stands in juxtaposition to my own feelings.

The sight of his face makes the tiny pool of hope that I carry within me—the one I can only summon after several hours away from his company each night—evaporate. His dark gray eyes are so different from his son's. Devoid of humor, they look nearly black in spite of the well-lit chapel.

"There is a seat for you here."

He doesn't raise his voice this time. He doesn't have to. A hush has fallen over the other worshippers so that it carries easily to my ears. It's not a request, but a veiled order. I push myself to my feet and pad forward, my quiet footsteps resounding in the silent chapel. I fix a strained smile on my face.

Caden nods in acknowledgement as I pass him. Lady Kat smirks at me, arms crossed over her chest and tapping a finger in the crook of her elbow impatiently.

The open seat is between the king himself and the girl with the peridot eyes, whose name I still don't know. I stiffly kneel beside them. It feels a little too much like bowing, like my body is telling a lie in which I swear fealty to this man I hate.

"Lady Breena, I don't believe you've had the pleasure of being introduced to the Princess Aleta," the king says softly. His whisper is a scythe through leaves, slicing through the air with a dangerous bite as he watches me closely for a reaction.

I do a double-take. The princess? I'd been so sure that Caden was the only heir to the throne. I didn't know he had a sister.

"His Majesty neglects to mention that I am not a princess of these lands." The princess's tone is dry. She must be very bold to feel secure enough to correct the king. I'm sure people have been executed for less.

"You will be." Inclining his head conspiratorially toward me, he explains. "Her Highness is my ward and betrothed to my son. She'll be a princess of Egria soon enough." His fingers squeeze her shoulder tightly, her skin paling around his grip.

Princess Aleta's fist clenches in the folds of her dress but relaxes again so quickly I think I might have imagined the movement. "Indeed, Your Majesty. The day shan't come soon enough."

I notice the barest emphasis on "shan't." As though Aleta doesn't want the day to come at all.

Caden cranes his neck around the figures between us. "Loathe as I am to interrupt my lovely bride-to-be—and my father's wedding dreams—I think we can save such talk until Her Highness and Lady Breena are better acquainted."

"Where are you—what lands do you hail from, Your Highness?" I inquire, my tongue fumbling the more formal speech.

The king answers for Aleta, though the princess looked ready to speak for herself. "She was born in Nereidium. But it was a land torn in chaos and tumult. Her Highness has resided in Egria since she was a babe after my emissaries rescued her during a riot and we provided her with asylum within our borders. We couldn't leave the only heir to their throne in such dire straits. Egria has been her home ever since."

Her home. I have a sneaking suspicion that between the king's condescending tone and the way the princess's eyes are locked on the crease where wall meets ceiling without blinking that she regards the palace as her home about as much as I do.

Which is to say, not at all.

The chapel chimes abruptly cease, and three clear gongs sound. A priest and priestess of the Makers dressed in white robes that slink along the floor take the stage, and then silence rings out as clearly as the bells.

I rest my hands on my knees and let myself focus on something bigger than my problems for a little while.

Stepping out of the chapel after the service, I squint, raising a hand to shield my eyes. Perhaps someday I'll grow used to the beacon of light that is the sun here in the south, but that time has yet to arrive. If I have my way, it never will.

People still mill about, discussing the sermon. It had been…interesting. The priest and priestess talked about the incarnations of the Makers. How the Father embodies air and earth, oscillating between solid and invisible, while the Mother is flame and water, flowing over the land, peaceful when it suits her and burning rage when it does not.

The service hadn't been as bad as I'd expected, given my previous conversation with Caden, but then again, I'd not paid as much attention as I should have. I'd been preoccupied by the pressure of being thrust into the center of attention in the chapel.

I made my getaway quickly when they concluded with the customary "And by the ether, let it be," excusing myself outside before the king could stop me.

"A word?"

Taken by surprise, the maneuvers Da taught me to dissuade overzealous patrons in the tavern take over. I lash out as a hand falls on my shoulder.

The king catches my fist in his. My quick movements were for nothing. More still, they'd been downright foolish. My heart pounds. I've all but attacked the king, and I stand on precarious ground with him already.

"A word," he says again. Menace lives in the growl of his words.

Unable to speak around the weight of my tongue, I nod, following him to the side of the chapel. He waves his guards, Lady Kat included, off. The countess frowns and stomps away. I'm relieved. The king is bad enough. I don't need both of them at once.

Against the side of the chapel, the cliff winds seize at my skirts.

The king gazes out at the horizon, pensive, and turns his dark gaze onto me contemplatively.

I find my voice. "You wanted a word with me, Your Majesty?" And that would imply *using* said words.

"I did." He clasps his hands behind his back and surveys me.

I fight the urge to squirm under that intent gaze. My eyes fall to the grass he treads beneath his polished shoes. What does he want with me now? Is this confrontation because he wants me to be uncomfortable, like the dinners? He can consider his task achieved. I've never felt more out of my element than I do here, with my words held captive by etiquette before a man I detest.

"Your father," the king says abruptly.

I start, eyes flying up from my study of his stance. Whatever I'd been expecting, it hadn't been that. "What *about* my father?" I hear the defensive note in my voice and do my best to correct it with a subservient "Your

Majesty."

"What do you know of the last mission he was on in service of the crown? The treasure he sought?"

What is this treasure the king's after? A weapon? Whatever it is, he can't want it for anything good. Embarrassingly enough though, I can answer his question with complete honesty.

"Nothing," I say. "In truth, Your Majesty, I know nothing of any of his missions. I only just learned of his abilities as an Adept a few weeks ago."

"Yes, he was one of the greats," the king muses, lost in thought. "A most valuable asset. It was a pity when we thought him lost to us. And it is a pity that we cannot trust his loyalty now."

I fixate on that word—asset—and my blood boils at the turn of phrase. The king speaks as if people are things he owns that add value to his estate. I draw my lips tight to keep from telling him how wrong he is. He doesn't own Da, and he certainly doesn't own me.

"Your mother?"

I don't bother asking what he wants to know this time. "Died birthing me, Your Majesty."

He nods, taking this information in, and rocks back on his heels. His boots shine in the sunlight. "It's wrong for a child to be parted from a father," he says.

"Your Majesty?" The odd jump in the conversation throws me. I don't dare let cautious hope creep into my voice. It's too much to hope that he may free Da. Free us both.

"I shall arrange for you to visit him," he says. "A half hour's time twice a week is fair, I think."

"I am…grateful, Your Majesty," I say, struggling to form coherent words, coherent thoughts. Visits aren't what I'd prefer, but they're better than nothing. Better than not seeing Da at all, not ever again.

"There is a caveat or two." He lifts one finger in the air in warning. "First, I may make certain requests of you during your time here. It would do you well not to pretend at defying me.

"During your visits, you may discuss whatever it is that fathers and daughters discuss. I do not care for your petty remembrances and the minutiae of your day that I'm sure you'll share with him. In return, you must investigate the matter of his last mission. The treasure he was sent to retrieve, the details of the mission. If you fail…" He smirks. "Well, I stand by what I said: it's wrong for a child to be parted from her father."

My throat is dry. I'm not sure what the threat is exactly—that I'll join Da in prison? More likely, the king plans to unite us in death should I fail. But I know before he's finished speaking that I'll assent to the king's terms, despite the fact that his unmentioned "requests" make me uneasy. My ladies are nice enough and Caden seems a pleasant sort, but they aren't my family. My only link to who I really am is locked in a jail cell. I nod my agreement.

"I am glad we have managed to strike an accord, Lady Breena." His lips curve up slowly, pleased. He holds out his hand, glittering with rings, and I hesitate, taking his fingertips in hand and bending at the knee, hoping that I've struck the right chord of deference.

"He may not tell me anything," I blurt. Shame burns through me at the admittance, and I drop the king's fingers, straightening. What if Da still clings to his secrets? "He kept all of this from me for the whole of my life, Your Majesty. It might be beyond me to get to him to reveal anything now."

The king turns away, lips still curved. As he leaves me, the wind catches his parting shot, tossing it over his shoulder to me as I stand with the ocean at my back, waiting to catch me if I fall.

"Try."

Seventeen

Days pass and I hear no more from the king on the subject. He's absent from dinners, something I'm not inclined to complain about. Despite his claims that the king is a good father, Caden is noticeably relaxed when the king isn't around. He jokes more, laughs often. Princess Aleta acts as she always has and stays silent, speaking only when spoken to as Lady Kat watches us. As far as I'm concerned, the fewer meals I have to endure in the king's presence, the better. Though I *am* anxious to see Da again.

I'm thankful when my ladies tell me I'll be permitted to take luncheon in my rooms. I haven't quite adjusted to thinking of them as mine. The dusty gold plating surrounding me is uncomfortably distant from the small room where I'd had one wooden chest and a pallet on the floor drowning in quilts.

After a meal of tea and chilled cucumber sandwiches, Gisela rings for maid service to fetch the dirty dishes and practically pushes me out the door. I need to attempt to socialize with others in my class, they tell me. They think that joining in on the ladies' sewing circle is the best way to do that.

"I don't really know how to sew."

I figure it's best to tell them now before we walk the entire length of the castle to get there and they have to stand in the corner, embarrassed for me. It's a thing I've discovered they do, my ladies. When I can't find it in me to be embarrassed over something, they suffer the emotion in my stead. Last week, when I'd confused an ancient knight's young wife for his daughter, Gisela looked as though she'd melt into the floor.

The ladies halt, turning to me with heads tilted like dogs who have heard a curiously new sound.

"You cannot sew?" Emis asks. "You jest. Truly?"

"Really, truly," I confirm. "I can sew a patch onto clothes, fix a tear, or attach a button. That's about it. I assume the sewing that you mean is more of the embroidery sort?"

They don't answer but turn to each other, silently conferring. Gisela frowns, shaking her head. Emis sighs. I study the vaulted ceilings and wait patiently.

"How do you feel about gardening?" Emis asks finally.

I perk up. If it'll keep me out of the sewing circle and in the open air, I feel *excellent* about it. "Better than sewing, that's for certain. I used to take care of a few herbs for Da. I'm still a novice, but how hard is it to pick up a trowel?"

Gisela nods decisively. "It's decided then. We'll

escort you to the garden."

They make me change first, into a plain dress made of a stiffer material. Emis stands before me and mimes for me to hold my arms out so that she can slip the sleeves over them. I groan, fidgeting, and receive a lightning-quick pinch for my trouble. Right. Groaning isn't ladylike. My arms grow heavy from hovering in the air.

"I'm nearly seventeen. I can dress myself." The complaint is one of habit now.

"Lady Breena, there are twenty buttons on the back of this shift. They lead from your waist all the way up to the back of your neck. How, pray tell, do you propose to contort yourself in order to do them up?" Gisela asks me with exaggerated interest.

I still in response.

They take that as a signal of my cooperation and hook the buttons hurriedly, affixing the skirt over my shift. A hat is pinned to my head. "To protect you from the sun," Emis explains.

Upon our arrival, I learn that the so-called "garden" is no simple patch of herbs. Blooms burst out at me when I come upon an iron gate. Ivy twines itself around the bars. The plants and flowers come in all colors and shades imaginable. A clean, fresh scent floats from a delicate periwinkle blossom. A slightly more earthy one from a lavender bloom.

"I get to work with these?" I ask, heady with the scents and sights before me.

"Unfortunately, no. These are the duties of the king's

garden staff. He employs several Shakers that he allowed to retire from his forces. It's the more delicate side of their gift. *You* will be working with the roses alongside Princess Aleta."

Just Aleta? It occurs to me that it's odd that it will be only the two of us, and I wonder at it aloud.

"The princess is…particular," Emis says. It takes her a moment to find the right word. "Her garden is a small bequeathal that His Majesty bestowed upon her. She permits only one lady to assist her at a time, so that she may monitor her work. In such warm months as these, most prefer the shade of the indoors, so her schedule has been quite free."

After equipping me with a small trowel and shovel, some miniature garden shears, and a watering can, they show me the way to the flowers in question: white roses. Intricate things, the petals spiral in on each other. The lithe figure of the princess is crouched in the dirt, hands busy with the shears as someone holds a parasol above her. Her dark hair spills over her back, loose and unbound.

My ladies nod at me encouragingly, and I kneel beside the princess. "Good day to you, Your Highness," I say.

"Good day," Princess Aleta says without moving her eyes from her roses. She examines the roots critically and paws through the fresh dirt with her trowel.

This is a different sort of gardening from my herbs, when simple watering and trimming would do. I tentatively reach my trowel into the dirt and sift through it, careful not to disturb any of the roots.

"It's a lovely day, isn't it?" *Wonderful way to make friends, Bree. Comment on the* weather.

Aleta only trims a few leaves from the bushes.

I lick at the beads of sweat forming on my upper lip, trying not to be obvious about it. It's so *hot* here in the capital. I'd been thrilled to get out of the confining walls of the palace after spending the past few days holed up inside but hadn't thought forward to the sweltering heat.

"It's a bit warm. I'm from the north, you know. It's probably snowing there now. I don't know *how* it's so warm here." I feel as though I'm chattering on, but no one stops me.

"It's likely you passed the Makers' Margin on your trek. It accounts for the barriers in seasons in the realm," she says shortly.

"Oh. Yes, I guess that must be it."

She turns back to her roses, and I rack my mind for something else to say. If I can make a friend out of anyone, it should be the princess. She doesn't seem like she wants to be under the king's thumb any more than I do. Though she doesn't seem particularly eager to be my friend either.

"I thought that roses were red," I say, a half-question. The flowers that Da middle-named me for look pale and unassuming without the scarlet color to them.

"*These* are white," the princess snaps.

A stab of irritation gouges me. "Yes, I can see that," I

say waspishly. She doesn't have to be so curt. "I wondered why."

"And, had you asked, I would have answered you."

I stake my trowel into the dirt and face her. The princess is carefully toeing the line of rude and polite, slipping ever closer to rude. I don't need friends like her. "Have I done something to offend you, Your Highness?"

"Your very presence offends me."

Curses rise to my lips, but I stifle them. I *had* wanted honesty from someone in the castle, and here I've found it in the form of a girl who glares at me, the sun shining into her eyes so brightly that they seem yellow.

"You wonder why there is a lack of red in my rose garden. Look around you. Do you see red blossoms anywhere in the king's gardens? Have you seen it *anywhere* in the palace decor in the time that you have been here?"

I open my mouth, but close it again, a fish tossed onto dry land. No, I realize. The flowers in the royal garden had been purple, blue, yellow—but none were red.

The look on my face answers for me. "There are two colors to which specific meanings are assigned by the Egrian king. Violet—all shades of it—are reserved for the royal family. Red roses grow only outside the dungeons. Red means death. Murder. Someone who has taken another life."

No wonder Lady Kat wears the color so often. She's boasting.

Aleta pushes herself to her feet and nods to the

attendant behind her, who hurries to her side with the parasol. She's ready to leave. I scramble to my feet as well, absorbing this new information. In Abeline, colors are just colors. It's not a custom—or law, whatever it may be—that's made it that far north.

"But you must know that, surely," Aleta says. Her words are an innocent bundle of firewood in a hearth, safe until the wood shifts and the embers still glowing beneath it leap out to burn me. "Your father must don red quite often."

A rushing sound fills my ears. How dare she? The princess doesn't know Da. She knows *nothing* about him to throw out accusations like that as it pleases her.

"My father is *not* a killer." I don't mean to shout, but I *do* mean to say it. The people here expect too much of my silence. I won't stay quiet on this. Da is many, many things. The longer I'm here, the more I learn about him. But a killer? I refuse to swallow that elixir. I may not know all the facts of his past, but I know his heart. He's a good man.

"Oh, but he is," Aleta says. She moves her attendant aside with one hand and pushes close to me, a finger prodding my shoulder. She moves so quickly, almost eagerly. Like she's been *waiting* for this confrontation. My ladies don't stop her, and I don't think they should. I want to hear what she has to say, so I can tell her why she's wrong. The princess stands a head taller than me. She breathes hard, like a dragon. I half-expect smoke to unfurl from her nostrils. "And if you wonder why your presence offends me?" Her whisper is dangerous. "You may think on your parentage, Lady Breena."

She backs away before I can demand her meaning, back into the shade of her parasol, and spins sharply on her heel, retreating down the dirt path, her attendant struggling to keep pace with her.

I realize I'm panting as if I've just run up a flight of stairs.

"Ridiculous," I mutter, swiping angrily at the dirt on my knees to occupy myself. I wipe a hand along the back of my neck to catch the sweat that drips there. Tears sting my eyes, an after-effect of the anger that's beginning to ebb, and I press the heel of my palm to them.

The princess left her tools behind, and Emis and Gisela are collecting them silently, not responding to my comment.

"Ridiculous," I say louder, wanting their confirmation. "Can you believe her?"

They avoid my gaze.

Doubt drips into my thoughts. *No.* Horror brushes over me. Do Aleta's words have some credence?

I snatch the princess's gardening shears from Gisela's hands and hold them behind my back, waiting for her and Emis to meet my eyes. They couldn't be more unwilling, but both do so and there's pity in their eyes.

"Is my da what she says?" *Please,* I think desperately. *Makers, please give me this.* I dearly want them to contradict me.

A breeze blows past, pulling at their hair. They don't

answer, and my heart sinks.

"*Is* he what she *says*?" I raise my voice, not liking the harsh, commanding tone that emerges. But I *will* have an answer, one way or another.

"We don't know, my lady," Emis says, finally. She puts a placating hand on my wrist and gently takes the shears from my hold. "The matters between the Court Rider and His Majesty were kept quite confidential. There were rumors, of course, but…" She trails off.

"What rumors? What did people say?" I demand. I have a right to know, don't I? He's *my* father.

Emis shakes her head. "I'm sorry. I'll not cloud your judgment with unsubstantiated claims." She retreats into silence and busies herself with opening a parasol to shade me. "You're flushed, my lady."

They've given me the honesty I wished for again, but somehow, Emis keeping quiet on the subject of rumors does nothing to assuage my fears. I leave the parasol's shadow in a daze, collecting my things to go inside, my movements jerky.

Wishes, I am finding, are fickle things when they turn on you.

Eighteen

The next day, my "education" begins.

Perhaps the king has forgotten his talk of allowing me to speak to Da. Perhaps he's given up on the idea that I'll be able to wrangle information from him. Regardless of whatever thoughts whirl about his head, he sends a summons to my room after dressing one morning that I'm to meet with a tutor named Larsden "or face difficulties."

I scoff at that. As if I don't already face difficulties. The threat's nonsensical.

This must be the first of those "favors" he mentioned, but I've never resisted learning, even if that learning has been limited to things like stews, ales, and letters until now. Da didn't have much in the way of books beyond the Creation Scrolls, and I didn't care to study those. Anything else he had was a study of the political history of faraway lands like Nereidium, Clavins, and the wars across the nations.

I'd teased him about them. "Live in the present, Da!" I'd said a few times, closing his open book and shoving it behind my back with an impish grin. "Isn't it better to focus on the war we're to wage on Jowyck's profits tonight?"

That, of course, had been before I'd understood so much of our present to be tied up in his past.

The king doesn't realize it, but he's done *me* a favor. My ladies are at a loss as to what to do with me. I can't go to the sewing circle, and I'd rather sit in the cells with Da than endure another prickly meeting over thorned bushes with Aleta.

That thought gives me pause as I set off for my lessons. I wonder how Da's doing. Are they feeding him decently? Is it dark in the cells? Hot? Damp? Despite how hard I've tried not to let myself wallow, my thoughts have a way of turning in on themselves, back around to Da.

I push open the door of the room where I'm meant to be meeting Tutor Larsden and shiver. Whether or not Da's cell is dark, *this* place is. And cold, too. Colder than I've been since my journey south. I sneeze.

"Hello?" I call. "Tutor Larsden?"

A scuffling sound comes from below me as I descend the stairs. It's dark as pitch in here, the stairs swallowed up by cavernous blackness. I trace my hand along the wall as I feel tentatively for the step below me. The ground evens out.

What is this? I wonder. I rub at my arms to ward off a sudden chill. I hadn't been sure until this moment that it could even *get* cold in the South.

"This is hardly an effective teaching method," I say,

determined not to sound as unnerved as I feel.

"I disagree."

I whirl. The voice is a vapor, surrounding me and disappearing again. It echoes, and I can't pinpoint its location.

There's someone in the room with me. "Tutor Larsden?" I ask again. "Is that you?" I've never met the man and can't recognize the voice on sound alone.

Tutor Larsden—I assume that it's him, anyway— ignores this. "A shame you can't see down here, isn't it? To know for sure?"

"Yes. It is," I say, annoyed.

There's a hint of a giggle in his voice. "It's cold, too."

I sneeze again, wrapping my arms around myself, longing for Da's bear-like coat. "Quite cold, yes."

"Why don't you light a torch?"

"I haven't a flint. Why don't *you?*" I ask pointedly.

"Light one anyway."

What? This man is insane. No wonder the king enjoys working with him; they're kindred spirits.

It slowly dawns on me what he's suggesting. Light one anyway. The only people who can do that are Fire Elementals. "I'm not a Torcher, sir."

"Aren't you?"

"No, I'm not." I snap at him this time. Will people never stop assigning unwanted and, moreover, unrealistic labels to me?

"But you could be."

"*No,* I couldn't. Look, would you kindly light a

torch?" I ask, exasperated. "It's disconcerting to address the shadows this way."

A small flame flares to life ahead of me, igniting over a lantern. I shuffle toward the source of light. A shadowy figure walks toward a wall and draws a pulley. Light floods into the room as a curtain flies upward.

Tutor Larsden stands before the window. He's not a large man. In fact, he looks rather frail. His olive skin is wrinkled, hanging off of his bones in a way that suggests his age. It flops at his arms as he lights the candle. My impression of him clears as my eyes adjust to the sudden influx of light. His eyes are a ruddy brown, emphasized by the bloodshot quality to them.

"His Majesty has asked me to see to your studies."

"Yes, I gathered that," I say. The note said as much. I find a chair and settle into it. Exactly what these studies are to entail, I've yet to figure out, but I'm beginning to doubt I'll be learning arithmetic.

"Have you ever Torched, Lady Breena?" Larsden circles a table and leans against it, studying me.

"This again?" I swear, it's like speaking to a child. And as if I *am* explaining something to a small child, I speak distinctly, enunciating every word. "It's as I told Lady Katerine when she retrieved us *weeks* ago. I'm not yet seventeen. Even if I *was* an Elemental, I wouldn't know. My birthday and Reveal haven't arrived."

"That is, by and large, the popular school of thought." he agrees somewhat cryptically. "But I do wonder. How could an ability as powerful as that of an Adept hide within someone for so long without any hint of what's to come?"

What in Egria's green pastures does he mean? That's just the way things *are*. It's the natural order of things. Elementals aren't Elementals until at least their seventeenth birthday. Until then, they're just like the rest of us. Even common folk like me know that.

"My...shall we say, 'flexible' way of thinking is why His Majesty has asked me to work with you. Torchers are the most common of the Adepts in Egria. We'll begin by assessing your affinity to the flames."

At this, alarm stirs in me. "And just how do you intend to do that?"

He sighs, the points of his shoulders descending as he exhales. "I had hoped it would be easier than you're making it. I thought that perhaps if it was colder than you liked or darker maybe. I had hoped that if I simply *unnerved* you enough, the ability would light around you."

"But it didn't," I finish. My voice is flat. It doesn't betray how wary I feel, the degree to which I really *am* unnerved. "So what will you do now?"

His teeth are blindingly white as his lips spread in a grin. He holds up a candle.

"Well, that's simple, really, Lady Breena. We have to see how you burn."

Nineteen

The door bangs behind me as I flee.

Have the lessons or face difficulties is it? I'll handle his difficulties, then. I let rage envelop me. Fear will soon encroach if I don't. Whether or not it was a part of our bargain, I'll not allow the king's mad "tutor" to *burn* me in the name of science. They're playing a sickening game. I wonder if I'm the first they've played it with, and the thought makes me ill.

No one knows if the Elemental gift is passed from person to person or at random. The heredity is sometimes thinly linked through families, but not always. I feel queasy thinking of other "lessons" that may have taken place in that cellar or elsewhere in the realm with people who weren't able to flee as quickly as I had at the intimation of torture.

My thoughts pause in their restless circling as I wonder why they'd want to begin with Torching for me anyway. In the case that the ability *is* inherited, testing me for an affinity to fire would be useless, wouldn't it? Why should I be able to Torch if Da's an Air Elemental?

Shouldn't their hypothesis be that I'm a Rider?

Maybe my ma had been a Torcher? Da never said. I add it to the list of questions I'll ask Da if and when the meeting that the king said he'd arrange ever happens.

I'm still storming through the castle under a cloud of anger, climbing staircases and turning corners at random, when I hear footsteps heading my way. I'm not in the mood to curtsy and pretend at politeness if I happen upon someone. My steps slow as I realize the hallway surrounding me is unrecognizable. I barely resist the urge to scream. Without my ladies to guide me, I've gotten myself well and truly lost.

I slump against the wall. What a disjointed place this palace is. I'd fled stone corridors, dark with dangerous intent, but now find myself standing on marble floors, bright and polished. This must be a newer addition to the castle. Do the royals just add rooms on when they get bored?

"Enough!"

I straighten, startled by the nearby shout and subsequent crash that follows. Was that the king? Have I really wandered so far from my rooms as to find the advisory hall?

"I tire of the excuses, Adept Tregle," the monarch of Egria says menacingly.

Tregle? Creeping closer to the open doorway where the voice came from, I flatten myself to the wall. Pacing footsteps echo in the room I hover outside. Tregle's been gone since the day I arrived. I haven't seen even a hint of him or Baunnid since Tregle left us in the dungeons with that cryptic statement.

They're going to kill us anyway.

I doubt that very much.

"I'm sorry, Your Majesty. I'm merely stating the facts as my commanding officer has given them to me to deliver unto you. We are still unable to take Nereidium by force."

There's a clatter, the distinctive sound of a metal bowl as it crashes to the ground and spins around and around. I wince. A result of the king's temper, no doubt. Tregle's lucky it wasn't thrown at his head.

The name "Nereidium" plucks a chord in my memory. That's Aleta's kingdom, isn't it? What does the king want with it? *Why* would he need to take it by force when he has a presumable marriage contract with Aleta and Caden's pending nuptials? Why would he waste the military resources?

"As it was last time, it's their navy, Your Majesty. It's too formidable. Their Throwers number too many, and as they're an island nation, we cannot take such forces on without control over the waters. Egria's scouting ship was destroyed. Again."

A chair's legs squeal along the floor, followed by a *wuft* of air as someone sits down.

"If we were able to arrive at their shores, this wouldn't be the issue that it is. My Torchers and Riders would trounce them."

"Indeed, Your Majesty," Tregle says tiredly. I take a guess that he's heard these disgruntled rantings before.

"If I had a *damned* Thrower—" The king stops. There's only silence. And then: "What of the girl?"

"Her maids report that she's done as you ask. They've kept her busy with etiquette, and she's with Larsden now."

"Do we trust the maids? Or is it your belief that they'd benefit from a little...incentive?" The king's voice trails off suggestively.

Tregle takes a beat to answer. "As far as we can tell, they're Egrian loyals."

My pulse pounds in my throat as they pause. Why all of this talk about my maids?

"Dismissed, Adept Tregle."

They're finished talking, and I press myself beside a tapestry of the first Elementals, heart pounding. Should I run before the king realizes he's been overheard? This scene is too familiar. I've stumbled upon hearing something I shouldn't have again. If the king sees me... I relax when Tregle leaves the room at a soft clip, alone.

His tall figure retreats down the hallway. I bite my lip indecisively and then, cursing my curiosity, follow him past the open door. I chance a glance inside and am thankful to see that the king's back is to me.

He studies something on the table. I'm dying to get a look at whatever it is, but all I can see is the curled corner of a paper around his side. I decide not to press my luck and slip by, praying that the king is too preoccupied with his papers to notice, to hurry after Tregle.

"Tregle!" I hiss, feeling foolish. I don't dare raise my voice any louder. The marble in the hall echoes, and the last thing I want is for the king to hear me milling about, where he'll surely reach the conclusion that I've been eavesdropping.

The long black robe that marks Tregle as an Adept catches on a windowsill as he turns.

"Lady Breena," he says, voice surprised. "Good day."

"I am begging you," I say, skipping all greetings. "Please call me Bree. I'm going mad in here with all of the 'ladies' and 'lords' and 'pleases' and 'how do you dos.'"

His mouth twitches. "*Lady* Bree, then. I can't overstep any more than that. If someone overhears me, I'll be in a heap of trouble"

"It'll do." I'll take what I can get. I fall into step beside him, hoping he'll lead me out of this maze. The last time we walked together, I'd been bound up and trying to keep pace with him.

We're quiet. The only sounds are our footsteps as I struggle over how to bring up the conversation that I heard. I don't know how to bridge the silence or where he stands in the king's good graces. Tregle's loyal to the king—at least, moreso than I am. He gave Tregle a better life than he'd had when they found him. I'm not sure he'll be forthcoming with me about the details of the conversation.

When it comes right down to it, I barely know him. We only travelled together for a few weeks. I wonder: *are* things better for him here? Now that he has some measure of control over his abilities and all. Does he have friends? Do they go into the city and lark about from time to time?

I envy my imagination's version of Tregle, even without knowing the answer. I miss joking around with people without having to worry about saying the wrong thing.

"Haven't seen you about," I say finally.

"Yes. His Majesty sent Baunnid and I to confer with the navy. They were off on an exploratory mission toward Nereidium."

"Then Baunnid's back, too?"

"No," he says. "He went along for the ride." He's struggling to keep a serious face but obviously happy about being rid of him. The king said that his navy can't take on Nereidium's, I remember. And I wonder if Baunnid will be coming back.

I decide I don't care. He didn't show even a hint of remorse for everything he put me and Da through, and he probably tortured Tregle more than what I saw. I'd just as soon put him out of my mind.

"I'm glad to see you looking well," Tregle says.

"You seemed so certain I would be." Again, I remember the way he'd left me and Da, how he'd said that he didn't think the king would kill us.

He shrugs. "I didn't think the king would slay you or your father without trying to get information from him first. Besides, I heard the guards whispering about His Highness being retrieved. He tries to intervene where he can with his father, so I thought..."

Caden works *against* his father then? And so overtly that even the Adepts are aware of it?

Tregle rubs at the knuckle of his pointer finger absentmindedly.

"Well, you were right." I spread my arms sarcastically and drop them at my sides. "Here I am, as much good as it does me."

"Don't be so glum, Lady Bree. Better alive than dead. Better trapped in the castle than in a cell."

"Better even than being experimented on?"

"Experimented on?" Tregle missteps as he swivels to look at me. His mouth is open, and his eyebrows shoot up into his forehead.

"His Majesty has commanded me to 'work' with Tutor Larsden," I say bitterly. "He seems certain that I should be able to manipulate an Element, never *mind* that I'm not even old enough. They have theories on how to test it."

Tregle hesitates, his face frozen in an expression like he has something to say, but he's thought the better of it.

"Say it," I say, feeling exhausted. I'm emotionally wrung out today, and it's not even time for dinner. "I can tell you want to. Go on then. Put it out there."

He hesitates. "You won't thank me for it."

"Say it anyway. Really."

Tregle looks away. "Let him."

"Let him—*let* him?" My voice climbs the octaves into something rather like a shriek. Whatever work Tregle's been doing involving Nereidium, it's clearly *addled his brain.*

He winces, holding up his hands in a placating gesture. "It sounds awful, I know. But if you want to do yourself the smallest of favors, you'll take my advice. They're going to test you one way or another. If you appear compliant, they're much more likely to relax the watch on you."

My breath catches. "What watch on me?"

Tregle winces again. "I shouldn't have said—"

"*What* watch on me, Tregle?"

"Your lady's maids," he says in rush before he thinks the better of it. "They have to report to the king's advisors when you exhibit unusual behaviors throughout the day. Who you see, who you talk to, what you do... Actually, I'm surprised they're not with you now."

There it is. I'm a void of emotion. I can't even bring myself to feel surprised, but I'd dared to hope the reports the king asked Tregle about were the vague sort. I should have known. I remember how they inched closer when Caden and I spoke during our ride in the pasture. The few people that I've begun to think of as my allies in this are nothing more than the king's spies.

And Tregle knew about it. "If they report to the

king's advisors, what does that make you?"

"I work for Lady Katerine. She's his right hand." Quietly, he adds, "The maids may be in trouble for letting you wander about."

"They were meant to retrieve me after my 'lessons,'" I say dully. My eyes are curiously dry, like their moisture's been drained away along with any hopes I had of forming real friendships here. "I left early."

The hallways change again. The marble disappears as it gives way to a more populated wing of the palace, where girls in dresses that consume doorways are busy leaving sewing circles and dance lessons. The doors are framed in mahogany wood, and I blink, stopping short as Caden exits through one of them.

"Ah, Adept Tregle!" he says with every appearance of delight when he spots us. "And the Lady Breena." He executes a sweeping bow as people maneuver around us.

I'm mute. I've barely spoken to him lately, and I'm not sure I ought to now after everything I've learned today. I think of my ladies. I'd been so sure we were becoming friends—or something like it anyway. If *they* have ulterior motives, isn't it likely that the prince of the realm does? Whether he opposes his father or not.

Stuck on the idea, I fumble a curtsy at him while Tregle gives a perfunctory bow beside me. I try for a smile, but it wavers and falls instantly. Caden takes in our expressions, the pair of us wearing deep frowns, and his grin fades, gray eyes flicking between the two of us. "What's happened?"

"Not here," Tregle says. He jerks his head down a separate corridor, and Caden shakes his head briefly, his brown hair swinging with the movement.

"Too easy for someone to overhear us. Perhaps we should…"

"Yes," Tregle says immediately, catching his drift. "I think that that would be best."

They're so *familiar* with each other. I look back and forth between the two of them. A prince and a peasant Elemental. What ties can they possibly have? And both of them are too preoccupied with whatever it is that they're saying without *really* saying anything to bother informing me what it is.

"Yes," I mock, frustrated when I find my voice. "Of course *that* would be best. Why didn't *I* think of *that*?" I lift my skirts—the better to stomp away—but Caden catches the crook of my arm.

A rush floods through me, making me lose my breath. He drops my elbow like he's touched a hot pot, just as I jerk it from his hold. Caden shifts his weight to his other foot, clears his throat, and steps away. Tregle's knuckle goes to his lips thoughtfully as he considers the prince.

Avoiding my stare, Caden glances off into the dwindling people around us, who are more worried about their next destination than whatever it is we're doing.

"I apologize for my vagueness. I promise you, it's necessary. I wouldn't be so deliberately rude otherwise."

My heart is in my throat when he meets my gaze again and I look into his earnest gray eyes. The milling crowd, Tregle, and everyone else seems very far away suddenly.

"Easy enough to forgive, Your Highness," I say around the pulsing lump in my throat.

He smiles, and my lips curve up to match it before he breaks our eye contact.

"Lady Breena," he says formally, with another bow.

"Your Highness," I return with a curtsy, back to pretending.

Whenever I slip into the facade of this Lady Breena person, I'm beginning to feel like nothing but a marionette doll, lurching about on invisible strings.

Twenty

Later that night, after a dinner during which I was unable to swallow more than a few bites, I retire to my rooms. I fall asleep quickly enough and am dozing fitfully when a hand claps itself over my mouth.

I come awake instantly, screaming into the palm, but the sound is muffled by my captor's hand. It's dark. I can't see, I can't catch my breath, and I'd been dreaming that Tutor Larsden was burning me alive. The blood roars in my ears as I flail wildly back at my assailant. I buck, reaching behind me to gouge my fingers into their eyes, when a voice I recognize pleads, *"Please* stop screaming."

Tregle? I still, and the hand drops from my mouth. I wipe at it with the back of my palm. "What are you *doing* in here?" I say furiously. My voice is a whisper and a yell meeting halfway.

His features, barely visible in the darkness, arrange themselves into a worried expression. "His Highness sent me to fetch you. I had to wait until your lady's maids had gone to their rooms for the evening, and I didn't want to startle you so that you'd alert the guard."

"Did it ever occur to you, Tregle, that practically suffocating someone in their sleep is not the most ideal method of instilling a sense of calm in them?" Suffocating is probably stretching the truth a bit and dismay lines his features at the word, but my heart still hasn't recovered from the fright.

Moonlight drips into the room, lending just enough light for me to see once my eyes adjust. I process what Tregle's said. My ladies have gone. And Caden sent him? Why?

I start to voice the question, but he cuts me off. "We felt it would be safe to bring you into things. Given the circumstances."

"What 'things?'" It seems that every time I get information, it only leads to more questions.

"It's easier to let him tell you."

I sigh in annoyance and push my covers back. It's not that I can't understand a certain amount of showmanship, but everyone here is entirely too willing to cling to their mystery.

From my limited experience, I've learned that guards patrol the corridors of the palace constantly, so I assume that Tregle's bribed the one outside of my door to disappear long enough for us to slip outside. He gently closes my door behind us and motions for me to follow. His movements are swift, and I wish that I'd had the forethought to at least grab a robe. If we're caught wandering the corridors so late at night, it'll look indecent. Particularly since I'm only in my nightdress. The nobles talk about me behind my back enough as it is.

The halls are quiet as we leave the wing that my suite is housed in. The weight of Da's talisman is comforting in my pocket. I no longer hear the measured steps of guards the next hallway over or even the occasional clink as one of their weapons clips a wall.

When we've walked for a while in a vacant section of the palace—with me muttering and cursing when I stub my bare toe on an uneven stone—Tregle stops at a nondescript wall. He pulls a wall sconce, and the cinder blocks before us descend to reveal a spiraling staircase that leads into the depths of the palace.

I look at him for an explanation as to where we're going or how he'd known that was there. He reaches for a torch inside the staircase, and we step inside. "Prince Caden knows the castle almost better than the Shakers who helped build it."

I shadow Tregle's back as the wall closes behind us. The staircase ends at an iron door with the simple shape of a hand where a lock should be.

I'm struck with recognition. Hands shaking, I fish in my nightdress's pocket for the medallion that Da gave me. The symbols are identical. Each finger on the hand depicted before me has a flame, leaf, teardrop, swirl of air, or heart. Just like Da's medallion. One mystery solved: the smudged symbol is a heart.

Tregle sees me staring at the dark metal on the door, and his attention snags on the object in my hand.

"Where—?" He shakes his head. "Should I ask?"

I ignore the question. "Do you know what it means?"

"It's meant to depict the unity of all forces: all Elementals and mankind. Only someone who knows the proper order of which finger to press can unlock the door."

I nod. Da must have known about this room somehow. Why else would he have given me the medallion? I wonder if he'd know what to expect inside here. I wonder if it means anything else.

Tregle pushes each symbol, and he recites the order as if it's a script. "First, the heart, our fellow beings before all. Then earth, for the life it holds; water and then air, which sustain it; and fire to burn it all to ruins again should the need arise."

I shudder. I remember the Bridge and Duchess burning to ruins, and I can't see why anything else should need to suffer the same fate. Tregle catches my cringing, hastening to add, "Only a ritual, Lady Bree. No one here intends for the world to end in fire, I assure you."

He pushes the flame, and the mechanics of an internal lock click into place as he pushes the door in.

Shouting reaches my ears almost instantly. How thick *is* that door? The voices cut off as we step inside, and I'm surprised to see Princess Aleta standing next to Caden. Nothing I've seen has betrayed such a degree of warmth between the betrothed couple that I would suppose them to be getting together for clandestine meetings.

I quell a flicker of emotion that I won't let myself

name.

The prince and princess are clearly in the midst of an argument. Caden's cheeks are red, and Aleta chews the inside of her cheek as she whirls to face the doorway where Tregle and I stand.

She glares at me. "What is *she* doing here?"

"I have to say I wondered the same about you," I say, glaring right back. I don't need to mince words here. It's obvious that the king has no idea what they're up to, and the princess can't complain about my rudeness when *she's* not where she's supposed to be either. I have no desire to keep company with her after what she said about Da. Whether it's true or not.

Tregle slouches next to me. The room is cylindrical but with a ceiling so low that his tower-like height necessitates the bad posture. It's practically bare inside, with just a simple wooden table and a few mismatched, flimsy chairs, along with a haphazard stack of books.

"Because," Caden snaps, raking a hand through his hair so that it sticks out at odd angles. "We need her." He rubs at his temples. "Makers deliver me from bossy princesses," he mutters.

"I can *hear*—"

"I am aware." He exhales heavily, trying to compose himself again. He and Aleta eye each other with annoyance.

For my part, I'm feeling some sympathy for him— and Aleta, too, much as I'd rather not feel anything for the girl. It must be miserable to be betrothed to someone that you argue with like this.

"Sorry to interrupt," I say. Caden's eyes flick to mine, and I cross my arms over my chest, suddenly more aware than ever that I'm in my nightdress. "But why, exactly, *am* I here?"

"Bree, I—" He gestures to the chair. "Would you sit? Please. Sit."

Aleta raises a brow challengingly. My arms shoot to my sides, fists clenched. Sit so Aleta can look down on me? I don't think so.

"Thank you, but I'd rather stand," I say firmly.

He doesn't press the issue. Tregle slides a seat out from the table and takes it for himself. Caden's hands leave his hair to fold behind his back.

"Tregle told me about your meeting with Larsden."

His look is expectant. Is he waiting for confirmation? After a moment's passed and he doesn't say anything else, I nod.

Caden paces a small area of the room. "And he wanted to test you?"

Aleta's suddenly paying attention. "Test you for what?" Her eyes bore into me like they're trying to dig the answers from my mind.

"Elemental abilities," I say, surprised that Tregle and Caden hadn't told her when they invited me here. "Torching, to be specific."

Aleta examines me closely, scrutinizing me like she'll be able to see it if fire crawls beneath my skin. "You can't be—can she?" She looks at Tregle entreatingly.

"Adept Tregle? Can she?"

He shrugs. "That remains to be seen, Your Highness," he says.

Some note in his voice makes me look between him and Aleta. They're looking at each other fondly. The princess turned to him first, rather than her betrothed, and there's something...*tender* in Tregle's eyes.

Oh. Comprehension washes over me. Tregle *likes* Aleta. Maybe even loves her. It's obvious when I see the two of them together. *Aleta* is the reason that his step quickened eagerly as we'd gotten closer to the castle, all those weeks ago. I'm sure of it.

As for Aleta, it's hard to say where she stands. She doesn't wear her feelings as plainly as Tregle does, but there *is* a degree of care etched across her features.

"I doubt that I'm a Torcher, princess," I say, focusing on the matter at hand. "Besides the fact that I'm not seventeen yet, there isn't any Torcher in my bloodline." That I know of.

Aleta is less than convinced. *What do they all know that I don't?*

"There's a reason the three of you have this little group," I say. "And a reason you had me summoned here." I address Caden. "Do I get an answer or am I going back to bed?"

Caden sits beside Tregle and gestures to the chair. I turn my eyes on Aleta, waiting. Before long, the princess rolls her eyes, perches in a chair, and I'm satisfied enough to take my seat.

Caden steeples his fingers below his chin, eyes on mine. I hold his gaze. I won't break it this time. Whatever the matters are that we're about to discuss, it feels too important.

"It might not surprise you to learn that my father and I rarely see eye to eye," he says softly.

I snort. That's putting things mildly. "I had inferred that, Caden."

"We cannot overthrow him," Aleta breaks in. "Yet. He has too many allies, too many powerful ones, and nothing that we've done—"

"I'm not sure we want to actually *overthrow* him," Caden hastens to add. "More...keep his power in check."

Aleta shakes her head. "I've told you, it's going to have to come to that one day. You must reconcile yourself to the idea." She turns to me. "We've debated the merits of an assassin—"

"—*we* have not," Caden says. "He's hardly my favorite person, but he's still my father, Aleta."

"I said '*debated,*' didn't I?" she shoots back.

"Ultimately, we felt that any assassin would be doomed to fail," is Tregle's quiet contribution. "Excepting Lady Katerine or—"

Caden shakes his head sharply. "All of this is beside the point," he says. "Which *is* that we strive to keep my father from seizing more power than he already has in hand."

I marvel at the situation. Caden plots against his own father. It's beyond me to understand the breaking of his filial ties in such a way. No matter what Da's done, I'm not sure that working against him is something I could ever do. Then again, I'd had a mostly happy childhood and enjoyed a healthy dose of friendship with Da. I don't know or understand what Caden's upbringing might have been like, but I know their relationship must be complicated. I've seen the kind of man the king is. He destroys homes. He tears families apart. He chases after war like a dog after its favorite bone.

Upon further reflection, I think, contemplating Caden, if I'd been the heir to the throne of Egria, I'd like to hope that *I'd* have the courage to make sure the people are safe from the king.

"If you're against the king, I'm for it," I say firmly.

Aleta crosses her arms. "I'd like to state for the record that *I* am against bringing her into this. Will the two of you kindly think who her father is?"

"I am already *in* this, *Your Highness.*" I inject as much venom into the title as I can. "Regardless of whether you involve me in your plans."

"And we are grateful for the help." Caden says placatingly. He spreads his hands between the two of us. "Adept Tregle mentioned that you overheard his earlier conference with my father."

"Right," I say, remembering what I heard as I lurked behind the tapestry. "They were saying that the Nereid navy is too strong. Too many Throwers."

Caden nods an affirmative. "That's right. And we have none in Egria."

My brow furrows in confusion. "Surely there's *one*— "

"There isn't." Aleta throws her arms in the air. "If it's going to take *this* long for her to grasp every little thing, I hardly think it will be worth the trouble."

If Aleta doesn't stop interrupting people and treating me like a rat she's found in her wardrobe, I'm going to throttle her. "I grasp it. No Throwers. Understood."

"You've had the advantage of growing up here, Your Highness," Tregle says.

"I would *not* call it an 'advantage.'"

"In the way of *knowledge*," Caden says, exasperated. He looks toward the ceiling in a quest for patience. "You know how my father works. How things are here. Adept Tregle is right. You have Bree at an advantage there. Please may we move on?"

"By all means," Aleta says, examining her cuticles.

Yes, halting my impulses to throttle her are growing more difficult by the minute.

"There hasn't been a Thrower Revealed in Egria for about sixteen years," Caden says. "Right around the time your father disappeared. The ones who were left were older, and they've since passed into the arms of the Makers."

"And..." I prompt.

They look at me, waiting. Some expressions are more patient than others. It clicks, and I straighten.

"The king thinks Da knows why," I say, filled with horror. No wonder the king is so bent on breaking down

Da's secrets. He believes he holds the key to making his army an even more formidable force. But how could Da know the answer to a freak turn of nature? How could anyone? "It must be a fluke. A strange coincidence."

"If it weren't for the fact that it was *Nereidium* that your father last attended as an ambassador, I might agree with you. But they are the land most closely associated with Water Throwing." A blank expression must show on my face for Caden sighs and puts a hand to his forehead. "I forget that you are not versed in the Creation Scrolls."

"Your poor country upbringing," Aleta says sweetly.

I bare my teeth at her, and Aleta jerks away. How is *that* for a country upbringing?

Tregle shakes his head, but Caden seems determined to press on without acknowledging this. "Though Adepts occur with some frequency in all realms, it's thought that certain countries have stronger ties to certain elements. I'm sure you've noticed the frequency with which Torchers are Revealed in Egria, for instance."

I hadn't, but I nod as if I know exactly what he means.

"Our central cities Reveal Torchers fairly often. Northern nations like Clavins have a slightly higher number of Riders. Landlocked nations seem to have more Shakers. There are several schools of thought on this." His tone grows excited and his eyes glimmer. "It's actually very interesting. Those who are more scientifically-minded claim that there are atmospheric trends that dictate what a person possessing the acumen of an Adept may become and one theory specifies that—"

Tregle clears his throat meaningfully, and Caden is shaken from his excited contemplation of science and continues.

"Conversely, those with close ties to the service of the Makers have adopted the philosophy that these individuals are specifically born into such regions by the will of our creators. Though they're named differently in the Creation Scrolls, historical scholars have determined what each land is called today by analyzing the details of the text." He waves his hand. "Whatever the reason, the country with the most Throwers has always been Nereidium, which likely has something to do with the fact that they are an island nation, surrounded on all sides by water."

I understand all of this and even think it makes a modicum of sense, but… "How have they managed to shut the abilities of latent Throwers outside their borders down?"

"We don't know," Tregle says. "But the king has grown increasingly obsessed with the idea of adding Nereidium to his empire."

"When he grows…impatient," Caden says diplomatically, "I try my utmost to advise him before other influential parties have their say." I'm sure he means Lady Kat. "And thus far, I've managed to convince him to contain his missions to exploratory terms rather than risk the loss of an entire fleet. He sends a ship here and there to—forgive the pun—test the waters."

Caden's mouth twitches at the joke, and I find myself smiling back despite the gravity of the situation.

"That's where I was," Tregle puts in. "Overseeing the navy exploration with Baunnid. I don't know how they all bring themselves to get on board. They know what happens to naval vessels sent to Nereidium. But there's something about the glory of battle to some of them."

"Then Baunnid...?"

"He won't be in the king's service any longer."

Caden sobers quickly. "It's a difficult decision to make, but we managed to keep the number of Egrians that we lose considerably lower this way. However, my father now believes that *your* father knows how to reverse whatever it is that's happened. That whatever this 'treasure' he was meant to retrieve holds the key to my father's victory. He'll use any means to get that information, and so must we."

Something about this bothers me. That's all well and good—except that really, if Caden's father succeeds, he'll only be ensuring more power for Caden someday. Why should the prince sacrifice that so willingly?

"I don't understand what *you* stand to gain from it," I say, unable to stop myself.

"Gain?"

"Well..." I interlock my fingers and study them, not meeting his eyes. I feel a little guilty accusing him of ulterior motives when he's done nothing but be kind to me, but I'd thought that my ladies had nothing in their thoughts for me but kindness, too, and look where that got me. My resolution firms. I have to ask. "Why should you want to stop your father when it would only mean a bigger kingdom for you? What's your ultimate goal?"

He pulls away like I've slapped him, looking stricken. Aleta's quieter than she's been all evening, and Tregle rocks back in his seat.

Caden draws himself up stiffly. Miles away from the charming prince, he now looks every inch the king he'll someday be. His voice is just above a whisper, and the insult is clear in his tone.

"Quite apart from making certain that my father doesn't run Egria into the ground before my reign even arrives, we're talking about a *war,* Bree. I have no interest in inheriting an empire at such stakes. Hundreds, likely *thousands,* of lives would be lost over my father's quest to obtain the Nereid throne and retrieve water abilities in Egrian Adepts."

I turn my head to the side, ashamed. The idea of profiting from his father's machinations obviously repulses him. "I had to ask," I say quietly.

No one speaks for a moment. "Why *does* he want Nereidium so badly?" I ask when I can make myself look at him again.

Caden shrugs, willing to let it go. "I don't know." He looks uncomfortable about admitting it. I'm familiar with the embarrassment that comes with too little knowledge of one's father. "But in truth, it's been a blessing that he's so fixated on it, since there's been little he could do about it over the past several years. I shudder to think what he'd be able to do to some other nation if his attentions shifted."

"What of Aleta?" I ask him, pretending that the princess isn't in the room. "Won't your marriage to her be enough to secure Egrian rule there?"

"Not for the king," Aleta says flatly, answering anyway.

Caden takes over the explanation. "To hear him tell it, he wants Nereidium by contract *and* combat. We've done all we can to avoid the farce of a marriage. It was already supposed to have occurred on my birthday—" Caden trails off, realizing that he's shared a bit more than he intended to.

Caden's birthday had been the day he'd felt that "pressing need" to attend to some of the other provinces. He hadn't been avoiding a party. He'd been avoiding a *wedding*.

That's not the point I should be focusing on now though, I think, trying to scoff at myself. The image of Caden and Aleta standing with clasped hands before a priestess persists in my mind, and my stomach churns unpleasantly. I worry the medallion between my fingers, feeling the imprint of the etchings against my thumb and try to focus on things that *actually matter*.

The only thing that I think is a certainty is that Da *knows* about this room. And to this day, it's been kept a secret from the king. Is that enough for me to go on?

"So what do you say Lady Breena? Will you help us?" Caden extends his hand to me. I stare at it. His hand is steady. Calm. Sure of itself.

They're against the king. That decides it for me. That *has* to be enough to go on. I seize Caden's hand and shake it, willfully ignoring the eyes that drill into mine like he can weld the promise between us that way.

"I have conditions," I say, jerking my hand away and wiping the sudden sweat that sprang up there on my nightdress.

Aleta pushes herself away from the table, her chair screeching. "Of course you do." She leans against the stone wall, ankles crossed.

The longer I spend in Aleta's presence, the easier I'm finding it to brush off her hostility.

"The first," I say, ticking it off on a finger, "is that, if it's ever possible, I want to get out of here. *With* my da. And the second is that I tell you only what I think you need to know. Not every bit of my conversation with Da is going to be recounted for you."

Caden nods. "The second is easy enough." Aleta opens her mouth to object, and Caden holds up his hand. "As long as you'll consent to let us ask you questions about said conversations."

It's my turn to try to object. Isn't recounting my meetings for the king enough? They're supposed to be working in *opposition* to him. They don't need to borrow his methods.

"We'll only ask if we feel it's necessary," Tregle assures me softly.

That's slightly better. "Deal," I agree quickly, before

I have a chance to change my mind.

"But your first caveat is a bit more of a conundrum." Caden sighs, looking at me regretfully. "You have to understand that the guard on you is difficult enough to work around. Your father is a considered a traitor to the crown, and thus his guard is even more difficult. Certainly, we have people that can afford you some protection, but... I don't know if we can do it, Bree. I don't know that I can just let you go."

I raise a quavering hand to shake on our bargain anew, ignoring the cold feel of my palms as air brushes sweat. I take a leaf from Caden's father's book and whisper: "Try."

Once the accord is struck, Aleta takes her leave. Good. I've had my fill of the haughty princess and can tell that the feeling's mutual.

Caden and Tregle quiz me on my current interactions with the king. But first, they ask me whether there's anything my ladies may have already given away.

"No," I say. "I don't know anything for them to betray me with."

I'm keenly aware that we've been there for an hour or more, so I try to answer their questions as quickly as possible. Better that I should get back before a particularly dutiful guard decides to do a sweep of my chambers to "ensure my safety."

Has the king threatened me? Caden and Tregle want to know.

"Only vaguely."

Does he intend to let me visit my father?

"Yes, but it hasn't happened yet."

Does he have me meeting with anyone else?

"Larsden." That brings us back around to how I've been pulled into this meeting in the first place.

"I have to agree with Tregle," Caden says with a thoughtful grimace on his face. "It pains me to say it, but you're going to have to let them test you. It will make them believe that you've bent to my father's will."

"That's *just* what Tregle said," I say glumly.

"I can try to arrange for someone else to sit in on your lessons," Caden suggests. "I know it's far from a perfect solution, but it may stop Larsden from taking his...tests further than he might otherwise."

That tips me off immediately. "And how far do you think he might go?"

"I've heard stories about the man," Caden says grimly. "I'd really rather not find out."

Twenty-One

They fetch me three more times that week, but we really don't have a lot to discuss, as I still haven't seen Da or been sent to Larsden again. The ladies have kept me busy, but though the king returns to dinners, he doesn't address me. I suppose he prefers for me to stew in my own worries.

I live for the nights now. The castle is my adversary in the daylight when every stray wind feels like Kat breathing down my neck. But it's friendly when all of the servants and nobles are tucked away in their beds. Tregle fetches me each time, and flames dance on his fingers like little fireflies to light our way.

Aleta mostly ignores me to tap a bored fingernail against the wood. Caden uses the meetings to educate me on the realm and the capital, with his explanations supplemented by Tregle's knowledge of the military situation.

The look on Caden's face when I tell him I can't pick Abeline out on a map is so dismayed, it's almost funny. I've never seen someone scramble for a book so fast.

His finger traces the yellowed page. "You said you're from the northern province?"

I nod. "The High North. A town called Abeline. You won't find it on there though. It's teeny."

"No, but I can approximate it." He's engrossed in the maps as his rough fingertips flip through pages. The speed of Aleta's tapping increases, and Tregle juggles a fireball out of boredom. Caden smacks down his thumb. "Here, I think. You mentioned a river, correct?"

I lean over. The top of my hair brushes his chin, and I look up into his eager eyes. He thinks he's given me a gift, but this is just ink etched across paper. The river is just squiggly lines winding into a book's crease. It doesn't capture its gentle rushing sound. I can't feel the cold that squirmed its way into me most days. There isn't a depiction of the Bridge and Duchess or the people in the village, who can't be confined to a simple portrait.

But I can't say that to Caden, who's so proud to prove himself a friend.

My mouth quirks up. "What else do you have to show me?" I ask softly.

He's thrilled with the question as the answer is, apparently, a great deal. I learn things like the ocean's name (Remediant); that Caden and Aleta aren't permitted to be seen by the general townspeople except by a distance; that Caden's house—Capin—hasn't borne an Elemental in five generations. Maybe that's why such strict laws were developed over them—fear of something the royals couldn't ever truly understand.

"And—" Caden hesitates. The page he's turned to is a new map. It's filled with tiny triangles symbolizing a mountain range. "These are your lands. Duchy Secan."

I recoil like the points of the mountains are about to impale me. "Those are *not* my lands." We've already seen *my* lands—the river and Abeline—and they brought me no feeling. "My history is back with the ashes of The Bridge and Duchess. I want nothing to do with Secan."

Tregle twitches, but I hadn't meant it as a dig at him for burning it down. Just that if The Bridge and Duchess is gone, so is my land really.

"Ridiculous," Caden says.

"Ex*cuse* me?"

He pushes the book toward me, poking sharply at the spot where "Secan" is scrawled. His frown carves a V between his eyebrows. "Just because you are ignorant of the history you have there doesn't mean it ceases to exist."

"It doesn't tell me anything about who I am either," I point out.

"Our history tells us where we come from," he insists. "Knowing our people, our bloodlines—it's *important.*"

"I come from *Abeline,*" I say. "None of the people who come from Secan affect *me.* I can't put so much stock in history, Caden. If I did that, I'd have lost myself already."

The book slams shut, and dust flies from its pages. Caden yanks it toward him and deposits it back on his stack of texts with a loud thump.

"Caden," Aleta warns.

"*Aleta,*" he mocks, running his fingers through his hair. This makes me hide a grin. The two are more like brother and sister than anything else.

She ignores that poor verbal parry, and he turns to Tregle. "How long until sunrise?"

"Still some time yet."

"Fantastic. Come on then."

His hand at my back enflames me, and I jerk away, annoyed. It's gentle, but I still feel like I'm being manhandled. "Where are we going?"

"To show you how history can still affect you."

After that tease of information, what else can I do but follow him? His steps through the hallways are presumptuous, taking little trouble to quiet his travels. Such is the luxury of being the prince, but I'm twitchy with worry. At least I'm in a simple brown dress this time and not my nightgown. Still, I don't want to be caught out of my bed with the betrothed prince. His little-used sword clatters at his hip.

"Here." He waves me inside a room and yanks a torch from a wall so that we can see. Aleta and Tregle haven't followed us.

"I still don't understand what we're doing he—" I stop short as the light dances over gilded frames. We're in a room filled with formal portraits. Hard-eyed men with steel at their sides, women with pursed lips and glittering with pearls and gems. But I only see one.

I know Caden's watching me as I take a step closer to

it. He's at least twenty years younger in this portrait, but I'd recognize Da anywhere. He has the same brown eyes, but the mischief in them is tamped down.

The woman at his side has to be my mother: Lady Corrine. Her lips are thin, but smiling. It seems genuine. She's a freckly blonde, with happy green eyes. Her curls are pinned up, and Da's hand rests on her shoulder.

My fingers run along my collarbone as I study her. "I don't look anything like her," I murmur.

"But she made you," Caden says softly. He crosses his arms. "I told you: our people are important. Without her, you very literally would not be who you are today."

True. As I stare at the mother I never knew, I have a strange longing in me, and it doesn't go away when I turn my eyes to the likeness of the father who is now a stranger to me.

Then I realize: Da's hair isn't auburn, like mine, like he'd said it used to be. It's black.

"Bree?"

Of all things, why would Da lie about that? I swallow the lump of confusion in my throat. "Take me back to my room, Caden."

Twenty-Two

Days later, the king enters my rooms without so much as the courtesy of a knock. Taken aback, I put aside the book I'm reading: *A History of Nereid Waters,* borrowed from Caden. I'm trying not to think about the lesson I have with Larsden in a few hours. And I've given up protesting Caden's insistence of understanding how history shapes our circumstances, but I'm not going to dwell on my own—at least not until I can ask Da about it. The first step in assisting with the group's plans is to really understand how Egria and Nereidium got to this point, but the text is so dense that I haven't gotten past the first paragraph. I rise from my chair to curtsy.

"My lord," I say.

Inwardly, I seethe. I know what this trick is about, entering my rooms without waiting for my permission. For all he knows, I could have been changing. It's just another way to show me that he doesn't *need* my permission and that he can and will do as he pleases.

"Lady Breena." He clasps his hands behind his back and nods to me. He sends a meaningful look to my ladies who slowly stop what they're doing and file out of the room.

I plead with them with my eyes not to leave me alone with the dreaded king, but Emis and Gisela won't even look at me. Maybe they feel guilty. And they should. I'd thought we were all friends—or as close as I could get to friends here, at any rate—but I see more and more where their loyalties truly lie.

"I've done you the discourtesy of neglecting to make the arrangements we spoke of when last we met, just the two of us."

The biggest discourtesy you've done me is continuing to breathe. Aloud, I protest mechanically, staring at the floor. "No, my lord. 'Twas no inconvenience to me."

"Yes, well. I've done as I said. You'll be meeting with your father before supper."

My eyes fly from the floor to meet his. "Truly, my lord?"

He nods. "You are to be waiting at the dungeon gates at dusk, after your lesson with Tutor Larsden today. A guard will escort you to the cell. You will have thirty minutes. After which, you will dress for dinner and attend me in my chambers."

Attend him in his chambers. My insides flip. Is that where he'll wrest a report from me?

"We will arrive at dinner together after you have given me the summation of the important matters you and your father discuss." A self-satisfied smile plays at the corners of his mouth.

Dinner isn't until moonrise. I do the math quickly. Da and I will have thirty minutes, I'll be in the king's rooms after that, and he'll have plenty of time to quiz me on the conversation. Then I'll have to have dinner and find some way to alert Caden of what's happened. I resign myself to the fact that I won't be asleep until very late this evening.

"I'm thrilled," I say, realizing that he's waiting for a response. "Thank you."

The words sound hollow. I *am* happy to be seeing Da, but less so to recite the content of our discussions. And it grates on me to pretend humbleness to the king for anything. Not when I know that I'll be spending the next several hours with Tutor Larsden as the man experiments on me, without proper time to mentally prepare myself for a meeting with Da.

He turns to leave, pausing at the threshold of my door. "I have been thinking over your living arrangements. I feel that it would do you good to spend time with someone your age closer to your station."

"Sire?" I feel the beginnings of dread. Maybe my ladies are more loyal to me than I thought. Why else would he be taking them away?

"Somewhere I can ensure your protection at all hours."

Now that's odd. He should be secure in the idea that I'm under watch. Has he somehow learned that I left my rooms last night? The only person of noble rank and my age in the palace, the only one who won't cause a scandal at least, is—

"You'll be moving into a guest room in Princess Aleta's suite."

Wonderful. My huff of displeasure refuses to be contained. I'll have to spend most of every day and every night with the person who glowers at me whenever we cross paths, flickering hatred whenever I enter a room. As strenuous as the idea that my ladies report on my actions is, being constantly at Aleta's side will be worse. The princess is never without an escort—though she does seem to know how to slip about the castle after-hours.

"All right, Your Highness," I agree warily.

"And Lady Breena?"

"Yes, my lord?"

His gaze is steely when I meet it, cutting me like a dull sword. "Knights are lords. My son is Your Highness. *I* am Your Majesty."

His tone lets me know I'm not to make the mistake again.

I have no time to pause and think about the fact that I'm moving rooms to be examined like a specimen beneath a glass, nor that I'll soon be reuniting with the only family I know.

I head to Larsden's laboratory, determined to stay focused. My fists spasm at my sides. If need be, *I'll* stop Larsden from going too far. I know the basics of defending myself—I'd had to, working in a tavern where occasionally the ale was a little too good for the patron consuming it. Thumb outside the fist. All of my weight goes behind a punch. A swift instep to the groin.

Comforting as my thoughts of violence are, I can't help but eye the flames dancing on candlewicks with trepidation. The tutor himself hasn't arrived yet, so I have some time in which to make my examination of the room.

Now that the curtains aren't drawn and light can sashay in as it pleases, it looks like an ordinary study. There's a workbench with several books stacked upon it. A few of them lay haphazardly open, like the tutor had been distracted by something one text said and flown to the next one in order to confirm it.

They're books centered on the Makers' myths, historic Elemental figures, and the elements themselves. I see the lands Caden mentioned as being particularly tied to one element and another copy of the same book I'd been reading earlier. Ink blotches have dripped, staining the wood of the table, but the quill at fault is currently housed in an inkpot.

There are notes scratched onto the sheaves of paper, and I bend to examine them.

"Subject shows ability to Torch nearly a year early. Might this be the evolution of Adepts that has been speculated upon?"

A Torcher before their seventeenth birthday? I whistle lowly.

No wonder they're testing me. If someone else's

powers have managed to defy the rules, that Makers-given assurance that Elemental abilities show up on the day of the seventeenth anniversary of one's birth and not one day earlier is no longer a certainty. My birthday is still almost two months off, but they must have discovered that things are changing in Egria.

I jump as the door bangs open, and Tutor Larsden stalks in, scowling. He halts before me, eyes flicking between me and the notebook that lays open.

"My lady," he greets me curtly. I step away. He brushes his hands together as though dusting them off and looks at me. "We must get started."

Belatedly, I realize that the supervisor Caden promised me has yet to make an appearance. "Certainly, Tutor Larsden," I agree. I paste a placid expression on my face. I can't let panic fill me or I won't be able to remain calm. Hopefully, whomever the prince is sending is only running late, or I'll be forced to take action myself. They'll never believe I'm submissive if I run again.

Larsden pulls a large bowl filled with water from a shelf next to the window and sets it on the table. Lifting a torch from the wall, he uses it prod the bowl's contents.

Not water then, I realize, recoiling instinctively as the surface of the bowl bursts into flame. Oil.

The fire licks toward me dangerously, and I stare at it with wide eyes, certain that the light of the flames is reflected in my pupils.

He looks at me expectantly. "Well?" he asks. "Are you going to stand there, or am I going to be allowed to progress my research today?"

I shake myself. "I—of course, Tutor Larsden."

He surveys me with satisfaction as I cross the side of the table to stand beside him. He hasn't given me further instructions yet. I need to stall for more time.

I can feel the heat from the fire lapping toward my skin. It's thirsty, begging to be quenched, and I'm its beverage of choice. I lick my lips.

"Could you tell me about the science behind your work today, Tutor Larsden?" I put as much sweet curiosity into my voice as I can.

He's startled that I've asked. I suppose the question must not come up much. The king's ready enough to put forward any experimentation that the tutor asks for, regardless of its merit; he's that desperate to find a way to his war. He doesn't bother asking about the science behind it.

"I suppose." He looks at me suspiciously out of the corner of his eye. "Recent scholarly findings have led me to believe that the trait that allows someone to use an Adept ability has advanced. You know that Adept Reveals used to occur no earlier than the seventeenth anniversary of one's birth, but one subject of experimentation was Revealed nearly a year before hers."

"How interesting," I say, filing away that "hers" for later speculation. Of course, I already know most of this from the notes I spied. "Do you think it has to do only with the particular element that she controls or simply with the powers themselves?"

He grows animated, moving away from the fire-laden bowl. I allow my shoulders to relax a bit. "That's the thing—it's hard to say!"

His voice has the same zeal of a Makers priest in the throes of a sermon. Tutor Larsden may not be devout in midweek services, but he worships *something*: he's a fanatic of what he considers science, his experiments with Elementals. He flips through one of the open books, its pages nearly ripping in his eagerness. The pages are thin, delicate things, and he swears when he tears one.

The door pulls open, letting a draft of air in.

"Sorry to be late," Aleta says drily. Her skirts trail on the floor behind her as she sails in, making her way to one of the stools.

This is who Caden sends? Aleta hates me, and I'm no great advocate of hers either. Why would he send *her*? I look dubiously between the princess and the fire. I can't decide which is worse.

"His Majesty has requested that my guards and I *see* to Lady Breena. I believe he intended for us to bond, noblewoman to noblewoman."

Other ladies might accompany such a statement with a girlish giggle or a bat of the eyelashes, but Aleta is stoic. I have to wonder what her version of bonding actually entails. Probably not squealing over the village boys. The mental image of Aleta squealing over anything makes my lip twitch.

She doesn't look at me after uttering the ludicrous idea that we'll bond, but I catch her light emphasis on the word "see" and understand. She's using the fact that the king constantly has her under some supervision. No one can claim I haven't cooperated if Aleta's guards and spies see me doing as I'm commanded.

The presence of another person draws Tutor Larsden out of the trance of his impassioned tirade, and he stands before the fiery glass bowl again.

"It's simple, Lady Breena. I want you to put your hands in the fire."

I'd known the man was mad, I'd known to expect pain, but putting my hands in a bowl filled with flames goes against childhood law, against basic instinct. If something is sharp, you don't poke it. If it looks too heavy, you don't lift it. And if it's hot, you don't touch it.

Despite knowing that it's something I have to do to throw the king's suspicions off of me, I hesitate.

"It's going to hurt," I say aloud firmly, more as a way of convincing myself than anything else. "I'm not seventeen, and odds are I don't have that ability. So I might as well just get this over with?"

Something like sympathy shines in Aleta's eyes when I look at her for a confirmation. It isn't comforting.

"Yes," Larsden says impatiently. He reaches across the table and grabs my wrists, pushing my hands into the oil.

And I scream.

The fire's been waiting for me and sears over my sleeves, burning, burning my skin, eating me alive. It chews at me with fiercely sharp teeth, clawing its way over me, into me, under my skin. I try to pull away, but Larsden moves his arms to my shoulders, holding me there. My throat is ragged. The screams cleaves my voice apart. I am nothing but pain.

"Give it a moment," Larsden insists, shouting to be heard over my cries. "The fire might just need a moment to recognize you."

I'm going to pass out. I have no voice left to scream, and I waver on my feet, still trying uselessly to pull away from Larsden.

Arms grab me around the middle, yanking me away from Larsden, and patting the flames down. "*Enough*," Aleta says emphatically.

I'm left panting and sobbing. I wrap trembling arms around myself and bite down on a scream as the light touch of my dress slices into the burns. I hold my arms stiffly away from my sides, trying not to let them touch anything that will magnify the pain.

The entire thing lasted only seconds, but my skin is charred, puckered, and pinkened. My arms are alien things. They ripple with discord, blistered, there only to cause me pain.

Aleta rubs my back soothingly for a moment, while I fight to catch my breath. I don't care that she doesn't like me right now. I'm just grateful to have someone here who doesn't want to burn me alive. Tears blur my eyes as Aleta glares at Tutor Larsden.

"It doesn't work that way, Larsden," she tells him. "The elements recognize their brethren instantly. If I'd realized *that* was your intention, I could have *told—"* Her voice is biting, furious. She takes a deep breath to steady herself, and when she speaks again, it's even. "Lady Breena is neither an active Adept, nor is she a Torcher. She needs a medic."

"Oh, very well," he says in disgust, turning away from us and suffocating the flames with a careful blanket placed over the bowl's surface. "You may escort her."

Aleta drops her arms from my torso, and I sag under the weight of my own agony. I lean on the table to support myself, but anguish carves its way up my arm when I put weight on it. Wavering at the edges, the chamber looks steamy. I shake my head, trying to clear it. I feel heady. The pain's so intense that I'm not going to be able to remain standing unsupported much longer.

Aleta's eyes burn him. "You may do well to remember that it is *I* who outrank *you*, Tutor Larsden. You do not give me permission to do as I see fit. Your studies appear inadequate. Lady Breena will most assuredly *not* be returning."

She whirls. Larsden looks at her with hate-filled eyes, but I can't watch the scene play out any more. I close my eyes as spots dance and fight to keep my balance.

"Why are you helping me?" I gasp out as Aleta hustles me up the stairs and out of the room. A guard follows in our wake.

She casts a glance at me from the side of her eye. "I volunteered for the task. Whatever you may think of me, I am not heartless. You're not the first to be subjected to

Tutor Larsden's scrutiny. I'm finished standing by, so I do what I can."

She brings me to a room in another wing of the palace, where a medic swipes a soothing salve across my burned arms. I sigh with relief. The salve is cool and smells like grapes. My arms tingle as numbness spreads through them, and I'm able to gather my thoughts.

The sleeves of my dress are in tatters, and my flambéed skin peers through. I'll need to change into something with long sleeves before I see Da. Under other circumstances, he'd be the first person I'd tell about a horrible experience like this, but when I speak with him now, my focus needs to be on discovering what happened sixteen years ago.

Da. My eyes flick up to meet Aleta's, who waits for me in the doorway, arms crossed. That haughty look of hers is back, but there's something else, too. Is it understanding? Wariness? I'm not sure.

"Why do you think that my father's a killer?" I ask softly. Maybe I shouldn't ask, but I need to know. Aleta's convinced that he is, and I just can't bring myself to believe it. Da's not that kind of man. He's a good person.

Her harsh attitude fades further. "I don't *think* it," she says. "I *know* it."

"How?"

She's not gentle. Her edge remains and her voice is brittle as she explains. "Have you never wondered how I came to be in my current position? Don't you wonder at the fact that I am the Egrian king's ward when he is constantly trying to sabotage my kingdom? Hasn't it crossed your mind that it's a bit odd that my parents would abandon me to the whimsy of such a man?"

Her parents. The words are so bitter. I'm staring at her, arrested by her story, by the evidence she's putting forward to condemn Da.

He couldn't have…

The question must show in my eyes, for Aleta nods slowly.

"You see now why I take such offense to you. You have lived happily these seventeen years with a father who must care for you a great deal, judging by the way you remain loyal to him. How could I believe the Makers to have handled the world fairly when my parents are dead and their murderers live on? *You* have a father who loves you. The only family *I* have is an aunt who rules in my stead in my kingdom—one whom the king won't even allow inside his borders."

Her lips are pursed. It's cost her something to admit that she envies me this way, and my heart sinks. She isn't lying about this.

I don't know what to say. I mean, by the ether, what *can* I say to such a reveal?

But Aleta doesn't expect much from me in response. "Come along, Lady Breena," she says. "I will deliver you to your lady's maids that they might properly attire you once more." She indicates the salve on the bed beside me with a pointed finger. "You'll want to bring that with you. I'm told burns have a way of flaring back up. That will be rather handy."

I grip the salve container in an iron fist and stare down at my knuckles.

How could Da do such a thing? He's the one who taught me right from wrong. Is his definition really so flexible?

"Come along, Lady Breena," Aleta repeats, standing aside in the door. Her guard waits to escort us. His helmet's visor is pulled down over his eyes, but he's watching us. There are eyes on us everywhere.

Aleta's given me a lot to think about and not much time to do it. I have only hours until I'm to confront Da.

And I don't know if I can forgive him that soon.

If ever.

Twenty-Three

Is it even possible to forgive someone I've never truly known?

Because that's how I feel. The man I thought I knew would never do what Aleta's said he's done, but I know she's not lying. I'm still thinking about it hours later, my skirts clinging to my sweaty legs as I follow a step behind the dungeon guard. His keys jangle at his hip.

Far from worrying about making our escape, I'm back to being angry with Da. Not only has he lied to me about our past, but he's just *so* far from the man he's pretended to be. I don't have any idea what to say to him.

The sun was setting in the sky when I'd followed my escort to the dungeon gates. Upon my arrival, I tried to ignore the red rosebushes marking the entrance. I'd been too preoccupied the last time I was here to notice their presence, but now that I know their significance, it's as though their stems stake into my heart, thorns and all.

The heat's been bad today—I noticed it this morning when I cracked open a window for fresh air. The palace is cool, but it's kept well-ventilated by a series of ducts that

Lady Kat monitors. I'd wanted a break from anything to do with her.

She doesn't handle the ventilation of the dungeon, but this escape doesn't bring me relief. It's terrible down here where the sun doesn't dare tread—suffocating.

It smells rank from prisoners' waste, and I gag, making a note to smuggle a packet of cinnamon from the kitchens to hold to my nose for future visits. If I can manage to give my ladies the slip long enough to get down there. I take only shallow breaths and cover my nose with my hand.

I keep my eyes ahead, locked on the bobbing head of the guard. The bony, sallow-skinned hands of the other prisoners—ones who aren't Da—reach out to me through the cell bars. Some are clawed with vicious intent; I skitter away to avoid their grasp.

The spindly fingers of others entreat, their dirty palms hungry for acknowledgment. These hands make me *feel* too much. Has Da been reaching out to strangers like this? Despite what I know now, it makes my heart twist to think of it. Aleta's evidence has changed both everything and nothing. I still need to get Da out, even if he's not who I thought he was.

"You've got a half hour," the guard says as he comes to a stop in front of one of the cells.

He pulls a three-legged stool from its spot against the wall and sets it before the iron bars. The huddled figure inside does a double-take. He faces me but doesn't speak.

How can he stay silent? I haven't seen him in weeks,

and I've been *ill* over what they might be doing to him. It seemed like I was important to him when we were separated, but now there's nothing but dispassion in his eyes. Did he bother thinking of me at all?

I sit down gingerly, positive that sickness and grime float about the dungeon and rest on my seat. But it's not as though disease can waft about on a gentle wind down here; there's not much spare air to be had. How does that affect a Rider like Da? To be deprived of his element?

His hair is growing in patchy. My insides coil at the sight of him behind the thick black bars. I'd never before considered the idea that he didn't come by his baldness naturally, that he *chose* to have a shaved head. Does he prefer it that way or was it another of his tricks to disguise us? Maybe he started shaving it when I was young to hide his lie over his hair color. Was everything he'd done just another shard in the broken glass of my childhood that I'm trying to piece together, or had at least a few of his actions had other motivations?

I second-guess every memory I have now.

Prisoners are a noisy sort. Curses, sobs, and screams bounce off the stones between cells. A palatable air of despair surrounds me, but it's the silence that stretches between Da and me that is the most stifling.

I'd felt such *relief* when the king had first told me I'd be able to see Da. Yes, there was anxiety at first, but it had been such welcome news that I would be able to see him with my own two eyes. After this latest revelation from Aleta, I don't know what to think. Much less what to do, what to say, how to treat him.

A lantern, mounted well out of reach of grasping hands, casts a dim glow.

"I see they've given you some hay," I try after several minutes. It dusts the floor and, to a certain degree, masks the odor emanating from him. It's a bit less privy, a bit more stable. "That should make it more comfortable when you sleep—instead of just the stones, I mean. Really brightens up the place, too."

One leg stretched before him and an arm flung over the other knee, Da flicks his gaze over to me and away. A dismissal.

Well, fine. I can dismiss him, too. I don't understand why he's had such a change in attitude toward me. It isn't as though *I've* lied to *him.* And after the scene in the throne room, I'd thought he would at least be glad to see me.

I pull my shoulder blades together. My stare fixes itself on a crack in the mortar. It cuts through the stone like a lightning bolt, exactly the way a crack in our hearth at The Bridge and Duchess used to look. Da and I used to joke that a baby bolt had found its way into the stone during a particularly bad storm after the other lightning bolts had chased it there.

I soften at the errant memory, sneaking a look at him. Da's posture is as stiff and confident as it's ever been. He wears the graying criminal rags as if they're an ordinary pair of breeches and tunic.

I should have *guessed* that there wasn't something

right about Da. He's a good actor, but he's never acted like the other men in the village. Most of them are beaten down by life and slumped over. *Da,* on the other hand, had been vain about his fingernails, keeping them trim and clean. Vain about holes in our clothes, where the other men's children had run about without patches sewn on. We're not beggars, he'd often told me when I'd protested after jabbing myself with a needle trying to fix a patch to a dress or pair of breeches. The Bridge and Duchess could get as raggedy as it liked, but we wouldn't go about with holes in our clothes.

There had always been a tight strain to his words.

How many times had he had to stop himself from saying that we weren't *peasants* and said beggars instead? Why is he stopping himself from saying *anything* now?

"Da, please." The plea chokes my voice. I hate that, that he's reduced me to begging. Damn him, he's the one who's lied to me. If anyone has the right to ignore someone here, it's me. He should be asking me for forgiveness, should be spewing *over* with answers for me.

"Tell me why you ran. Tell me why you lied to me about it. What treasure does the king think you stole?" A thought occurs and I voice it before I have time to think too hard about it. "And what about my mother?" Seeing him blanch, I press. "What about my *ma*, Da? I doubt it was just the corsets that spurred her to leave. Did she know about any of this? Did she even know that you were fleeing, or did she think the two of you were just going for an evening *stroll?*"

The silence persists. It's an annoyingly stubborn creature that way, choosing now for a nap and laying down for a good spell between us. Lazy, rotten, ridiculous silence. Tears prick at my eyes, and I yank them in. They're always trying to escape these days.

I stand, leaning my forehead against the iron bars of his cell.

"It's not fair, what you did to me. We had a good life there back at the inn, but it's spoiled now, all of it. If you hadn't stolen me and Ma away in the night, what might my life be like now? Would I married? With child? Would I like sewing? Would I be ready to govern a duchy, having prepared for it all my life? Would I be a completely different person? There's no way for me to know that other Breena, the girl I should have been." My voice rises to a frustrated shout and fractures. I clear my throat, still sore from Larsden's torture session.

If we'd been back at the inn, Da would have spoken up by now, told me to mind my tongue, watch who I'm speaking to because no matter how old I get, he's still my father. But the man who sits in the cell before me looks at me with the careless stare one would give a bug crawling across the room, as though he has neither the energy nor the inclination to deal with me.

My hands and arms throb. The medic's salve is wearing off. I carefully adjust my sleeve, and the burn peeks from beneath the lace.

Da's eyes catch on it, and he leaps to his feet. The hay

rustles with his movement and flies about in a sudden gale that sweeps in. A question burns in his eyes as he starts toward me, but I shake my head angrily.

"Not your business anymore, is it? You've got your secrets, and now I've got mine. If you had an itch in your boots, you should have left me and Ma behind." He winces at my bitter tone, one of the few reactions I've managed to garner from him. I won't apologize for it.

These pitiful "conversations" won't do the king or me any good. Likewise, this meeting will be useless to Caden and the others. We'll never break free of the palace like this.

The king's hopes that Da will share the secrets of his treasure with his *daughter* are unfounded. His wishes won't help him get his war. I'll be lucky if I can pry even few words from the lockbox of Da's mouth.

I'm finished for the day. I've had quite enough of this.

"You still refuse to admit that you were wrong," I whisper, rising as I hear the clink of the guard's steps coming toward me.

Why prolong the silence? I turn to leave.

"I wasn't." Da's voice is hoarse and cracked from disuse. I whirl at the shock of his voice as he clarifies. "Wrong." He finally meets my eyes and holds them. "I wasn't wrong, Breena Rose."

He'll say no more, and the guard leads me away.

Twenty-Four

"Honestly, my lo—Your Majesty, that's it," I say tiredly. I had only a scant moment to rush back to my room to apply the salve as the burning in my hands intensified before having to meet the king in his chambers. "I asked about your treasure and he wouldn't say anything."

The king rolls up the scroll he's reading and flings it into the hearth. "I refuse to believe that I've kept you and your father apart for weeks and he wouldn't say a word to you. I was given to understand you get on well."

"It's not that he wouldn't say a *single* word to me," I say. I'd gotten a solid eight actually. "But nothing that is pertinent to your kingdom."

But it's pertinent to me. How could I have come from a man who killed people in cold blood and still claims he isn't wrong?

The king collapses in a settee like an overgrown and petulant child. He curls his fingers at me. "I must know all then."

"Well, he did seem a bit put out when he saw the

burns Tutor Larsden's work had left behind on my arms."

The king waves that away like an insect that buzzes too near his face. I'm sure my injuries are *most* inconvenient for him. "We must all sacrifice in the name of progress."

Of course we must. I contain my retort and instead agree with the king. "I grew frustrated and told him that he was wrong for taking me and my ma away from the palace. And that it was worse that he'd hid the secret from me for all of those years."

The king is amused by me, a finger to his lips hiding an almost-smile. "What did he have to say to that?"

"He said that he wasn't wrong, my lord."

And therein is what perturbs me most about this entire situation. Da's never been too proud to admit his faults. Why does he cling so stubbornly to *this* mistake?

"How very interesting," the king murmurs.

That's all. I don't see *how* it's interesting, unless he sees it as confirmation that Da is still like *him.*

He rises, and I hurry to do the same. "To dinner then, Lady Breena. I require sustenance to ruminate on all that you've told me."

But I'd been so certain that I hadn't told him anything. I place my arm carefully on the king's offered forearm, trying to work it out in my mind.

He thinks it's important that Da still believes he did the right thing? Or is it Da's stress at my injury he finds interesting? But that's stupid. Of course a father would be upset to find his child injured when there's nothing he can do to prevent it.

I bite back an exclamation of pain when the king jars my sleeve. My arm is nestled in the crook of his arm—insomuch as a rope can nestle the thing it binds.

It's odd to think that I hope to topple such a powerful figure. After all, if Tregle, Aleta, and even Caden can't affect his plans much, what can I hope to achieve? The king looks at me from the corner of his eye, and I try to quiet my thoughts, struck by the insane notion that he can hear me.

We stop short of an arched opening. This isn't the dining hall. Beyond, there's a low murmur.

"Our dinner this evening will be a bit more intimate." The king's voice is a caress, and I shudder in response. Intimate. I don't care for the sound of that.

When we enter and there's only a simple table around which Lady Kat, Caden, and Aleta are seated, relief burgeons out from me. At least I'm not to be alone with the dread king.

I nod coolly at Caden and slip into the seat the king holds out for me beside him. It's not where I'd have chosen to sit, there at his side like a puppet on hand for his amusement, but it helps to have people nearby who are…if not friends, then something rather like it. Allies? Certainly, the title fits Caden well enough—he aims a quick smile at me—but whatever Aleta is remains to be seen. It's a shame Tregle isn't here. I think I can safely call him a friend at this point.

It's not the sort of group that lends itself to the chatter

and laughter of ordinary dinner conversation, but then again, I haven't enjoyed a dinner like *that* since leaving Abeline.

I indulge myself in imagining a reality where I have the courage to share the dirty Earth Shaker joke I'd overheard last night and indulge myself still further by dreaming that the king and Lady Kat burst with laughter, clutching their stomachs, their faces turning red between gasps of glee. It's strange to imagine them as such, taking a small pleasure in the company of words that serve no purpose but cheap entertainment. I glance at them as they sip their soup from their spoons. No, if they were to laugh now, it would ring false, like they're lording it over someone.

It's even difficult to imagine it of Aleta, despite traces of humanity creeping in from her. She may not burst with pealing laughter as I once would have, unreservedly, but I picture her hiding a small smile behind a napkin.

Caden would laugh at my joke, I'm sure. He's perhaps the only one who would join me in it, though it would take him by surprise. He'd cough, choking on the laughter and his food. In spite of the severity of his self-appointed task—to keep his father in check, if not overthrow him altogether—he takes joy where he can find it. If it's through an afternoon spent riding with the court pariah or an inappropriate joke, so be it.

I envy him that. Any joy I feel is instantaneously squashed by guilt that there are more important things that I should be doing, should be concentrating on. It's no joke that my father is imprisoned in a dungeon and I'm in what amounts to a very large cage. My tether might be looser and with a longer reach, but that doesn't change the fact that I'm as much a prisoner as Da is.

But what exactly am I doing about it? Joining Caden in his cause, as much as that is. I'm as submissive to the king's whims as I've ever been. How is that helping anyone?

These are the thoughts that occupy me as I plod through the soup and vegetable courses. Prepared properly, I'm told that eggplant is a royal Egrian delicacy. After finishing it, I decide that's due to the fact that it makes one's stomach feel exceedingly delicate.

As the servants replace the eggplant with veal covered in a creamy sauce, the king holds up a hand. Shame. The veal looks vastly preferable to the eggplant. A scintillating aroma of cheese and spices wafts from it, and my mouth waters.

"I have been thinking," he says.

Kingdoms have been known to fall in the wake of his thoughts. My salivating abates. He has my attention.

Caden exchanges a glance with me and Aleta. We don't want the king thinking about anything but his agony over the Thrower problem and the Nereidium situation. Caden's managed to convince me that *that,* at least, his group has under control.

"It seems a shame that you missed your wedding date." He addresses his son with a flair of innocence that's ill-suited to the poorly disguised taunt in his eyes.

"Quite the shame, Your Majesty," Aleta drawls. Seeming oblivious to the tense cloud that fills the room, she picks up her fork and knife and begins to slice into her veal. Her knife screeches across her plate. "Words will never express how I pined for my betrothed in those lost hours."

Caden's cough does little to hide his laughter, but it's wise that he's at least made the effort in this case. His eyes dance away from mine at the mention of the wedding. "Yes, regrettably unfortunate. How the date could have slipped my mind among my travels, I'll never know."

"It was your birthday," says the king.

"So it was!" Caden snaps his fingers, like he's lit upon an epiphany. "I knew something about the day seemed important. Aleta, it's your birthday soon as well, isn't it?"

"Mmm." The sound she makes is noncommittal. "My seventeenth. There's to be a banquet."

"Indeed." The king swirls a tornado into his wine. "But back to matrimonial matters. We shall simply have to examine other options. I'm certain we need not hold off on rescheduling much longer."

The smile curls across his face, but the emotion that a smile is meant to convey is missing. It's like the muscles in his mouth remember the movement, but not the intent. The sentence is a threat, a vow, and it hangs over the room like a heavy veil. I clear my throat, wanting to rid the atmosphere of thinly disguised amity and make it...if not truly friendly, then a bit more believable.

"His Majesty tells me that we are to room together going forward, Princess Aleta." I think I say it pleasantly enough, without the contemptibility I found in the idea only that morning.

"Yes, I'm told the same," Aleta says after dabbing at her mouth. "You may accompany me and my guard following dinner if you wish. Your maids have already been so kind as to deposit your things inside my rooms."

My things don't number many. I came to the palace with nothing but the clothes I wore and my father; neither were returned to me. Da's medallion is stuffed inside my bodice. All that could have been taken to Aleta's rooms is the few gowns that Emis and Gisela have procured from the seamstresses during my stay.

"That's kind," I say, not sure that it is. "Thank you."

"I'm sure Lady Breena will be thankful of the rest," the king says to Aleta.

Rest? Real rest, in this palace? I'd laugh if that veil of tension didn't cling so stubbornly to the room. Instead, I make a comment that passes for my agreement: "Rest would be a dream."

"I'm certain that's true after your strenuous day."

I stiffen, a bowstring drawn too tight. Strenuous? Yes, after he set his man to the task of burning me as some sort of twisted test. I've never hated someone so much. I am a roiling sea of wrath.

"She conversed with the traitor she names her father today," says the king.

That's his game then—to bring Da into it. I'm no less tense. He thinks to draw everyone into my affairs. He won't even let me have the *charade* of privacy and discretion. Sure, I've already shared the details of the less-than-fruitful meeting with the king and I intend to do the same with Caden at some undetermined time later. It's a given that they will, in turn, each share it with their own people, but that's different, somehow, than presenting it before them all like a winning deck of cards.

Caden's eyes are quick to light on mine, and I give him a barely perceptible shake of my head. To let him know I've gotten nothing from Da. Not yet.

"It was trying, to be sure," I demur through gritted teeth. I take a steadying sip of the wine at my right and blanch at the taste. It's never been my preferred beverage.

"I doubt he took well to being reminded of the life he took from you." Katerine brings her first offering to the evening's conversation, and I start. It's uncomfortable that Kat's remark aligns so closely with what I said to Da earlier. The hairs at the back of my neck raise. Had she been listening? If that's so, why does the king even need my reports?

And *is* that what the problem is? Seeing me in the gowns to which I would have been accustomed if I'd grown up as Lady Breena settles oddly with Da? I mull the thought over as silence falls and we move to dessert.

It doesn't feel exactly right, and yet…it seems close. Da had done a double-take when he'd seen me perched on the stool in my gown. But he's seen me in a gown already—and a finer one—upon our arrival to court.

Aleta, in an uncharacteristic moment of comfort, rejects Kat's claim. "I feel sure that Lady Kat is mistaken."

The words are awkward, like Aleta means comfort but it's a task she's yet to perfect and needs a great deal of practice with.

I barely taste the dessert, which is a true tragedy. It's a study of artistry in chocolate and berries.

Afterward, the king rises from the table, and all of us stand with him.

"I bid a good evening to you all." He says the words as he's turning.

Katerine follows behind him. She bears a sneer as she curtsies to the table, but her expression changes as she falls behind the monarch. She reminds me of someone, her expression eager, devoted. It clicks into place. Katerine follows the king like Baunnid had followed her. A dog eager to please its master.

I hope it works out as well for her as it did for him.

Twenty-Five

After dinner, I'm just thankful to exit the room unassisted. My arms are aching again as they hang limply at my sides. I move them cautiously, careful of bumping them against errant corners as I pass the rooms I slept in only last night and trail in Aleta's shadow to the princess's suite.

I'd thought my rooms were grand, but they're a hovel when compared with Aleta's. Strands of gems dangle from her ceiling in lazy spirals. The walls are painted with swirls of gold that hold a telltale shimmer in their depths. Real gold paint? I don't dismiss the notion. The paint in *my* rooms had been only gold plating, and they'd missed that shimmer.

Aleta seems to have forgotten me as she disappears behind a heavy set of double doors and closes them firmly behind her.

"Um…" I knock hesitantly. "Your Highness?"

"Your room is at the opposite end of the suite." Aleta's voice comes, muffled. I'd missed the set of doors she mentions, but I see them now and follow Aleta's directions.

Unlike the opulence of the rest of the suite, this room is meant for a servant—a lady's maid, most likely. A small twin bed takes up the majority of the cramped quarters. A singular tiny window allows only a tiny slat of the moon's light to enter.

I back away, unable to fathom sleeping there. It's not the small space or bed that I protest—they still beat my old pallet—but unless I'm able to obtain a lantern or a torch, I'll be making my camp on Aleta's sitting room floor. The dark never gave me cause to fear until Elementals had come creeping out of the night and hands, friendly or otherwise, had clapped themselves over me as I slept. A light would be a small comfort.

I had hoped to talk with Aleta, to understand more about her knowledge of Da's past, but Aleta's door remains closed. I sigh and flump down onto the settee.

How can I impress upon Da the urgency with which I need this information about his past, his last mission? I'm afraid to come right out and tell him, lest I be overheard. My thoughts fly again to Kat's cunning comment.

But it may soon come to that. His cooperation is the key to our freedom.

After several minutes, it dawns on me that I haven't heard so much as a stirring from Aleta's bedroom. I strain my ears.

"Your Highness?" I call. "Are you all right?"

No answer. She can't possibly be asleep yet. I deliberate with myself for a moment, then push the doors open.

The room is empty.

⤜⟨⟩⤛

A creak wakes me from my position on Aleta's bed, where I'd slept fitfully after pacing the room and debating the merits of calling for the guard.

What if she'd been kidnapped by enemy forces? The princess could be in serious trouble, in which case, calling for the guard and alerting the palace would be the right decision. Then again…her window was sealed firmly shut, so if she'd been spirited away, that wasn't the escape route. If she'd simply managed to evade her guards for the evening again, she's *not* in trouble, but she *would* be if I alerted them.

I told myself that if she hadn't returned by morning, I'd find someone. Still uneasy with my decision, I was unable to rest my mind enough to sleep.

I wore a tread pacing the plush rug that lined Aleta's floor, and then, when my feet refused to cooperate with me any longer, I'd sat down on Aleta's bed. Out of habit, I touched my nightdress pocket where Da's medallion rested. Just to remind myself that it was still there.

At some point, I'd drifted off, and I woke at the sounds of a thump, hurriedly wiping traces of sleep from my eyes.

Aleta stands before me, hands on hips, indignant. "What," the princess demands, "are you doing in my quarters?"

"I should lower my voice if I were you, Your Highness," I whisper. So glad I'd wasted my time with anxiety for her. "Think of your guards. Where have you been?"

"That's none of your concern," Aleta says breezily. She lights a torch and retrieves a poker from the fireplace to shift the kindling. The fire's nearly out. I blink as my eyes adjust to the change in lighting.

"Maybe not," I say, annoyed. "But did it occur to you that I might be so concerned over your disappearance that I'd alert a guard?"

Aleta whirls, clutching the poker to her chest. Her eyes are wide with fear so blatant that I feel bad for worrying her needlessly.

But that's before Aleta's nightclothes begins to smoke.

"Aleta!" I rush over to her and snatch the poker, dropping it instantly. It's red-hot and my puckered hands are further seared, blinding me with pain for an instant.

But before it can set the room on fire, I kick the poker into the fireplace. It can be retrieved later, in the morning when the fire has burnt itself out. The maids will find it and put it down to someone else's clumsy fingers—not this occurrence, which grows stranger by the minute.

Aleta pats down the flames on her chest

absentmindedly. Her attention is solely focused on me.

"You didn't," she begs. She seizes my hands, dropping them when I yelp. "Please tell me you didn't."

Aleta's hands had been as hot as if she'd held them in a pot of boiling water. I can't focus on her question. "Didn't what?" I ask faintly.

"Alert the guard. You didn't, did you?" This is a side of Aleta I never expected to see: vulnerable and terrified. The princess usually stands so cold and aloof, like nothing has a hope of touching her, not even the king who's little more than her warden.

"I didn't," I say softly. Aleta puts a hand to her heart as the fear dissolves from her eyes. She leans against one of the columns of her bed for support. "But…Aleta. How did you do that?"

She's a Torcher. There's no other explanation possible. But that should be impossible. Like me, she hasn't yet reached her seventeenth year. The ball celebrating her birth is still several weeks away.

Trepidation leaps back into her eyes as she looks from the poker sitting innocently among the flickering flames to me.

"I don't know," she says, resigned. "It began to happen several months ago. I didn't have nearly as many incidents as most Adepts when they first Reveal, but Larsden—he's not truly a tutor, you know; little better than a madman, really—assumed that was owed to the unique circumstances surrounding my gift."

Now I understand where Larsden and the king have

gained the assumption that Reveals no longer necessitate the previously requisite seventeen years.

"No one knows," Aleta says. "That is, no one excepting myself, Larsden, and the king. And now you, I suppose. They wish to keep it quiet, and I have no reason to wish it otherwise."

"I won't say anything," I say and mean it. I can't say what Larsden and the king's motivations are, but if I were in Aleta's shoes, I wouldn't wish to be watched any closer than she already is. I wonder why she hasn't told Caden and Tregle.

"I thank you for it." Aleta, relaxed now, stretches her arms above her head and yawns exaggeratedly. "However, I am quite exhausted. If you wouldn't mind?" She inclines her head toward the bedroom's door.

"Of course," I say hastily, making for an exit. I hesitate, remembering my thin slat of a window. "May I borrow a torch?"

"Certainly." Aleta waves her hand at the torch, and the flames leap to meet her. I jerk back.

It's only after I shut myself in with my cot and dancing torch that I realize Aleta never told me where she'd been.

Twenty-Six

When I was very small, no more than five summers, I ran away from home.

I can't remember why now. Probably Da had scolded me for something, and to my mind, the argument had been simple: I was right, Da was wrong, and if he didn't see that, I wouldn't stay with him.

What I *do* remember is trudging out of the house, determinedly throwing my knapsack over my shoulder. There'd be no sneaking for me. If Da saw me leave, so much the better and served him right.

I'd been outraged. He hadn't seemed concerned at all that I was on my way out. Just stood there, wiping down the bar, an amused quirk tugging at his mouth.

The door had slammed behind me as I left.

I'd been fine until darkness hit. My anger at Da kept me big and tall in the daylight, but after the sun fell behind the horizon, I shrank. The forest grew. Spindly branches transformed into shadowy witches' talons, reaching for me, determined to cook me and have me for their next meal. I thought of my bedtime stories, of the land that comes alive against trespassers.

True summer only lasts about a month in Abeline, but that night was warm. I'd shivered nonetheless. Huddled in the gaps between the tree roots, I'd tried to sleep, to wait out the long hours that stretched between darkness and light.

The normal forest sounds had turned sinister. The innocent birdcalls turned to hunting hawks. The movement of the grass was probably due to the same wind that rustled through my hair, but to my mind, it was a snake, venomous and evil, winding its way toward me. The thoughts kept my eyes open. Wide open.

Gradually, terror had loosened its grip, and sleep took a firm hold. When I'd awoke, I was back at The Bridge and Duchess, bundled in blankets on my sleeping pallet.

I'm still not sure if Da followed me the entire time or somehow tracked me later. We didn't talk about it much—not at all, come to think about it. When I'd gone downstairs that morning, opened my mouth to speak, to ask questions, Da beat me to it.

"Don't you have chores that need doing, Breena Rose?"

I haven't wanted to run since. Until now.

The thing is, I can't see how that will help anything. Da will still be locked away, I still won't have my answers, and—worse—the king might get closer to the war he wants with Nereidium.

I leave the dungeon after another visit with Da, more frustrated than ever before. It's my sixth visit in a month, and they're still fruitless as ever. Oh, sure, Da's uttered the odd statement:

"Your hair's gotten longer."

"There's a spot on your collar."

"Don't suppose you could smuggle some roast pheasant in? That's one of the few things they get right here."

But ultimately, I've gotten nothing from him, and I'm beginning to lose the ability to *care*.

I'm *tired*. Every day, I slip away from our rooms with Aleta for clandestine meetings with Caden and Tregle in the middle of the night; evade more lessons with Tutor Larsden; match wits with the king; and, sometimes, try to find a glimmer of my da in the prisoner behind the cell bars. It's exhausting. And it's taking a toll on me.

I fall into step behind the guard sent to escort me, and we make our way up a flight of stairs. I falter as we hit unfamiliar territory. There are portraits of nobles I've never seen before lining the hallway. A thick-set man stares me down from behind his frame. And I don't remember that oil painting of the weeping Makers. This isn't the way back to my rooms. It would seem that even long exposure to the castle halls doesn't guarantee you manage to learn them. The guard's led me the wrong way. I turn, intending to march my way back to Aleta's chambers, but stop short. Two guards I don't recognize bar my way. Tension threads through me.

As best as I can, I channel Aleta, nose in the air, and stride up to them. "Let me pass."

"I'm afraid they're under orders not to, Lady Breena."

The voice creeps from the hallway. *Kat,* I think, as a shiver climbs my spine like a ladder.

"Whose orders?" I demand.

Kat languidly runs a finger over a curl, watching me. Has she been here waiting for me this whole time?

Larsden steps forward from Kat's side. "His Majesty's, of course."

By the ether, my arm's only *just* healed. I'm finally able to stop applying the salve, and the skin bears only faint scarring. It barely pains me at all anymore, and I've been successfully dodging Larsden for weeks now to avoid a repeat performance.

"This again?" I try to sound impatient, dismissive. "I proved that I'm not a Torcher the last time we met, Larsden."

"True enough," he agrees. "But I'm unconvinced as to your other talents."

Kat's presence. *That's* why she's here.

I take a backward step, holding a hand out to keep them away. "No matter what my da is, I'm not a Rider either. You saw that well enough, Lady Kat, upon our first meeting. It's as Princess Aleta said, right, Larsden? The element would have recognized me?"

Kat's lips curve. "I don't recall that incident," she says. "You'll have to refresh my memory."

A gust of wind slams into me, knocking me against a wall. My back vibrates with the impact against stone. A hairbreadth of a moment later and Kat meets me there, impossibly quick, hand at my throat as my breath is stolen from my body.

She snaps her fingers with her other hand. "Well, this *is* a familiar sight! You were right, Lady Breena. I remember now."

Suddenly, I'm filled with something besides exhaustion. I'm angry. And *anger* I can use. I make a fist. My vision is going and so is my energy now, but I have enough left for this.

Thumb outside my fist. All of my weight behind the hit. Just like Da taught me. I lash out, landing a square punch on Kat's eye. The hit reverberates through me as I make contact.

Kat shrieks, letting go. Air *whooshes* back into me, but I can't pause to steady myself.

"You *wretched* little—" Kat clutches at her eye with both hands. She lets out another angry shriek, sounding like a bird of prey.

The guards look stunned and level their weapons at me. That's fine. I turn quickly and run in the opposite direction where none of them bar my way. This castle is large and meandering enough. It will spit me out *somewhere* familiar if I take another route.

I race toward a staircase, but Larsden catches me, seizing my upper arms. A swift jerk of my knee to his groin, and he releases me instantly, sinking like a stone.

I'll pay for the hits later, I'm sure of it, I think as I fly downstairs and melt into a crowd of other noblewoman, wheezing and short of breath. But I'm no longer interested in appearing obedient.

Twenty-Seven

The evening of Aleta's birthday banquet is an excuse for the gossips of the court to watch the girl who holds herself so aloof from them. And for those who *don't* know one of her best-kept secrets, it's a chance to keep an eager eye on her to see if the Nereid princess will have her Reveal.

My ladies have returned to attending me after I escaped my guard so overtly, but they're cautious with me now, like they can sense how I've closed myself off from them. They fill my ears with their meaningless rumors, hoping to ingratiate themselves back into my good graces. Chief among them is the speculation that, owing to her country's tendency toward Water Elementals, Aleta will be a Thrower, the first to grace Egria in sixteen years.

If only they knew. The princess is her country's opposing force: fire. Could it be owed to the fact that she's been in Egria since she was a babe? I doubt we'll ever really know. The science of the elements isn't something I can hope to understand when I have bigger things on my mind.

The ladies dress me in a heavy, green silk brocade. I put a hand to my stomach. I've felt uneasy ever since waking up, like my insides are sloshing about. There's nothing in particular I can attribute it to, but I just can't shake the feeling.

When Aleta and I leave our suite for the ballroom, accompanied by a veritable posse of attendants, my discomfort only increases. I've managed to adjust to the royal dinners of veiled threats and icy pauses, but I feel far from prepared for this. The "banquet" is a banquet in name only, Aleta told me a few days ago. Certainly dinner will be served, but it is, for all intents and purposes, a birthday ball.

"Why don't they just call it a ball then?" I'd asked, stumped.

"I suppose they believe a banquet sounds more dignified."

It sounds *quieter* and I long for it to be, but strains of music reach my ears already. Stately drums pound evenly, keeping time with the meandering strings and horns. It won't be the music and dancing I'm familiar with. I'm likely to make a fool of myself tonight, drawing more attention to my upbringing than there already is. Most of the king's court will be inside. It's a chance to make good on my declaration to defy the king, but I don't know if I have the stomach for it tonight. The nausea makes my breath shaky.

The nobility already swirl around the room, flitting from partner to partner like butterflies to blossoms, past the large window that consumes the far wall. The ocean's whitecaps are silvery in the pale moonlight. The waves look rough tonight. Violent.

I'm surprised when Aleta and I are able to sidle into the room without much notice.

"They don't announce you?" I ask.

"Only at state dinners." She sweeps her skirt aside to gracefully descend into a chair.

"Ladies."

As if flown in on a Rider's wind, Caden appears at my elbow. He drops a perfunctory kiss on his betrothed's extended hand and then takes mine. My heart pounds. Is it my imagination or do his lips linger a moment longer on my knuckles?

Aleta murmurs a greeting and picks at the food on her plate, some mangled sort of meat drowned in a brown sugar glaze. It's likely delicious, but my insides lurch at the thought of taking a bite.

"Your Highness." I manage the hello, sounding strangled. I eye my meal with trepidation. I'll never keep it down.

"Are you well, Lady Breena?" Caden's gray eyes are alight with concern.

"Fine," I assure him. I'm anything but. "I feel a bit queasy, that's all."

A warm palm covers my forehead. My skin is clammy against Caden's fingers, and I fight back the sudden heat that wants to rise in my cheeks.

"You do look a bit flushed," he says. He motions over a server. "Sparkling wine for the lady, please." Turning back to me, he explains, "The bubbles will calm your stomach."

"Oh, no." I rush to correct him. "Honestly, Caden— Your Highness, I'm not one for wine. I think it'll make things worse."

"Trust me. Just one glass and a bit of sweetbreads. It will settle you."

I don't feel like protesting, don't have the energy it requires. I take a half-hearted sip of the sparkling wine like a dutiful child with a spoonful of elixir.

Caden nods approvingly, a mother hen. "You should be resting."

"I don't have a great deal of say in my activities. You might have noticed?"

The room dizzies me as people swirl around, a typhoon of bodies. My skin flashes hot and cold. I close my eyes to fight off the spell of the nausea.

"I'll escort you and make your excuses." He puts a hand to my elbow. "Come."

Aleta watches us with an interested eye, sipping at her wine nonchalantly. For the guest of honor, no one's troubling to make themselves known to her, but I see the way they eye her, whispering behind their palms.

I capitulate, thinking of my small bed and the relief of sleep. "You're all right?" I check with Aleta.

She scoffs. "Please."

It had been a foolish question. If there's anyone I'd expect to be able to hold her own alone in a room full of catty nobility, it's Aleta.

Just as I let my arms be tucked into the protective embrace of Caden's, we're stopped short with the appearance of the king before us.

"Lady Breena!" he greets me delightedly. "Son. Leaving so soon?"

"Lady Bree's taken ill, Father," Caden says stiffly. I feel the tension drawn through his body. His muscles go taut.

"Lady Breena is made of very stern stuff." The king stresses the final syllable of my name, emphasizing the formality. "I'm sure she can muster the strength to attend this banquet."

Again, I'm given no choice in my activities. I slither my arm from Caden's hold. "Yes, Your Majesty. I certainly can."

The sea inside of me thrashes. I inhale deeply through my nose to calm it. Perhaps in the open air that would do me some good, but in the crowded ballroom, the scent of sweating dancers mixed with food only makes me feel worse.

"Lovely. Then I'm sure you won't object to favoring your king with a dance."

My entire body objects. Caden's hand finds mine hiding amongst my abundant skirts and gives it a rallying squeeze.

"A pleasure, Your Majesty." I'd do Aleta proud with the evenness of my voice. The lack of emotion in my tone masks a fair amount of disdain.

The king leads me to the center of the floor, and Caden disappears into the crowd, returning a moment later with Lady Kat on his arm. It's an easy enough dance to follow, so I try to focus simply on the arm that leads me and the music that guides us both. The music is merry, the horns moving quickly as the strings wind themselves around their tune.

The king doesn't speak.

I feel the eyes of the nobles on us. I can guess at what their whispers say. The king is parading me like the prized carcass from a hunt. "Look," he seems to be saying. "Look at my pet duchess." These thoughts and the spinning required as the king loops me in a circle around him don't do my stomach any favors.

There's a brief moment of the dance that requires the male beside us to spin me, and I swoop with relief into Caden's arms, grateful for the respite.

"You're doing fine," he breathes into my ear. His breath is harried. "It's almost over with."

He hands me back off to the king.

I feel many things, but fine is not among them. This dance needs to be over with soon. It's *already* lasted an eternity. The music swells in a final crescendo, and I wrench myself from the king's arm, putting space between us to curtsy shakily.

The king lunges forward, and for a terrifying moment, I think he's going to attack me.

Instead, he picks up my hand and drags a kiss along my knuckles. His mouth is wet, slimy. This time, I can't suppress a shudder of revulsion or the instinct to yank my hand away. I wipe it surreptitiously in the folds of my dress.

"Thank you for the dance." The tremble in my voice is loathsome, but I explain it away. "I'm afraid His Highness Prince Caden was correct, however, Your Majesty. I do feel quite ill." A hand flits to my midsection. "I hope you'll forgive my rudeness if I retire for the evening."

"I am a charitable ruler, Lady Breena, and not unreasonable." He smiles a shark's smile. "Of course you may retire to your chambers."

"I'll escort you, Lady Breena." Lady Kat must have been listening to us the entire time. She appears at the king's elbow, resplendent in red silks, but for the purple that darkens her left eye.

I cringe at the bold color of her gown. I know that Katerine's killed, but I can't believe her audacity—to declare it for all to see.

"That isn't necessary," I protest. Even to my own ears, it sounds weak. "I'm certain I can find my way on my own."

"I insist."

The two of them look at me with matching grins, ones that could devour me whole. I acquiesce with curt nod, turning away from Lady Kat. She tucks my arm in beside hers and beams at me. To view us from a distance would be to see us as friends, about to share a giggle of secret confidences.

Instead of leading me to the suite I share with Aleta, she winds me through the crowd. I mumble apologies as I jostle ladies' fans and stumble on the hem of my dress.

"I believe there's been a mistake. I was to return to my rooms. Perhaps you failed to understand that, Lady Kat. How is your eye, by the way?" I infuse the words with as much sweetness as I can muster.

Abruptly, breath abandons me. Kat prods me with a finger until I stand with my back against the wall.

We're in a corner of the ballroom, practically hidden behind an ornate sculpture of a giant stone flame. The countess smirks, exceedingly pleased with herself as I gulp soundlessly for air that will not come.

My heart crashes against my chest as I'm suddenly back in the hall the other day, then back in the woods of Abeline the day I was thrust into this mad world where people threaten me wearing smiles. I raise my fist for a punch, and Kat pins my wrists to my sides.

I force myself into calmness. Panicking will do little but waste the precious little oxygen I have left, and the burning in my lungs now is nothing to what it had been when I'd been on the forest floor. Nothing to the flames that raced up my arms at Larsden's behest only weeks ago. This is pain I can withstand a while longer.

Besides, I think on a weak wave of confidence, Katerine won't kill me. Not in the midst of all these people. Not when the king's made it clear that he still wants me alive.

"It's you who fails to understand something, Lady Breena. It is not wise to bait me. My *name* is Lady *Katerine*. I won't tolerate anything else from a girl who may as well be a peasant. Is *that* understood?"

I nod frantically, wanting only to have breath back in me.

Katerine steps back, and air—delicious, life-sustaining air—rushes back into me. I gasp down lungfuls and press a shaky hand to my diaphragm.

"Understood, Lady Katerine," I say. I meet Kat's stabbing gaze, despite the room swimming around me. I'll use the woman's given name, but I refuse to be completely cowed by her. Katerine will not own me. No one will.

Like she's been issued a challenge, Kat's lips curve up approvingly. "Very good, then. Tell me, Lady Breena, how is your testing going?"

"Inconclusive thus far, my lady." As if she hasn't seen that for herself three times over, stealing my breath away.

She tuts. "I don't know *why* he's bothering."

"Do you mean the king?"

"Of course. I don't know why he's bothering to test you. I'm not certain why he's bothered to keep you alive at all, if we're speaking frankly."

"I do so enjoy your particular brand of honesty," I mutter.

"I wouldn't expect it to last much longer." Kat barely seems to have heard me, she's so wrapped up in her own musings.

"The honesty?" Her thoughts are difficult to keep pace with.

"No." Her attention snaps back to me. I start at the gleam in her eyes. She has a tenuous grip on sanity at the best of times, but the spark of madness truly shines there now. "Your life."

My nausea dissipates as a chill races over my arms. "The king won't kill me. He needs me."

Kat's laugh is shrill. "For what? The treasure your father is purported to possess knowledge of? His Majesty has *me*, Lady Breena. I have served him well in your father's stead these past sixteen years. We have done without this treasure he now seeks. If he desires it again, I'm certain that the solution lies with me and not with you. We'll be able to rid our realm of you *and* your father's scourge soon enough. And I *so* look forward to that day."

A flame the size of a fingernail shudders across my arm. Pain lances through me. Kat simply smiles.

It's her. Somehow she's not *only* a Rider. She's a Torcher, too.

Egria. This *place* and its secrets. This *woman* and her strange gifts. Why should the Makers give them to her when she only uses them to hurt people? It's not right.

I shove at Kat's shoulder, suddenly livid. "That's enough," I say, voice low.

A rivulet of water from a nearby glass splashes up, dousing the flame.

My laugh is one of mocking disbelief. She's a Thrower, too? Why not? Why *shouldn't* she have three powers, one of which is supposed to be missing from Egria altogether?

Kat takes a startled step away from me, eyes locked on my soaked arm. "How—"

"I don't care," I say, stepping closer and closing the gap between us. "Do you hear me? I don't care to know how it is that you wield three elements, Lady *Kat*. I care naught for your threats either. I may not be your definition of nobility, but like it or not, I *am* your peer now. I am finished pandering to your expectations. I am finished trembling in fear when you walk by. I hope we understand each other."

I make to turn away, but Kat's faint voice stops me.

"Two."

I turn back. "What?"

"Two," Kat says, voice stronger now, eyes still on my arm.

"I—two what?" I ask, momentarily distracted.

The color's drained from Kat's face, and she lifts her eyes to mine, searching my face as though it holds an answer to her question.

"I have power over *two* elements," the countess whispers, her voice steady again. Her gaze sharpens. "Unusual, yes, but Larsden has his theories. I wield only wind and flame, Lady Breena. So, pray tell, how is it that the power of a *Water* Thrower has come forth in such a way?"

I don't have an answer for her. My thoughts scramble. This is a trick. The water had been Kat's. It *has* to have been Kat's. How else—*who* else—?

"How, when it hasn't been seen in years?"

My eyes flicker over the crowd, still whirling about the dance floor, none the wiser to what's happening in our corner. I spot Caden arguing with his father at the throne, Aleta picking at a salad apathetically, and Tregle standing beside a guard.

They all think I'm back in my room. No one thinks to look for me at the edge of the room, to pull me from this conversation where I have no answers but a growing number of questions.

What Kat implies is impossible, yet I can't think of another explanation. *Why* can't I think of another explanation?

The hall goes curiously silent to my ears as I roil in my thoughts, unable to reel a coherent one in. I'm drowning in them. They're suffocating me as they tumble one after another. I clutch my head.

A rushing sound fills my ears. It's like my thoughts are all roaring at once as great emotion swells within me, rising up so that I can give voice to it.

Not sure of what I'll say, I open my mouth—

—and a frothing wave crashes through the dark windows of the ballroom.

The glass shatters, and screams echo around the room as the powerful gush of water knocks people to their knees. Dresses are weighed down with water, and still it floods into the room, whirling into the lanterns and plunging us into darkness.

I stare with wide, uncomprehending eyes.

The water pools around our knees, and bewildered shouts join confused sobs as people struggle to stand despite the force of the waves that thrash around them, receding and dragging them inexorably toward the jagged, gaping hole in the window that will send them crashing onto the rocks below.

Water still pours in, arcing up from the ocean itself.

I spy Caden hanging one-handed from a wall sconce. As Aleta is pulled past him, he grabs her around the waist. She pushes him off, scowling and holds onto the sconce herself.

The current of the sudden waters carries Tregle by them. Aleta shouts, stretching out her hand. Their fingertips brush. But don't hold.

Tregle's eyes widen as he's dragged away. Aleta screams.

It's a terrible sound.

"Breena! Get a hold of yourself! You'll kill us all, you stupid girl!" Kat screeches. She clings bodily to the statue we'd been talking beside only seconds ago.

I'm the only one left standing unencumbered. How is this happening?

I extend a cautious hand and dip it into the dark water. It gentles at my touch. Like an obedient hound, it laps at my fingers.

"We need a Shaker here," Caden bellows, gesturing with his free hand toward the window.

At his call, an Earth Elemental sloshes forward daringly. The current tries to down her, but she bends at the knees and pulls upward until the floor bends to erect a barrier between the ballroom and the outdoors.

It comes just in time. Tregle and a host of others crash into the barrier. They groan—smacking into solid stone can't have been pleasant—but they're alive.

I feel it then. The tie I have to the waters. I wiggle my fingers experimentally. Nothing happens but for a small splash.

I give it a mental push. *Go,* I think at it. *You need to go. Gently.*

The waters withdraw like a stopper's been pulled, draining out of the room through cracks in the tiles and around the Shaker's barrier to rush from the shattered glass.

I behold the room before me. People are weeping, confused and clinging to the nearest stable object they found in the madness. Water drips from the ceiling and chandeliers.

Torchers work to dry their hands so they can get flames and lights going. Everything's soaked and everyone's bewildered.

No one except Kat realizes that I'm the source.

"But I haven't even reached my seventeenth year."

The feebly whispered protest barely reaches my own ears over the roar of ocean pounding within me. By the ether, I can still feel the waves thrashing at the foot of the palace, meters below.

Kat's talon-like fingers squeeze my shoulders, and she breathes a hot whisper into my ear.

"Haven't you?"

Twenty-Eight

Water dripping from our sleeves, Kat drags me into the throne room, commanding a messenger to relay that we'll be waiting for the king. It's empty this time of night and all the more daunting without bodies to fill it. I haven't been in here since Da's sentencing.

The scene Kat and I left behind was a dream that had warped into a nightmare. My mind is still shrouded in fog, but it's dissipating rapidly, leaving me with a sense of horror.

I'm a Thrower.

Makers be blessed, *truly*? Because my life really requires further complications at this point. I shake my hands as if that will shake the abilities loose from me.

Even as I wish the Elemental powers gone from my fingers, I take it back. Maybe it's a curse, maybe it's not, but the gift is mine and it's not something that can be stripped from me. There's little else I can say the same of these days. A puddle of water pools beneath my feet, and my fingers absolutely itch toward it.

No, I amend, correcting myself. Itching isn't quite

right. There's a sort of…*current* in my blood now.

I take a deep breath to clear my head. Kat's beside me, watching my every move with the beady gaze of a hawk. I yank my arm from her grasp. She lets me go, but I'm sure she'll stop me if I stride across the marble floors in an attempt to flee. I *might* be able to defend myself now, but I still doubt I'd make it past the hall.

Kat taps a finger in the crook of her elbow and purrs, "I don't know what keeps His Majesty."

I wish the rocks below the palace had kept him. It's so little to ask in the wake of this discovery. If the water had to rear up like that, if I *had* to have a Reveal tonight of all nights, in the presence of the entire court, why couldn't I at least have managed to rid myself and Egria of the poison of the king's rule?

But no, the Shaker intervened before anyone had gone crashing below and I'd managed to pull myself out of it. For the most part, I'm thankful for that—I'm not sure I could have forgiven myself if I'd had a part in Tregle's death. Or anyone else's.

We wait, the drip-drop of our gowns the only sound.

I expect the double doors to bang open, announcing the king's entrance. For him to make a spectacle, cause a scene. Instead, the door creaks open, and the king strides in leisurely, Caden and Aleta following behind him. They're little worse for the wear—Aleta's hair sticks wetly to her cheeks and Caden looks like he hasn't had a moment to catch his breath in days—but I'm relieved to see they appear unharmed.

The three royals halt in front of me. Caden's eyes scan me, stopping at the puddle rippling around my feet. "You're well?" he checks.

I manage a weak smile. "Depends on your definition." I fight against the impulse to sink to the ground from exhaustion as I meet the king's gaze.

"It seems our search for a Thrower is at its end," he says softly.

I feign confusion, remembering that I'm not *supposed* to know of the problems he faces in his conquest of Nereidium. "I beg your pardon?"

"You've made things simple for me, Lady Breena. You are the second to Reveal before her seventeenth birthday. Your father holds the answer in the treasure he was supposed to retrieve for me, I am sure, and my patience is at its end. I have a Thrower now and—"

Makers bless, he does *not*. I can't believe he's already making plans, when my shock has yet to subside.

"You have nothing," I say. My words are tired but heated. "I've only just Revealed, and you've no one to train me. I'm as good as useless to you." I'll do nothing for him either way.

He cuts me with a glance and lifts a warning finger. "I. Have. A Thrower. Now." His raised brow dares me to contradict him. I keep my silence, but my puddle now swirls at my feet. I might be able to control it—maybe. But it seems more prudent to keep my connection with it strong until I see what his plans entail. He continues, "And I shall take Nereidium."

Aleta leaps in, expression fearful, but her voice calmly curious. "Your Majesty, you already have me as your ward." She forces a chuckle. "What more do you need to secure your rule in my kingdom?"

The king settles back on his heels and rocks once. I can't break his gaze. He holds me rapt, dreading the idea that I *know* what comes next. Caden and Aleta's faces reveal similar feelings. Caden's eyes are locked on his father. Aleta's mouth thins to a line. Lady Kat's grin is so wide it threatens to split her cheeks in two.

"My son and the princess will marry in a fortnight."

Twin hisses as Caden and I suck in our breaths whisper through the unfortunate assembly. Aleta's eyes shutter. Seeing her emotions there is an impossibility, but her hand clenches and unclenches at her side. The blood's all but drained from her cheeks, leaving them to match the bone china our meals were served on this evening. It's too soon. We haven't figured out how to stop his conquest of Nereidium yet.

"And, Lady Breena, you will wrest the secret your father keeps from him by the end of that eve. Elsewise, you shall find yourself both motherless *and* fatherless."

The threat hits a dull mark. I've always guessed that's where this would lead. Hasn't the king been making these threats all along? Only now, I have a definitive date for his agenda.

I nod, showing that I understand, but I'll get nothing for this hateful man. Any answers I seek will be for me and others like me. He's too confident in his power to recognize that I can be a threat to him, but we'll topple his rule.

"I thought to keep the young sweethearts waiting a bit longer, but it does seem as though the Makers are trying to usher things along with tonight's events."

"Father," Caden tries, splaying his hands wide. "This is so sudden. There are dignitaries to contact. Arrangements to be made. You can't—"

The king lashes out, his unnatural calm breaking. "I am the king of this realm," he spits, clutching his son's collar. Caden looks stricken. His hands go to his father's wrists, and the king comes to himself and shoves him away. Caden stumbles. "I can do as I wish. The arrangements that you speak of are mere trifles. The plans have already been made. Several months ago, in fact, when I first *thought* this marriage would take place."

Both Aleta and Caden look as though it's a fight to hold their dignified postures with the sudden weight pressing upon their shoulders.

"I so look forward to celebrating with you all," the king says. He offers his arm to Kat, who takes it smugly. The door *does* bang behind them this time, and the sound reminds me of a thrown gauntlet.

"What now?" I whisper.

"Nothing," Caden says shortly. "We wait."

My patience frays. The likelihood that the king will allow me to slip away from his guards for secret meetings now is slim, all but nonexistent. I highly doubt anyone— be they an Adept, nobility, *or* the crown prince—will convince them to abandon their posts.

"We had best address the situation *now*, Highness." I match him for tone. I understand that he's just been handed his wedding date, but the problems facing the kingdom and Da's life rather overshadow that.

"Lady Breena is right." Aleta's voice is hollow, empty of her usual confidence. "We'll have no other opportunities to speak."

I barely catch Caden's eye as he turns away from us. I've never considered him a spoiled princeling, but he's certainly acting the part now. I grab his arm.

"*You're* the one who wanted me brought into this. We can't just let this sit. We've got a fortnight to come up with and execute a plan. That's *two weeks*, Caden."

"I understand that," he snaps. He breathes deeply, calming himself. "I know what a fortnight is, Bree." He tries for a smile but doesn't quite make it. "I'm sorry, but I find myself ill-suited to continuing discussions this evening."

He's retreating. I feel it as certainly as I feel the ground beneath my feet. He may be plastering on a smile, but he's falling behind the guise of cordiality.

"I bid you both a good evening." He nods once, a quick jerk of his head, and then he's gone, turning sharply on his heel.

"*Caden*." I swear and make to follow him, but stop, Aleta's stance catching my attention.

She's not quite *there* anymore. Her eyes are straight ahead, but she hasn't said anything since voicing her agreement with me. Her shoulders are pulled back to her spine, and her fingertips are pillowed lightly on each other. But her picture of grace is ruined by the deep shuddering breaths she draws. Her hands begin to tremble, and she forms a fist in an effort to stop their quaking.

I should go up to my room, I think, a bit uncomfortable. *Leave Aleta to think in private.* She's never welcomed any words of comfort from me, and it's not likely she'll start now. Despite these thoughts, my feet carry me closer without my express permission.

"Are you all right?" I ask, after a great deal of subtle throat clearing.

Aleta starts. She turns to me, and I regard her warily. I don't want to spook her. She's got the look of a cornered animal, frozen in place before a desperate strike.

"Yes, Lady Breena. What is it that I can do for you?" Her voice sounds as if it hasn't been used in a long time.

"I think we'd best be returning to our rooms now."

Aleta blinks and looks around us, surprised to find that we're not already there. "Right you are. So we should."

She glides from the throne room in a daze. I'm at her side, flicking worried glances between her and the guard that meets us at the doorway.

Upon entering our suite, Aleta moves immediately to the sitting room, where an enterprising servant's left a carafe of red wine. She pours. The sound of the sloshing liquid fills the room.

Wine won't exactly elucidate matters. "Is that the best—"

Aleta flicks her fingers at me as if shooing away a fly from the wineglass's rim. I quiet. Aleta's need for something to wet her lips is greater than my need to talk just now.

"I'll join you then." I pour myself a glass to match and throw it back. Ugh. I've always preferred a hearty cider or even The Bridge and Duchess's watery ale.

Aleta's green eyes are fixed on some point in the distance that only she can see, but she gulps back the wine as if it's water. When she finishes, she breathes like she's surfacing for air, swiping her fine sleeve across her mouth. The red wine stain smears over the green of Aleta's billowing dress.

The palace is quiet around our suite. The banquet's attendants scattered after my Reveal like ants in a rainstorm. I can just hear the clinking of the guard's armor outside the door as he settles into position for the night.

Aleta cups the goblet in her hand, turning it so that the glass catches the light of the lanterns. There are tiny bubbles in in it and gold molded around it. Someone has been lax in their polishing duties, though. The embellishments are tarnished.

Aleta follows the path of the winding metal with a thoughtful nail. "I suppose you've never seen such finery before."

The usual mockery of my country life is missing from

her tone, but I bristle a little anyway. "No," I say curtly. "Not until I came to the palace, Your Highness."

"It's glass."

"We did have *glass* in Abeline."

It comes out in a snap, but I hadn't meant it to. I ease a deep breath out of me and settle my goblet back on the table. Aleta obviously doesn't have any further desire to talk about the evening or what the immediate future now holds.

"I think I'm for bed," I say, stretching. I start toward my tiny bedroom.

Aleta's voice drifts to me, poking me in the back. "Do you know how glass is made, Lady Breena?"

I do a half-turn. Aleta's voice still has an odd, dissonant note to it, like someone's standing on her throat and the result is this strangled croak.

"I can't say that I do," I say, inviting Aleta to say more.

"I meant shaped, really," Aleta amends. I wait in silence while Aleta stares, trapped in her own thoughts, at her goblet. "They have some glass, you see, and it might be any shape to start with—a really lovely vase or a misshapen mistake, a disfigured blob. But they can turn it into whatever it is they wish for it to become.

"They use a fire, temperature so high it'd forever scar your skin unless you're a Torcher. Even Egria's best healer couldn't help you. They blow at it and twist it and turn it until they think they have what they want. This beautiful thing that fits into their decor. Forged in fire.

But at the end of the day, it's still so fragile. Still so delicate."

Aleta's expression twists into something fierce, and the goblet is clutched in her hand so tightly I'm surprised it doesn't break. Suddenly, she hurls it at the stone hearth, where it shatters. I jump at the sound.

This is it. *This* is where Aleta finally breaks down. I ready myself for it, to care for the girl who had been an enemy and is now almost a friend.

Aleta's ferocity melts away as she begins hysterically laughing. "But despite all of the work they put into it, it can still be broken," she gasps out, clutching her stomach. Tears run down her face as she lifts her eyes to meet mine, a smile remaining melded to her. Her laughter sounds like a sob. Encouragement jumps to the tip of my tongue, but Aleta straightens before I can voice it. She wipes the tears from her cheeks. "They think *I* am glass," she says. She's hard again. "But I am not. I am not delicate. I am *stone.* If they want to break me, they will have a hard time of it. I am *un*breakable."

We say no more that night.

Twenty-Nine

The sun streaks in through my small window, prying my eyes open with intrusive fingers. It lights upon the chest of drawers on the opposite wall. The chest is weather-beaten but ornate, with swirls of blooms carved into it. Out of habit, I reach under my nightdress and withdraw Da's medallion, running the chain I've procured through my fingers and pondering it as I come awake.

My eyes are heavy. When I'd retired last night, I'd thought I wouldn't be able to sleep, but I've managed at least a few hours. I stretch in my bed, kicking a leg out from beneath the covers to cool off. A few hours might as well be none; I feel like I haven't slept at all. My limbs ache, and my thoughts are clouded with exhaustion again. My eyes weigh down more and more with each blink.

I Revealed last night. There's no time to waste on sleep. I have to wake up. Reluctantly leaving my bed behind, I move into the sitting area. It's brightly lit, even more so than my room. It has to be midmorning, at least. I'm surprised none of the servants have come to wake us to break our fasts.

The washbasin water is cold when I splash it on my face, but it does its job. I'm more awake now. More *alert.*

Aleta's large magenta door is firmly shut, denying entry to anyone who approaches. How lucky for me that I'm finding it a little more difficult to be intimidated by something so simple as a shut door. I'm a Thrower now, and whether the king tries to control me or not, I have an element on my side that I hadn't before. I feel stronger. I *am* stronger.

I rap on Aleta's door. "The day's a quarter passed, Your Highness," I call.

No reply answers me. She can't still be asleep? I push my way inside.

It's empty. Again.

How is Aleta doing this? How does she disappear at night, leaving me to discover her missing? And better yet, why does she leave me behind? I'd like to escape the guard just as much as her.

I search for her exit. There isn't a possibility that she's gone through the doors of the suite—the guard is still outside—and the windows are tightly closed. I open one to examine it just in case, sticking my head out. No ropes hang swinging in a breeze. That eliminates the idea that Aleta left that way for a certainty.

I take a deep breath, enjoying, for a moment, the wind that blows past me, ruffling my hair. It's grown quite a bit in my months here and hangs past my chin now. I look past the castle, past the gardens. In one direction, there are triangular treetops—the forest where Caden and his men hunted, where I'd had my first real conversation with him. In the other...

I straighten. The city lies beyond the palace grounds, a twisting and meandering series of stone buildings and cobbled streets. There are patches of colored fabric waving in the wind—green and blue, white with orange lining. I squint. Are those tents?

They are. It's a festival caravan. I went to a traveling festival only once, three years ago when I was almost fourteen. The caravan festivals almost never came as far north as Abeline. It was the bad luck of a mistaken route that had led them to the northern province in the first place, Da told me afterward. They'd landed themselves on the Chittering Pass and gone too far to turn around by the time they'd realized it.

The festival had been a grand time, even in a small village like ours. We'd turned a better profit than we had in ages with the new people in town, had barely been able to keep up with the demand. And the caravan had brought with it their own brew.

Da'd shooed me off to try it. "Go have fun, Breena Rose. And bring us back a sample of their wares."

I'd been happy to oblige. There had been games of strength and mysticism. A fiddler had pulled his instrument, and I'd whirled around the square in a mad, turning dance that I could barely keep up with. Their brew was excellent, something called Starter Cider. I'd drank too much, laughed a lot, and kissed a boy I liked—

the farmer's son—square on the lips. I could have gotten lost in it all.

Lost. My mind refocuses itself, fixing on the streets. *There's an idea.*

If we can somehow make it out of the castle, *could* I really lose myself in the city? More importantly, could the king lose me there? I can see the mass of bodies from here. None of them know me. They're not permitted in the palace, so they'd never recognize my face—or even Da's or Aleta's. Somehow, my intentions for escape have come to include her, too. If I escape the stronghold, maybe I can disappear, evading the guards and blending in with the crowds long enough to make contacts and save enough coin to hire a way out of Egria altogether.

Another breeze rustles past me, and I shiver. My skin is still wet from washing my face, and the breeze is cool, sending goosebumps skittering over my arms. I clasp the window shut hurriedly, rubbing warmth back into them.

A scrape sounds from Aleta's room. She's back…somehow. I dart into her room to see her throwing all of her weight against her wardrobe. I've never seen her in a state of such…disrepair. Her dress is rumpled and streaked with dirt. Her hair hangs loose in strings, some plastered to her neck, and her skin glistens with sweat.

I clear my throat loudly to catch her attention. "Pleasant night?"

"Help me with this," Aleta says, ignoring my sarcasm. She continues to strain against the heavy oak furniture.

"You could have picked a better time for redecorating," I mutter, but I join her. My back goes to the side of the wardrobe as I push against the ground with my feet. The wardrobe gives, sliding slowly across the floor until it occupies a new spot on the wall.

"Why exactly was that necessary?" I pant when we're finished, putting a hand to my side to ease a cramp. That's the most manual labor I've done in months.

"I needed to hide it better."

"Hide *what*?"

"The entrance, of course." Aleta eyes me in a manner that suggests I've forgotten which direction is up.

Of course. I could smack myself for being so obtuse. How else would Aleta slip in and out past the guards? Of course this doddering old castle has a secret passageway besides our meeting room. Probably multitudes of them.

I turn and examine the wardrobe with renewed interest. "It's behind that wall then? Where does it lead?"

"Underground. It deposits you just inside the city."

Inside the city? "Then we can—"

Aleta cuts me off by shaking her head, seeing where my thoughts are leading. "Using it to escape won't work, I'm afraid. It's near a post of the king's guards—Adepts, at that. There's always a man or two outside. I've never even opened the exit, just peered out."

I sigh, deflating. Another road that leads to nowhere. "Why the excursions into the tunnel then?"

She shrugs uncomfortably at my questioning look.

"It's nice to pretend that escape is possible, that's all."

Hours later, I pace. I tell Aleta that it helps me think, but she tells me to think somewhere else because I'm driving her mad.

So I move back to the sitting room and circle the sofa, skirt the edges of the room, and try the door, thinking to pace the halls, whether shadowed by a guard or not. The door's locked from the outside.

No charade of freedom left for us then, is it? My lip curls at the doorknob, as if it's responsible for my position. Pacing isn't doing me any good. My thoughts are a riptide, pulling me along. I can't direct them, only pray for release.

Da's still trapped, and so am I. So is Aleta. Da will be killed. Aleta and Caden married. And I'll be—what? The king's prized Thrower? Conscripted into his navy? I rub at my eyes. This is all wrong. *I haven't even turned seventeen.*

Haven't you? The echo of Lady Katerine's words come back to me. I jerk my head up, eyes widening.

Had Da lied about my birth, too?

My thoughts are interrupted by a click, a creak, a few footsteps, and then the clearing of a throat. My head whips to the door to see my ladies entering the suite.

Not your *ladies, Bree*, I have to remind myself. *The*

king's *ladies*. I haven't seen them since departing for Aleta's banquet last night.

"What?" I ask flatly. Before, I'd have been delicate. I'd have wanted to please them, to make them proud that I was learning their courtly ways. Now, I only want to repay them for making me trust them when my trust was unwarranted.

Emis winces at my tone, and I revel in it.

"H-His Majesty asked that we return to your service," Gisela reminds me, a nervous eye on Aleta's door. "And Her Highness."

"He asked that you return to reporting on us," I correct her. As one, their mouths clamp shut. "It's not as though we've a choice in the matter anyway."

Well, I intend to make their time *useless* then. No longer will I employ any sort of candor when addressing them. They want me to play the part of nobility so badly? They'll get it. I'll give them my orders, stay distant, and shut them out as soon as possible.

Gisela forces a smile. "Is Her Highness up and about? We're to escort the two of you to the docks."

I wave a hand at Aleta's door. "She's up." Wait. Had Gisela said—"*Docks?*" I try to tamp down the eagerness in my voice. Docks mean ships. Ships mean *water*.

A splash comes from the washbasin behind me, and it's like the cold liquid is tossed over my head as I come to a realization: if the king wants *me* around water after last night, I'm sure there's a reason.

Thirty

At the docks, the scent of salt tinges the air, and I sweat beneath my corset, cursing the sadist who invented it. With the weight of my perspiration soaked into the thing, it's a small marvel that I'm even standing.

The sun is a ball of light above us in a cloudless blue sky. Beside me, Aleta breathes easily in the stifling air. Even the rare breeze that blows by today just teases us with relief before snatching it away.

A ship stretches above us, its mast shooting straight up into the sky. Plum sails are bound around it. I shade my eyes against the sun as I look up. It looks a part of the atmosphere, there, like it's painted against it. I can hardly tell where the scenery ends and the ship begins.

It rests upon the ocean—a vast body of water that glitters with secrets. Well, not *exactly* the ocean, but a port to it. The water is corralled, a bit calmer than the wild sea at the foot of the palace cliffs. I've felt cowed before it in the past, with all of its varying shades of blue and gray, the crests that pop up unpredictably. Now it's like seeing an old friend. Its secrets are mine; we share them.

I slip from dock to sand. My slipper sinks, and I snatch my foot back abruptly at the heat that bolts through me. Da and I roasted a hen once by heating the stones around it. It feels like the same just happened to my foot.

I resist the urge to run forward, toss my slippers into the waves, and let the ocean break its fast on them. I've a wild craving for feeling the foam of the water lap against my toes.

Aleta nudges me. The king's approaching, Caden and Kat behind him like shadows.

"Lady Breena. Princess Aleta." He inclines his head. "Son, say hello to your betrothed."

Caden's face is expressionless as he executes a stiff bow. He says nothing.

I try to catch his eye, wanting to communicate some sort of assurance, but he avoids my gaze, moves his so it's trained on the horizon. There's something new in his stance, a pretense that hasn't been there before. Despite the heat, a chill goes up my spine as I realize what it is.

It's the first time Caden reminds me of his father.

"Come," the king says, moving swiftly up the plank to board the ship, Kat at his heels. Aleta, Caden, and I follow at a more sedate pace. Our ladies will stay behind and await our return.

"Are you all right?" I hiss in a whisper to Caden.

"Fine," he says dully.

The navy vessel's beams are dark inside the bowels

of the ship where we board. Gray lumps of cargo are secured with thick ropes. Here, the sway of the ship as it rocks in a still port can be felt strongly. Aleta's face takes on a nauseated expression as we move toward the steps to climb above.

The deck is polished to a fine shine, and sailors stand at attention, snapping their heels together and bowing from the waist to their king. It seems like a small amount to crew such a large ship. I count only twenty hands on deck including the captain. He seems a capable man, giving only the cursory bow to the king before filling us in on the ship with short, clipped phrases. I nod a surprised greeting to Tregle, who's standing alongside the seamen.

"We're going for a short jaunt, in and out of the harbor. Only need a few hands to lower the sails and go below with the oars. With such fine weather, we'll return just before supper."

He bids us to come up to his quarterdeck and observe as the crew descends on the ropes that kept them tethered to Egria's land. They cast off, tossing the thick braids into the water.

The ship lurches as we crawl away. I stumble on the deck, bumping Aleta's elbow. Her face has a distinct greenish tint to it now, and the glare she shoots me lacks its usual fire. I scramble away. I have no love for the dress I'm wearing, but I've no desire to wear Aleta's last meal instead.

"Steady," the captain says. "You'll get your sea legs

under you. It will be only a moment before the lads find their rowing rhythm and we'll be able to loose the sails."

True to his word, the ship's motion soon shifts. We coast along the waves, and Aleta's color abates a bit. She gropes behind her for some support, sagging against a railing gratefully.

I can't help but feel impatient. I'm right on top of the ocean, but it's as distant as ever. I need a better vantage point. That's when I spy the bow, leading the ship's charge over the water.

Pointing to it, ignoring the sharp eyes that rest on me, I look to the captain in question. "May I?"

"Want to get another perspective, do you? By all means, my lady."

My lady. I shake my head as I walk away. I'll truly never get used to that.

A breeze caresses me as I lean against the railing that prevents someone from rolling away into the ocean's depths. My wrists dangle over the edge. My cheeks still smart from the slap of heat I got before coming aboard earlier, but I'm considerably cooler. My corset's practically dry. My hair blows into my eyes, but I smooth it away. I don't want to miss a second of this: the churning of the ocean as the ship slices neatly through it, the shimmer of the water as the sun's rays spark on its surface.

And I don't just see it. I *feel* it. It builds up in me, fills me, exhilarates me. I've never felt so strong before. The temptation to test my new ability is irresistible here.

Slowly, I slide my palms against each other.

A thin sheet of water launches from a wave like a javelin. Whoops. Not the graceful movement I'd intended, but I grin as it catches the sunlight and casts off a rainbow. It's amazing that only yesterday I hadn't known I had this in me.

Someone sidles up beside me. "Don't get comfortable." Tregle barely moves his lips.

The arc falls back into the ocean as I glue my palms firmly to my side. "I'm not," I say, defensive.

But I am and I shouldn't be. The memory of a tidal wave crashing through the ballroom windows sweeps over me. How *can* I get comfortable knowing what a lack of control could lead to? Shame courses through me. I need to remember that I'm untrained. I could easily have capsized the boat with my actions.

Tregle's red-faced beneath his Adept robes and looking fixedly out at the ocean, tension lines his face.

My consternation fades. I suspect my lack of training isn't what he means. "Comfortable how?"

His eyes are fathomless and haunted by a past I can't see. "Steel yourself, Lady Breena. His Majesty does little without reason."

I know that. I'd thought the same myself when Aleta and I were summoned to the docks. But when the king hadn't actually explained his motives, I'd assumed that he was just showing off. Showing me what he has at his disposal, how powerful he is, to further intimidate me.

Tregle seems to think otherwise.

He leaves my side wordlessly as we slip farther out to sea. The harbor is a distant blend of indistinguishable buildings in the distance.

A few deckhands mill about the ship. Aleta's where I left her, leaning against a railing. Her hands are clasped in front of pursed lips. Probably praying to the Makers that she can hold it together and this trip doesn't last any longer than strictly necessary. The king is with the captain, gazing out at the horizon. They're talking, motioning out at the expanse of water. Caden is his father's silent shadow, his hands linked behind his back, studying him. He's looking at the king the way I look at Da: like he's searching for his father in someone he doesn't recognize.

Abruptly, the king points decisively at something I can't see. I crane my neck, but there's only the sea.

"Port!" the captain yells. "Hands to port!"

I descend from the bow as the crew hurries to heed their captain's call. The ship banks to the left.

"What's going on?" I ask the captain as I approach.

"His Majesty is desirous of further exploring today," he clips out.

Exploring? The king surely already knows the port in his own capital, but it seems harmless enough. I shrug a dismissal, but Tregle's warning reverberates through my thoughts. I know not to trust the king's actions without questioning his motivations.

"Why?" I press.

The captain taps a foot impatiently. "Hell if I know—

" He catches himself, sweeping his hat from his head in an apology. "I mean, I don't rightly know, my lady. I'm sure His Majesty has his reasons."

I'm sure of the same thing. That's what worries me.

Without answers, I can't shake the feeling of dread that squeezes in on me, but there's no sense in useless anxiety. I retreat, making my way over to Aleta. The seasick princess has found a bench to sit on, and Caden joins us, collapsing beside me.

"Having as much fun as I am?" I ask them.

Aleta withers me with a look, indicating the pail set beside her. "What gave me away?"

Peering in, I recoil, throwing an arm over my nose to cover the stench of vomit. "What's wrong with you? Toss that overboard!"

"It seems to be providing Father with some amusement to keep it onboard," Caden says. It's the most he's said all day. "He's forbidden it." He winces as it sloshes against the side of the pail.

The ship rocks, and Aleta throws herself toward the pail, gagging uncontrollably. Her hand trembles as she raises it to cover her mouth, leaning tiredly on the arm of the bench.

"By the ether, Aleta." I swear, jumping away from the ominously sliding bucket. I usher her to the ship's railing. "Don't give him any more to sicken you or the rest of us with. If it happens again, you just let it out right over the side, understand?"

She nods weakly, glaring arrows. She's ill-suited to

taking orders. I take my seat on the bench beside Caden, keeping a wary eye on the bucket.

My heart pounds suddenly, and I find that I can't look him in the eye. We haven't had the chance to talk since he made his escape last night. Silence makes itself comfortable on the bench in Aleta's stead. Around us, sailors shout and run about, but Caden doesn't say anything.

"Have you thought any more on—on what must be done?" I struggle to form words that won't give our treason away. The wind thrashes all about us here on the water, and there's no telling if our words will be dragged back to Kat. Makers forbid the king have an inkling that he's been manipulated in any way.

"I have. And I'm giving it still more thought."

"And have you...come to any decisions?" I brave a glance at him, but I needn't have feared. Caden won't meet my eyes either.

"Not as yet."

His spine is ramrod straight. *Why* won't he look at me? I stare at him worriedly. "Caden, what are you going to do?"

"I will do what is best for my people. Even if that means I have to give something up."

That sounds like he's already made a decision. My stomach churns. He's going to resign himself to his fate, ally himself alongside Aleta and her kingdom because it's what his father wants and the king *gets* what he wants.

Caden sighs, his facade breaking, and lets his head

drop to his hands. He looks at me tiredly. Gray shadows hover below his matching gray eyes. Now that I can examine him more closely, it's obvious that he hasn't slept.

His hands fall apart in his lap, resting on his knees. "I just haven't worked out the details yet. It's a lot to handle and I almost feel... Things are moving too fast."

My palm covers his hand, wanting to comfort, but clumsy at it. "It's a lot to take in," I agree.

"No, Bree." He leaps to his feet, looking about in alarm. The wind whips his hair about. "The *ship* is moving too fast."

He's right. I fly from my seat. We *have* sped up. And the ship is going still faster. No wonder the wind has intensified. Sailors grab hold of anything within reach to stay on their feet. Aleta's bent almost double over the rail, trying to hold herself in place but being lashed back in the face with her sickness as the wind tosses it back at her. My stomach twists with quick sympathy, but there's nothing I can do for her.

Kat's at the helm, conducting the wild breeze into our sails with a peaceful expression, hands raised above her head. She alone stands unsupported, eyes closed as the air she controls thrashes at her dress, at her hair, pulling tendrils from its neat coif.

The ship races on, leaving the harbor completely. Caden falls back onto the bench with an oomph, and I lose my footing, crashing backward into his hard chest. Absent hands steady me, lingering on my arms. A quick glance back at Caden confirms that he's more concerned with what the ship is doing than what his hands are occupied with. I'm both glad and disappointed.

Finally, the wind slows. The people onboard right themselves. Caden offers me a hand as he stands up again, and I take it. Together, we check on Aleta.

She's covered in her sick, but ridding herself of everything in her stomach seems to have quelled her nausea. Her old fierceness is back on her face. "If you ever mention this, I swear, I will make you regret it."

"Mention what?" I ask innocently. A smile slips past Aleta's frown.

The ship drifts near a small boat, a two-man rowing canoe. A moment later, we're even with it, albeit at a distance as a wave buoys us about.

"Ahoy!" one of the men calls cheerfully, waving his arm. They stood upon seeing the violet sails that mark us as a royal vessel. We're far enough away that there's no cause to worry that our ship will somehow plow into the tiny canoe.

"Lady Breena!" The king calls my name, and dread floods me. Whatever he wants, it's surely nothing I want any part of. He crooks a finger at me, and I rise to meet him. I flick a glance at Tregle, who appears at my side as if Kat blew him there. A rancid stench emanates from Aleta, so I chance a guess that she and Caden are at my back.

A wave of gratitude washes over me. I may not have Da with me, but I'm not alone. Not by far.

"I have a bit of a test for you," the king says. He's got the look of an overly satisfied tomcat.

"Da always despaired of my test results during lessons, Your Majesty. I'm afraid you're going to be disappointed."

"Oh, I think you'll find a way to pass this one. Do you know what purpose Elementals serve in my realm?"

"They—"

He doesn't wait for my answer. "They are in my service. They run my armies, construct my forts, tend to my gardens. I've not had a Thrower in years, and my navy has suffered for it. But now that I have you..." His smile spreads. "Lands I wasn't able to conquer before will stand no chance once we make it upon their shores. And we will, with you as a part of my navy."

Be a part of his navy? I will *not*. "I'm not—"

"But first we need to see what you can do."

The words on my tongue sink back into me. What does the king want now? My eyes dart about for an escape route but find none. If I thought I could do it, I'd vault over the ship's railing and run straight back over the water to Egrian land.

I follow the king's arm as he indicates the small boat beside us. "Sink the boat, Lady Breena."

He keeps his words quiet, but he may as well have shouted them for as hard as they slam into me.

The men on the boat aren't even looking at us anymore; they've lost interest, casting a net. Fishermen. And not well-to-do ones either if they can't even afford a proper boat. Probably have wives, families, children. Sole bread-earners and tax-payers for their households. And the king wants me to kill them.

"I am not my father, sire," I say quietly, eyes locked on the small boat. It bobs uncertainly next to our ship.

"That is abundantly clear, Lady Breena. Your father at least had the good sense to hide his treasonous leanings until such time as I could do little about it."

Not for the first time, I think with a confused sense of pride of how well Da can play a part.

"Perhaps I was not clear," the king continues. "You will do this. Or not only will that deceitful excuse for a father that you have vanish, but I will send Lady Katerine back to your village to burn it into the ground."

A garbled sound leaves my throat without my permission.

"I will salt the fields so that the survivors—and they will be *few* in number—cannot even hope to rebuild."

"They've done *nothing*," I whisper. I lift defiant eyes to the king's, not bothering to hide the hatred that simmers there. "How can you condemn them all because of your lust for power?"

He snaps his fingers, bypassing my question. "All of them, Lady Breena. Gone. Two lives for the trade of…perhaps a hundred? I am unsure, I confess, as to how many people your village houses."

I tremble with barely suppressed rage. How I'd love to seize a handful of the water from below us and thrust it down the king's throat. It would be better than Kat's trick of stealing air from lungs. I'd trap the air there with water, where it's unable to escape. See how he likes it when the thing he cares most about—himself—is threatened.

I take a step forward, stalling for time. Caden and Aleta don't stir behind me. It's foolish of me to wish they would when they can't save me from this fate. No one can.

I study the expressions of the men below us impassively. They've turned back to the ship, seeming to sense the eyes on them. They can't know that their king has just given their lives away, but their grins fade as they sense something amiss.

There has to be a way out, a way to avoid becoming the king's puppet. Could I smash the boat and avoid their bodies? Then pull the men under in a pocket of air? I doubt I have the finesse for it as a fledgling Thrower. Even if I d, the bubble will pop under the ocean's water pressure. And pulled beneath the surface, where they're unable to escape the water's inexorable grip, their drowning will be more of a certainty than ever.

But all of those people back in Abeline, I think, grappling with myself. They don't expect to be pulled into this, have done nothing wrong. And there's so many more of them than these two men. I think of the children who dance in the village square and play in the fountain. Lady Kat would set her blaze during the night when most people are asleep and can't escape from the flames.

They'd burn to a crisp. Survivors would have to guess

at which bodies belonged to whom based on the rooms that they were found in. They certainly wouldn't be recognizable.

I picture it all: The ash raining down on them, coating the ground like gray snow. A foot planted on a shovel to drive it into the earth. A mass grave, the length of several houses, on a field that used to supply wheat.

Two lives…for all of theirs.

Could I live with it? Not well, I admit to myself, feeling shaky, but I could make it through. I *can't* shoulder the knowledge that everyone in my village is dead because of me.

"I grow impatient, Lady Breena."

My decision is made. Trembling, I step forward to the railing and start to raise my hands. I make myself look the men in their eyes. I'll remember my victims, carry them with me always, never allow myself to forget.

Circular ripples surround the boat, but the men don't notice, as their attention is fixated on the ship.

I take a deep breath, readying myself to feel that power again, to use all of the feelings swirling inside of me and send them crashing down into the boat. Readying myself for the guilt I'll carry with me for the murder.

It's a good thing, I try to tell myself, that it has to be a blunt strike because of my lack of training and knowledge. Maybe the men will avoid painful deaths through my ineptitude. But I can't let them avoid death altogether, not at the cost of the people I grew up with. I swallow hard, hesitating. I can do this. I *have* to do this.

Just like Da taught me. Count to five and—

Heat streaks overhead before I can act, taking the decision from my rising hands. I turn, uncomprehending as my hands fall to my sides, and follow the path of a second sun flying through the air—a massive fireball flashes past our ship and heads straight for the boat.

"Stop!" I yell hoarsely, sure that it's Kat wielding the blaze, but the flames smash into the tiny fishing boat like an angry fist on an irritating pest.

No. Horror fills me. There'd been no preparing for that, no way that I could muffle the cry that escapes or quell the sickness that rises in me upon seeing the fishermen's boat go up like a hearth's kindling.

I can't even see the bodies.

Tears clog my throat. My voice is husky when I spin to the king, my breath ragged.

"I was going to do it," I say desperately. My corset is too tight, my *ribs* are too tight for the shallow breaths that I inhale.

I loathe the truth in my words. I *had* been ready to do it, to trade those lives for the ones that I know. Now that they're dead, my only task is to convince the king of that fact. I have to save Abeline. My throat is closing in on me. The scent of smoke sears my nostrils.

The king's eyes are steely as he considers me.

"Please," I beg. "I was *going* to do it before Lady Katerine stepped in. *Please* don't punish my village."

"It wasn't I, Lady Breena." It's as though Lady Kat halted the wind completely to better hear the conversation. Her steps forward tap loudly on the deck in the stillness.

Then... I turn to Aleta in question, who shakes her head, mouth in a half-open O.

That leaves one person that I know of. Slowly, I turn to the first friend I made on this transition into my new life. The first person I'd let myself trust here. The first Elemental who made me consider that they weren't all bad.

The person I'd thought had grown from the cowardly destroyer I'd met in Abeline.

Tregle won't meet my gaze.

"It's nothing I haven't done before."

Thirty-One

So much for the idea that Tregle had been led to a better life after his Reveal.

He doesn't truly *believe* that, does he? I wasn't the one to take the lives of the fishermen, but even now that we're safely back in port, bile lies at the base of my throat from having been a party to their deaths.

And if it's not the first time that Tregle's done something like that... I forget sometimes that he's a soldier. No wonder he keeps quiet so often.

This is what becomes of the *good* Elementals under the king's rule. He presses them into his servitude until they become one of his *Adepts*. Until they become someone they'd hardly recognize.

I won't let it happen to me. Not like it happened to Tregle and Da.

From the ship, I'm escorted to Da's cell door. I hardly know what to say to him now that I'm close to understanding why his past shaped him the way it had. Why he'd felt he'd had to run. Maybe, like me, he'd had something to lose.

I still don't appreciate all of the secrets, the making of my entire life into a lie. But I can understand it now and that's something.

Da's as quiet as ever, picking at some dirt under his toenail, tongue twisted to the side. He looks like a wild man. Tufts of his hair protrude from his scalp like unruly weeds, and the clothes he's been given are gray with his own filth.

The pick of his nail is a bee buzzing at my ear, irritating me until I can't bear it any longer and I burst out with an accusation that's not really an accusation at all.

"You've never worn red."

He stops picking at his toes. I know he understands my meaning. If he's killed as many people as I think he has, why not acknowledge it? At least Kat does that much.

"Yet my middle name is *Rose.*"

His hands fall to his sides. He's made me wear the color in his stead, only I haven't realized it until now.

"I'm trying to understand," I say. My voice is strained, and I take a minute to calm myself. I don't want to accuse him anymore, but I can't go on ignoring what Aleta told me of his role in her parent's deaths. "You were his assassin?"

Da's mouth puckers at his toes. "Wondered when you'd get to that. Yes, I was his favored assassin. But what does that matter? I did right by you when the time came."

"*Lying* to me my whole life wasn't exactly *doing*

right by me," I bite out, losing my composure as quickly I gained it.

"You're still alive, aren't you?"

I try my hand at the stony silence Da's practiced so effectively during my visits.

He leans forward, resting his arms on his knees. "Think the situation's black-and-white, do you?"

"You either murder or you don't," I spit out without thinking. This is not how I'd wanted this conversation to go. I *don't* see it as black-and-white, not anymore, but he just refuses to give an *inch.*

Words can't adequately say how angry it makes me that *this* is the subject he finally chooses to have a conversation with me on. That instead of inquiring after my health or making plans for both of us to get out of here, he delivers a defense for murder in a voice just above a whisper.

"How about this scenario, Breena Rose? Imagine that you're a child. You think you're an adult, but really the world is so much bigger than you've ever known—more than court, more than fencing lessons, more than birthday balls thrown for nobles you don't even know."

He's talking about himself. He's finally going to tell me *something.*

"The *world* is more than you've ever known," he continues. "You've got a good head on your shoulders, but you're cocky. Too cocky. And secure in your station. And worst of all, you're powerful, which is a dangerous ingredient when combined with youth. You know only what your best friend tells you about the world." Da shuffles his feet and sighs. "Even back then, he wasn't the same boy I befriended as a child. There was a thread in him that had unwound somehow."

Best friend. He can only mean the king. The glimpse into their past that the king gave me our first night in the palace is enough for me to guess that.

"The way he saw it, it was Egria against the world. Us versus them." He shrugs. "I wasn't so sure, but then he showed me a list from another kingdom and told me that every name on the list had wound up dead. And I saw Corrine's name on it."

Ma. I'm afraid to even breathe too loudly, lest I stir Da from his fervor. We never talk about Ma. He scarcely seems to know I'm there anymore, trapped in his memories.

"I knew I could stop the rulers from moving down the list," he says. "I wouldn't have to use a knife or even poison. Nothing so crude as that. I could just steal the breath from their lungs, and it would look natural. Like they'd passed in their sleep. No one would suspect the emissary of peace from Egria as a culprit."

He stops, face paling at the remembrance. "It was different than I thought it would be. They woke up when they couldn't breathe. Struggled. Their faces purpled, and they fought me until…they didn't anymore."

I'm going to be sick.

"But I did it because I loved my wife." His face is fierce now, and he emphasizes every word. "And the man

I once called a friend promptly moved armies into a country too torn by chaos after the sudden loss of their rulers to defend against him."

Wait. He *hadn't* been speaking of Nereidium? I know that the king hadn't been able to get his armies onto the island after the slaying of Aleta's parents.

So the king has done this to other lands under his rule. No wonder Caden and the others are so determined to prevent it. They know his procedure, know how he works. Nereidium's the first land he's tried and failed to conquer, so of course he's fixated on it.

"But it was so easy that the king couldn't believe he hadn't had me do it before. He abandoned the excuse of a list. One never existed to begin with. I was almost relieved. It meant Corrine was safe. He told me it was for the good of the kingdom. He said, 'Those who are not for the good of the kingdom are against it, and we execute traitors to the kingdom here. As well as their accomplices.'"

Accomplices? Da's grim face says it all. He hadn't had accomplices. Just my mother. The king threatened Ma's life.

I feel vaguely guilty. If that part of my history is true, Da saved Ma only for his work to be undone when I was born.

"I was a coward. So I bowed to his will and executed those he chose. His enemies began to whisper of me as a shade, one who steals someone's breath away in the moonlight. Somehow, no one connected the falling kingdoms with my visits. I wish they had. I wanted a way out. And because I couldn't see another way, because I *was* a coward, I tried it on myself. If I tried poison, they'd get me a healer, and if I used a knife, they'd staunch my blood, so it seemed that depriving myself of air was the only solution. I blacked out before the deed was done. The traitorous air came rushing back to me." Da's eyes are flat. "How could I bring an innocent child into that mess?"

It's a good question. And it explains why he'd run with Ma—and me in her belly.

And yet, he *had* brought an innocent child into it. Aleta was stuck, bitter and mean and an orphan under the rule of her nation's greatest enemy. She'll be denied her rightful crown. None of it is fair, and it can all be traced back to Da. Despite how close I am to understanding, I can't forgive him for this. His actions affected far more people than they'd helped.

"Two nations are trapped in a deadlocked war because of you. Aleta's parents are dead."

"Who?"

"Aleta." He doesn't even *remember* the girl whose life he tore asunder? My sympathy is unraveling faster and faster. How could he just forget the girl? "The princess of Nereidium?" I remind him.

To my disbelieving ears, he actually laughs. "Right. Of course. *Aleta's* parents. The princess is *alive* because of me. I was the one who stole her away from the nursery that night while Kat set the blaze in the royal wing."

Kat killed the king and queen of Nereidium? She and Da had worked together—the two Riders under the king's command.

That title isn't quite right for Kat though. I dimly recall the chaos of my Reveal. Hadn't Kat sent a flame crawling across my arm? In fact, I'd been sure until Tregle stepped forward that Kat had been responsible for the fire that had taken the fishermen's boat today. I've been so concerned with the addition of my own powers, I've hardly paused to consider Kat's.

"She set the blaze. How can that be?" I broach the topic. "I mean—I know that she can both Ride and Torch, but *how?*"

Da laughs again, but there's no humor in the sound. "Sweet mercies, they *do* keep you away from the castle gossip, don't they? Lady Kat was birthed a twin, but her sister's abilities transferred to her...somehow. So they say."

I'm getting sidetracked. I drop my voice to a whisper, hoping that the stillness of the air means Kat isn't spiraling my words to her ears as I speak. "Tell me about that night. There's a deadline now, Da. The king'll kill you if you don't hand over this treasure he's convinced you have. We've got until the prince's wedding in two weeks."

"And you?"

I falter, noticing how Da's eyes have sharpened, his shoulders drawn in toward his spine. "I'll—I'm not sure. He wants to make me a part of his navy."

"Navy?"

"I Revealed last night." I shift in my seat—it's still so surreal. "I'm a Thrower."

He stills. "So you'll be in his navy. But you'll be alive?"

"Yes."

He relaxes, leaning back against the gray bricks in his cell. "You look nice. New dress?"

Trying to pin down Da for an answer is like trying to capture the air he's supposed to command.

"The king tried to have me kill someone," I shoot back. There. *That* will hold his attention.

The light of mild mischief in Da's eyes after his compliment fades. He wilts under the press of my gaze. "Did you do it?" he asks.

I, too, sag under the weight of the memory. "I was ready to," I say softly, feeling ashamed at the remembrance. "Someone else stepped in."

"You're making allies then." A half-smile lifts Da's cheek. "That's good."

"Don't talk of allies as if I've gone to war here, Da." I'm only trying to do what it takes to get by until I can get us both *out*. I want only to survive that long.

"My dear girl." He sighs. His voice is world-weary, and the exhaustion in it frightens me. "The minute Kat stepped into our tavern, you were at war."

Thirty-Two

They tell me I'm a Thrower, but that term implies that I can use my powers deliberately.

Da's words stay with me when the king assigns me a new tutor, one who is, thankfully, nothing like Tutor Larsden. Though I have no desire to give into the king one bit more than I already have, Da's right. I *am* at war with the king and have been for months now. I'll let them teach me how to Throw. Learning how to use my abilities is a wise decision.

Unfortunately, I can't seem to muster up a modicum of control in the days after my Reveal. Water responds to me in moments of heightened emotion, but making it obey my will is another matter entirely.

It doesn't help that I'm the only Egrian Thrower to be found anywhere. The new tutor is a kind Shaker, but she can only offer suggestions on how to concentrate or examples of Shaker methods. Maybe, the frail old woman suggests, I can adapt the movements to suit Throwing?

But I don't know *how* to adapt them.

Every day, Tutor Alys is very calm as she starts out with me. We practice in a secluded corner of the garden, where the Shaker can manipulate the earth and I can attempt to work with the water of a decorative fountain.

When Alys bids, a vine twirls from the ivy on a nearby arbor to whirl playfully around her finger before twining itself back about the arbor. A bud blooms slowly, like a palm opening, to reveal petals of pinks and purples.

When I mimic her motions, sweating yet again beneath the sweltering sun, the fountain's water surges up in a liquid tornado before splashing over my head.

At least it's cooled me off.

Alys sighs, raising her arms tiredly. The sleeves of her robe slide past her elbows. "Let's try again."

Her voice is encouraging as she entreats me to start over, but I'm irritated and verging on disgust with myself. I have no control. Can't even guide a stream of water from a bowl to my fingers, a skill that has to be the most basic Throwing method in existence. How is it that I commanded an ocean-filled ballroom with nary a thought, but a small *fountain* is beyond me?

"This is absurd," I mutter. Frustration scrapes its way through my voice.

"Lady Breena—"

"No, really!" I insist, wringing out my hair. "What does the king want with a Thrower who can't even master *this* much water?"

"I'll remind you again that the key lies in controlling your temper." Alys makes her voice soothing. "It is the same with all Adepts. I master my element by grounding myself, imagining the roots that tie me to this land. *You* must be still as ice. Calm and innocent as a brook. Placid—"

"Placid as a lake, I understand." It's the same list of trite metaphors she's spouted every time I grow annoyed. "What if I'd rather roar as the rapids? Or—or crash like the waves?" I throw my arms wide so she'll understand what I mean, and my frustration sends the water sloshing over the fountain's lip.

The soil drinks in the moisture greedily, and Alys watches in contemplation. Triumph fills me.

"See?" I ask pointedly. "*Finally,* results."

"I don't think that these are the results you seek."

"Perhaps they should be. It's the most I've accomplished in all three of our lessons."

"Lady Breena—" Alys stops, shaking her head, and pats the bench beside her.

I sit, feeling impatient. I want to get *on* with these lessons. I've finally managed to make some progress and don't want to stop now.

"You are rushing things." Alys's eyes are sympathetic, but her words are blunt. "It will take *time* to master these abilities. Years."

Years? I don't *have* years. I have *days*. I have a deadline that draws closer with every passing breath. I can't waste time fooling with gentle waterspouts when any semblance of an escape plan depends on me being able to *fight* my way out.

"Don't look at me so." Alys takes my hands in her wrinkled brown ones. "The name you Water Adepts are given—Throwers—is not still. It's not placid. It is made to remind us all of the force with which water can be wielded. Yet you are regarded as the pacifists of the land to all those outside the royal forces."

I most decidedly do *not* feel like a pacifist. I feel like I'd relish the chance to throw a few hits, toss a drink in someone's face. I miss my firewood axe. At least then I'd felt like I had something to do damage with, something I could really *control* and rely on.

Alys squeezes my hands, bringing me back to the conversation.

"But I know. I know that, as much as the ground beneath me can keep me calm, the ocean must roar in you. You cannot hope to master it by being just as unwieldy. It is like an untrained marksman loosing an arrow. Without proper direction, there is no telling who he will down."

Much as I'm reluctant to admit it, she makes sense.

"The king..." Alys hesitates, choosing her words carefully. "He will never think of you as a pacifist. He is mindful of your potential for power. He sees you trained to use you as a weapon. He sees you trained so that he won't lose a vessel to a tsunami when you grow upset onboard. Untrained or used against him, you are a dangerous liability that he would be...disinclined to put up with."

There it is. I'm no safer than Da when it comes down to it. The king wants to use me, but not enough that my life won't be constantly at risk.

And Alys must know of what she speaks. She's an Elemental, which means she probably served in the king's army before being selected for palace service. It's hard to believe that the woman's gentle hands likely once smashed earth down atop the heads of the king's enemies.

She lets go of me and stands, smile bright once more. "Let's begin again. Still as ice. Calm as a brook. Placid as a lake."

I push myself to my feet, take a deep breath, and try to picture her lake. Still. Quiet, with dark waters. I imagine it in the midst of a shaded glen, where a willow gently strokes its surface in a soft wind. Not a perfect stillness, but the image projects a calm over me that I haven't felt in days.

"Good," Alys murmurs. "Now. Lift your arm. Slowly. Think of it as a dance."

Cool sensation prickles along my spine. I feel a bit heady, like I'm floating. My arm glides out with two fingers extended.

The water weaves its way to me, a python slithering in mid-air. I laugh in disbelief before it reaches me, and it splashes down onto Alys's robe.

Alys beams with pride. "There, you see?" She thumps me on the back enthusiastically. "Progress. *Real* progress. The element was *yours.*"

I smile back but can't meet Alys's eyes, knowing that, despite this training, it will matter little in the end.

Because yes, progress is progress. But it's not enough. One week more and the waves will crash past any who stand in my way.

Whether I can control them or not.

Thirty-Three

Soon, the deadline is under a week. I have four days left.

I haven't gleaned anything further from Da, haven't made much more progress in my daily lessons with Alys, and Aleta and I haven't managed to escape Emis and Gisela for even the space of a quarter hour. I see no hint of Tregle; hear no whispers of Caden beyond wedding chatter; and if the two of them plan some escape from the king's machinations, I don't know about it. The prince is even absent from dinner.

Seamstresses join the ladies and guards in our suite every day now to ensure that Aleta's wedding gown fits her.

Though her fittings are rushed, Aleta is eerily relaxed during all of them. It alarms me to a degree. She doesn't even bother to verbally skewer the seamstress when she pricks her side with the needle. But I can't blame her. There's blood staining the matrimony already. What's one more drop?

I've seen Da every day and have all but given up

asking about the king's treasure or trying to pry more details from him about the night he fled Nereidium. It's nothing more than a half-hearted effort now, as my mind is more preoccupied considering what might happen when I try to escape. Just after the ceremony, I'll grab Aleta and run down to the prisons. We'll get Da out of his cell—somehow—and then—

I can't see past that. My mind circles itself like a dog chasing its tail.

We'll get out, I try to assure myself. There are three of us, three different sorts of Elementals. If the king sends a Torcher, I can hopefully do something about it, and it can hardly hurt Aleta. Da's air can blow away any earth Shaken toward us.

And if he sends another Rider? a small voice inside of me prompts. *What if he sends Lady Kat?*

The idea dismays me. As many times as I've now lived to tell the tale of a confrontation with her, I still go out of my way to avoid the Rider. If the king sends Kat... Well, if he sends Kat...

There are three of us, I tell myself firmly, trying and failing to convince myself it will be enough.

But at dinner the next night, I slip a knife up my sleeve. Just in case.

Before long, it's two days. And then it's the night

before the Bonding banquet, a formal ball during which Caden and Aleta will be formally presented to each other before their wedding day. As if they weren't raised within spitting distance of each other.

I can't sleep. Kicking off my blankets, I pace my tiny room, then transition to the suite. I peer into Aleta's room, which is dark save for the fire glowing softly in the hearth. The passageway remains safely ensconced behind the wardrobe, and I contemplate it for a moment, wondering. Could we truly manage to pull off an escape that way?

Shaking my head, I back away. It's not time. I've been afraid to even whisper my lopsided plan to anyone. I don't want to alert someone and ruin everything. Aleta showed me how to open the tunnel. That needs to be enough for now.

Finally, after a few more laps around the sitting room, I tap on the door—still locked from the outside—and ask the guard to escort me to the kitchens for an evening snack. Maybe a full belly will lull me to sleep.

"I'll send for a servant to fetch some food." The guard stares stiffly at the wall opposite our rooms. His posture indicates his reluctance to look at me, but his voice isn't unfeeling. He shifts his weight to his other foot uncomfortably. Mayhap even the king's guards aren't *entirely* on his side.

I press him, sensing that he's sympathetic. "Just an escort will do. Please? I think the walk would do me some good."

He gives in, as I thought he would. The man's armor clanks, echoing through the nearly empty corridors. This is my favorite way to find the palace: quiet and vacant. We walk in silence to the kitchens, where I ask a servant to fetch me some bread to fill my insistent insides, suddenly ravenous.

The guard waits at the entryway, and I move inside to await my bread.

The sight of Caden, already seated in the dining hall, brings me up short. His hair falls loose over his forehead, and his head is slumped into his hands.

"Isn't past your bedtime, Highness?" I tease in an attempt at levity.

I falter when he lifts his gaze to mine. Eyes bruised from lack of sleep, the prince looks like he'd barely be able to lift a spoon to his lips, much less twirl about the dance floor with abandon tomorrow night.

"Haven't you heard?" he cracks, trying—and failing—at a smile. "Heirs in this kingdom haven't time for sleep. We're much too busy wavering between familial loyalty and morality."

I hush him furiously, looking around the dark hall. The wooden tables are empty, shrouded in shadow, but in the castle, I always feel that there are eyes and ears on me that I can't account for. I indicate the guard watching us with a jerk of my head.

Caden straightens, his gray eyes sharpening on the man's form. He lifts his voice to carry. "Sir knight."

The guard stands at attention, feet snapping together.

"Your Highness."

"You may entrust the Lady Breena to my care."

"I must decline. His Majesty the king commanded that she never go unescorted."

Caden pulls in a haughty sniff, and I nearly laugh at his pompous attitude. "Are you inferring that my escort is somehow less than adequate, sir knight?"

"No, Your Highness, not at—"

"Then I bid you a good night."

Unable to argue with that, the guard marches away to return to his post at outside my rooms. Fleetingly, I wonder if he's realized that Aleta has gone unguarded while he's been away. I wait until the clinking of his armor no longer reaches my ears before speaking.

"Familial loyalty and morality, is it?" My eyes trace his face. He's been so closed off in the past weeks, but finally, he looks like the boy who greeted me in the dungeons again. Like a friend.

But those eyes of his still make me think of trouble.

"You should try to sleep," I tell him, settling on the bench across from him. "You've a big couple of days ahead of you starting tomorrow."

Caden snorts. "Big isn't the word I'd use, Bree. Monumental. Unthinkable. Either of those would be a little more apt. I'm to become a slave to my father's will and tie myself to the ice princess."

"I'll not hear you speak of Aleta as such," I warn. "We've become close over the past weeks."

He waves a hand in apology. "I'm sorry. You're right.

I didn't mean it either. We grew up together and she's a friend, but I just—*marriage.*" He rubs at his eyes, and lifts them to mine, a smile flickering at their creases as he steers the conversation in a different direction. "I'm not entirely surprised that the two of you have become friends, you know. You're more alike than you realize, and you've an enemy in common." His smile drops as he yawns, finishing it in a groan. "Ether and arrows, I'd give my kingdom for some sleep."

"So take it."

A shake of his head. "I can't. There will be time later. After."

I lean forward eagerly. "So you *do* have a plan?"

"Bree…" His tone is apologetic, and I slump.

"Pretend I didn't ask."

"It's just—it's not really safe to talk here. You do know that?"

"I know. I just let myself forget it sometimes." Is this the last time we'll be able to speak so informally with each other? Going forward, if my escape goes as planned, I'll never see him again.

The thought catches and sticks with me. I'll never see him again. We've hardly even had time to get to know each other, but already it's a wrench to think of the rest of my life without his encouraging presence, his half-smiles and sturdy shoulders that seem like they could help with my burdens.

This is the way it has to be.

"Whatever your plans may be, Caden, I'm sure they'd

be better served if you didn't look as though you'd fall flat on your face mid-sentence." I give his knee a joking prod with my toe.

"Perhaps you're right." He stands, and I follow suit.

We say our goodnights as I choke down the urge to tell him of *my* plans. I can't tell Caden. He already struggles enough with his own decisions about the wedding—that's evident.

"Caden…" His rebellious name swims to my lips. I put my palm to his forearm. "Goodnight." My hand refuses to move, and any other words refuse to come.

You're going against good sense here, Mistress Perdit. I've toed the line with Caden this long. It would be stupid to step over it now when I'm so near the end of our time together.

Before I can step back, Caden's arms come up around me and pull me into his chest.

This close, I can hear his heart, pattering against my ear. Its beat echoes my own. It's quick—a gallop. The tunic he wears is rough and scratches my cheek. His chin pokes into the top of my head. It's important that I focus on these more uncomfortable details. And not the fact that he's warm and smells of cedar and apples. Or how his hand smooths down my hair with a light touch, lingering on the nape of my neck.

It would be too easy to let myself soften, to fall into him and forget who I am now and what I have to do. It would be too easy to reach a mirroring hand up to his cheek and let my palm graze the hairs rising there. Too easy to look up into his open, honest face and finally understand precisely what trouble his eyes can bring.

There's too much at stake to explore here. I stiffen in his arms and give him a gentle push.

He releases me immediately, stepping away and putting some much-needed distance between us.

"I'm sorry," he says.

"For what?" I'll let us both walk away from this as unscathed as possible. Pretend I haven't let my thoughts lead me down the trail of what could happen next.

Gratitude shimmers in his eyes. "You've been a good friend to me, Bree," he says. His voice is the whisper of a cloud on the night sky.

I nod, understanding that this may be the closest that we'll get to a real goodbye.

"I'm to escort you back—"

I cut him off with a nervous chuckle. "Much as I appreciate the offer, my alone time has been scarce lately. If you don't mind, I'd love to seize the opportunity."

He nods, accepting that, and walks away.

I watch as the shadows of the hall swallow him up. *Someday, Egria will be in much better hands. Understanding hands.* But I can't stay and wait for that day to come. His footsteps fall away, and I stay behind, wishing for a life in which I could follow them.

I make for my rooms soon after, halfheartedly chewing on the warm bread the servant finally appeared with. I may need all of the sustenance I can get in the next few days, but I'm not all that hungry anymore.

Thirty-Four

By the time Aleta and Caden's Bonding night is upon us, I'm a bit more accustomed to the routine that precedes a formal event. I understand the customs of nobility now. They wear their gowns and jewels as a symbol of their status—like their own personal shields, protection from the swords of others' words or judgments.

And as Gisela arranges the hem of Aleta's Bonding gown, the princess might as well be wearing armor; she has the look of one going to war.

A battle *is* drawing near, though Aleta doesn't know it. But I do. I *know* that, by escaping, we're on our way to true war with the king. I draw a shaky breath from my position behind the group of women who have appeared to dress me and the princess for the evening. Tomorrow is the wedding. This will be my last night in the palace one way or another, I think grimly.

After the wedding ceremony, before the reception and the consummation of the marriage, Aleta and I will make our escape while everyone is occupied waiting for the new bride to appear. I can't leave my friend to the king's mercies, but I'm afraid to voice my plans aloud anywhere in the castle. Makers only know whether they'll be overheard.

Gisela yanks the princess's corset tight, and Aleta grimaces. The laces at her back cinch shut, and her shoulder blades nearly meet.

The gown is designed to show off the extravagant fortune at the king's fingertips, and it serves its purpose well, sewn with silver thread that catches the light as Aleta moves, encrusted with pearls and other sparkling gems that I can't put a name to. The traditional silver sets off her skin well.

Emis steps forward, armed with a crown of blue flowers. Aleta holds up a hand, halting her progress.

"The azulys make me sneeze," she says. "Perhaps something in red?"

Emis hesitates, and I'm pulled from my contemplations of escape, growing more attentive to the conversation.

"*Red,* Your Highness?" Emis asks.

Aleta knows the protocols involved in color selection. She taught them to me the first time we really spoke. As a princess and presumed future queen of Egria, she's safe in choosing any color, save red. The color of spilt blood.

The color of death.

"But—this blue would look so lovely on Your Highness," Emis tries. She holds the flowers up entreatingly. "And the king was quite clear—"

"If His Majesty protests, you may tell him that I

refused all flowers adamantly. He's not so unreasonable as to punish you for my misdeeds."

I hope she's right. I still smart over their betrayal but have privately conceded that Emis and Gisela had no real choice in the matter. To refuse the king's wishes is to invite his wrath upon yourself and all you hold dear.

Aleta finger-combs her hair as she examines herself in the mirror, lips pursed. "Besides, it's high time we threw away outdated customs. If I'm truly to be queen, I intend to push for the legislation."

"Your Highness...where are we even to *find* red flowers?" Emis, still polite, is growing more exasperated by the unreasonable request.

Aleta peruses her fingernails. "I'm told there is a bed of roses that grows outside the dungeons. You might try there."

"I'll go." I lurch to my feet. My mind scrambles to put together the layered meanings behind Aleta's words. She wants to wear a killer's colors. To throw away outdated customs. And...*if* she's to be queen?

Perhaps while I've been making my plans, Aleta has been busy with schemes of her own.

"Most kind, Lady Breena, thank you," Aleta says.

"It's nothing," I say, already heading for the door. "I'm due a visit to Da today anyway. I'll tell the guards they're for Lady Kat or something."

The less attention this stunt of Aleta's draws the better. What is she playing at?

"Such subterfuge. You needn't do that. Tell them I

requested them. By all means."

The smile Aleta unfurls is far more cutting than any knife I've ever held.

The guard at the dungeon's entrance is a new face and refuses me entry, saying that he needs express permission from his superiors.

As it would only aggravate me to remain there and argue with him until he capitulates, I decide to wait to see Da. Perhaps I'll get a guard to escort me for a visit after the Bonding banquet.

Or I can simply wait until tomorrow when I find a way to break him out.

The guard with me balks at entering the rose garden, telling me that he'll wait until I rejoin him at the dungeon's entrance. An unexpected blessing. I'm a little happier to be doing this for Aleta if I get some time to myself.

The paths in the garden are overrun and the bushes tower above me, but I go deep inside, forgoing the flowers at the entrance. The longer I walk, the more time I have to think. I gather a few roses, slicing them free of the bushes with my knife.

I carefully shift the ones I've cut into my other arm, wary of the thorns. My bouquet is made up of passable blooms, free of aphids and browning, but the red roses are so vibrant that they'll be striking against Aleta's dark hair—which, I know, is what the princess wants.

Aleta knows *what red means,* I think again. Does she only want to cause a stir? Or does she have other plans? Darker plans. Plans of bloodshed.

The branches of the rosebushes catch at my skirts as I pick my way through the garden, but for once I'm grateful for the dress. Breeches would be much closer to the skin, much more likely to end with me getting pricked.

Barring the red that's so rare in the palace, this garden isn't particularly special. Their placement is symbolic of blood spilled by the people held inside the dungeon, and the bushes full of thorns act as a deterrent should the criminals find a way to the southern wall. They'll find no escape that way. Beyond that, the garden is barely tended and mostly ignored. By the look of things, the roses are watered only when it rains and trimmed only to keep them confined within the walls of the garden. But some, inexplicably, blossom widely, opening themselves to the sun. I almost feel bad when I find those rare blooms and snipp them at their stems for Aleta's hair ornaments.

A rose near the ground catches my eye, and I crouch to get a better look. Looks about as nice as the rest. I slip my stolen knife out of my sleeve again and press it against the stem.

"Are you sure that you should be here?"

The knife slips and slices into my finger. I bite down on the curse that almost escapes, mouth instead opening with explanations, readying my defense. I'm *allowed* to be here, technically speaking. It just isn't…often done.

My words die in my mouth before I can give them voice. There's no one behind me, no one standing next to me. With a few more looks from side to side to confirm that, I carefully stand, keeping my head below the tops of the greenery.

A curly blonde head of hair stands several bushes away.

Fitting that Kat would be here. She must feel so at home surrounded by her favorite color.

Kat moves her hand, and I follow the shine of her ruby ring as she strokes it down a cheek—the *king's,* I register with shock, noticing him for the first time. I duck a bit lower, heart pounding.

"They can hardly stop me from roaming my own grounds. Even if it is the prison garden." The king's voice is a low rumble. "I rather enjoy…tending to my garden when I've the time."

There's an undercurrent to what he says as he steals Kat's hand from his cheek and drops a kiss into her palm.

Eurgh. Quite of its own volition, my nose wrinkles. I should have guessed that Kat's unholy devotion to him meant more than it appeared. They're lovers.

Kat's voice is uncharacteristically breathy and pitched lower than normal. "I only meant that I worry of someone overhearing us. Dissenters may use it to try—"

He straightens, his hand fisting in Kat's hair. "My reign is absolute. Do you doubt it?"

Kat's neck bends at an unnatural angle. "Never, Your Majesty," she chokes out.

The king looks reassured as he releases her to pat down his doublet.

Insistently, Kat presses herself against the king, and my stomach turns. Instead of fearing the king, Kat's basic sense of self-preservation is off. The forceful handling, the power... It excites the assassin. It's writ plain across her face.

Kat's arms go around the king's waist. "It won't be long now."

Long until what? I hold my breath. Have they somehow gleaned that I intend to escape tomorrow? I've been so careful, haven't said a word to anyone.

His hand falls to her shoulder and pushes her back. "Yes. We won't have time to discuss the timetable after the wedding, so pay attention."

I breathe a bit easier—but only a bit. Not about me or my plans then. About theirs.

Kat nods sharply. All traces of a lover's softness disappear as she focuses on her orders. She has a soldier's posture. Her mouth is a slash upon her face.

The wind sweeps past me, rustling the bushes, and I seize on the noise to cover my movements as I shift my weight to my other foot. It would have been simply *uncomfortable* for the king and Kat to see me in the garden before they'd acted so intimately with each other. Now that they've moved on to discussing secret affairs and plots, their notice would be disastrous.

I miss something of what the king says, his words lost to the breeze that carries them away, but then he continues. "...That should be enough time to legitimize the marriage. And even Nereid law is clear when it comes to succession."

Nereid law? I strain my ears. If it's Nereid law that they're discussing, then they're talking about Aleta. But enough time for what?

My heart drops as I process the last word.

Succession. Nereid *succession.*

If Aleta was free to actually *go* to Nereidium, she'd be the reigning monarch. If something were to happen to her now... Her closest relative is her aunt, who governs Nereidium for her. She'd assume the crown.

Unless Aleta were married, which she will be soon enough. Childless, the crown will pass to Caden. And the king is still arrogant enough to believe that his son is squarely under his thumb.

He plans to finally have Nereidium for his own. Ether and arrows, they're going to kill Aleta.

And only the Makers know when.

Thirty-Five

The instant the king and Kat leave the garden, I flee back to my rooms to warn Aleta, tripping in my haste. I burst into the room, slam the door shut, lean heavily against it—and stop.

My ladies and Aleta stare back at me. I gulp back the panic that threatens to choke me. I know what I must look like to them. My hair is damp with sweat. Leaves cling to my skirt. My hands, slick with blood razed by pointed thorns, clutch the roses to my chest.

I look like I've been through a battle, not off picking flowers.

Gisela takes in my disheveled state. "You still find gardening a particularly stressful pastime, I gather, Lady Breena?" she asks innocently.

Aleta retorts before I can. "Mind your manners. I'd like to see you return from the dungeons and thorn bushes looking any better. I daresay they'd improve you."

Gisela's mouth closes with an audible click of her teeth.

"Really, though," Aleta mutters to me as I bring the

lurid bouquet forward with shaking hands. She motions for Emis to take them. "You're bleeding, you realize. You might have been a bit less careless." She spares me a mirthless smile. "It is my Bonding night, after all."

A strange croak escapes me, and Aleta's attempt at humor falls from her face. "What in Egria's green pastures is it?"

I yank myself from my frenzied line of thoughts. Aleta will marry Caden. The king wants her throne. Kat and the king—and the Mother and Father only know who else—plan to kill Aleta. And there's no telling when.

But the eyes of my ladies and the other attendants in the room are heavy on my back. I can't tell Aleta what I overheard with them watching. Their past reports to the king reveal that none of them give one toss in the coffers for my or Aleta's well-being; only their own.

I let my lower lip tremble. I'm not Ardin Perdit's daughter for nothing. Toeing the carpet beneath my feet, I channel Da's ability to play a part. If I pull off a lie just once, it has to be now.

"It's nothing. It's just...my da, y'know?" I rub at my dry eyes, feigning the tears that came and went months before.

If anything, Aleta looks alarmed at this show of emotion. "Yes. Well. Steady on, Lady Breena." She gives my shoulder two brisk pats. "Things will work out as they must."

Dire as the situation is, I have to force myself not to roll my eyes. It's a good thing I don't actually require emotional comfort. Aleta would be a poor choice to turn to.

Aleta redirects her attention to Gisela and Emis, who are now affixing the roses to her hair. "Higher. Higher. By the *ether*, at least make them even, would you?" Slowly, their focus is drawn away from me and back onto Aleta

I turn my hands over and sigh at the sight of my filthy palms. There are two hours left to prepare for the banquet, and I can't tell Aleta of the plot against her with this many witnesses.

I slip away from the gown preparations. *It will be fine,* I tell myself as I slide the screen over the bathing chambers and pour the waiting water in. *Nothing will happen tonight.*

After all, they still need Aleta alive.

After preparing for public presentation all afternoon, Aleta is as placid as a lake as we stand outside the ballroom. The Bonding banquet is in a separate ballroom from the one her birthday celebration was held in. They've yet to repair the damage I did during my Reveal.

The princess's thoughts must be in turmoil. She's about to make her entrance with red roses wound into her hair. No one watching will mistake it for an innocent error, least of all the king.

I still don't know exactly what Aleta means by it. Is she accusing the king? Making a statement about her marriage? Only she knows.

But not a trace of that shows on her face. She's utterly calm. In fact, Shaker Alys would have held her up as an example for me—*this* state of calm is what I should be striving for in our lessons.

Aleta should be a Thrower instead of a Torcher.

I look to her. "Are you ready?"

"This is a state event," she says quietly. "The heir's Bonding night? It's ritual, not simple celebration. They'll announce us this time. You'll go in first, and I'll follow after. I'll be the last to enter."

My pulse pounds as the guards grasp the door handles. Aleta inclines her head to them in a nod. The guards pull the doors open, and I look forward with new resolve.

Am I a Thrower or aren't I? If Aleta can be calm, so can I. I look down the tall staircase I stand atop to the crowd below.

The ivory wall flickers with a multitude of colors, the source of it a candelabra that hangs above. If I squint, I can make out the tiny stained glass panes that sit in front of the individual flames. The effect is dizzying.

One noble blends into another in a sea of glittery jewels. Some foreigners are easy to spot—Clavish fashion favors the fur touches from the far north. A quartet on the strings is in the corner, finishing an elegant dance.

I swallow as the music dies to a smattering of polite applause. There's the king in the center, Kat at his side. Tutor Larsden lurks behind a table, his arms folded in, and Caden is nearby, too, still clapping lightly. Tregle is the first to spot me, hunched in his robe in a far corner, and disappointment fills his features. He must have expected Aleta.

The steward raps a staff smartly on the ground, and the room of expectant faces turns to me. My hand spasms on the stair railing as I stare back at them, dumbstruck.

Still waters, Bree, I remind myself.

"Presenting Her Grace, the Lady Breena, heiress to the Duchy of Secan!"

Heiress, my foot, I think with disdain. If I have my way, I'll never clap eyes on Secan lands. I take a gliding step forward, unable to will myself to look down into that mass of people. I choose a focal point where the wall meets the ceiling and school my features into a mask of coolness as I enter the ballroom.

When I reach the floor to a round of applause, I turn with the rest of the guests to where Aleta stands, bloodthirsty roses wound into her hair.

The princess looks expectantly at the steward. He falters, cringing away from her as though the roses will stain him as well. "A-and presenting Her Royal Highness Aleta Daphoene Nephele Cyrene, first of her name. The Crown Princess of Nereidium and the betrothed of His Royal Highness, Prince Caden Garrett Langdon Edric Richard the Fourth of the House of Capin,, Crown Prince of Egria—the future king and queen of our lands!"

A ruby glitters at Aleta's breast as she descends the stairs. I didn't notice it before. Wonder if she secreted it beneath her corset until I left her. Only the Makers know where she's found it. Miners don't typically waste their time with the near worthless red stone. Kat's the only one I've ever seen wear one before.

As mine were, Aleta's eyes are locked on something. I follow the grim promise glinting in her gaze to the king. His steely eyes are faintly amused as he awaits his ward's approach.

Kat sees me watching and holds my stare, a slow, predatory smile unfurling across her face. The guests are silent, waiting to hear any words uttered by the royals. Cutting through the crowd, Aleta coolly drops into a curtsy before the king.

"Your Majesty," she pronounces.

Her voice rings out over the tension-filled room. Hands choke their goblets. Jaws are tight and shoulders stiff. It's instinctual, like animals fleeing from a hunter's heavy footsteps. They sense the *wrongness* of this ceremony.

The king takes an echoing step forward to gently grasp her shoulders and pull her to her feet. "Rise, Aleta. You have been my daughter in all but name as my ward these sixteen years. And now you shall have my name as well."

The fact that the king and Da were schooled together is obvious to me now. They can play a part equally well.

The king is every inch the benevolent ruler from a child's tale. Aleta accepts the kiss he presses to her temple and turns as the king makes a formal presentation of his son. Aleta gives a perfunctory kiss to her betrothed in greeting.

Caden has an air of seriousness about him tonight. My eyes sweep over him. He looks like he's finally managed to get some sleep, but I doubt the worry over his next step is far from his mind.

I look back to where Kat still stares and allow a small smile of my own to spread across my face. Let her wonder at that.

Still waters.

The music restarts after the king takes his seat in the marbled throne. Situated on a balcony, he has a perfect vantage point to see everyone at once. I dart a look at the bottom of the king's beard—the only part of him that I can see from my position underneath his balcony.

I locate Aleta safely, if a bit reservedly, twirling with a minor lord and find Caden performing the same dance with a noblewoman.

I'm a bundle of nerves, trying to keep an eye on everyone at once. The blade up my sleeve serves only a small amount of comfort. It's doing me no good to be throwing looks around the room like this, like I'm already on the run.

I push off from my sturdy wall to steal the attention of a servant. I wouldn't mind a flute of the fizzy drink that they're serving. It's not my stomach I need to calm at this ball, but my mind.

"Imported from the shores of Nereidium," the waiter informs me as he hands me a glass.

Interesting. The king will allow Nereid products in his kingdom, but not a representative. At least not until he has a firmer claim on their government. It hasn't escaped my notice that even Aleta's aunt hasn't made an appearance for the princess's wedding festivities.

Thoughtfully, I sip at my drink, and my eyebrows lift in surprise. No wonder the king allows this beverage. The stuff practically sparkles on my tongue. My mouth twitches in amusement. The king *does* have a penchant for shiny things.

"*That* is not fair."

Caden slouches in on himself as he steps next to me, trying to appear smaller than he really is. I could have told him that it's useless. Any tricks for avoiding the audience's attention are wasted. There isn't a chance that the gossip-hungry crows of his court will miss one step of his tonight.

"What's not fair, Your Highness? That this young man doesn't have a flute left for you?" I allow myself a brief moment of levity, and my smile becomes genuine.

The waiter's eyes widen. It's obvious he's cursing himself—and me by extension—wondering how he could have let himself run out of drink right as the crown prince happens over.

"I can get more from the kitchens, Your Highness," he blurts. "They've got barrels of it. I'll just—"

"Don't be absurd," Caden dismisses. "I much prefer a hardy Egrian mead."

Not seeming to know what else to do, the waiter bows low and mutters an excusal as he backs away, nose practically scraping the floor.

One of Caden's hands rests near his scabbard. It's surely for show. I rarely see him with a weapon. His doublet is a stiff velvet, a dark gray-green with gold embellishments. The shoulder shells are two horns poking out of his torso, the customary style for Egrian formalwear. A reminder that even when participating in revelry, the soldiers of the realm remain sharp.

"That wasn't very nice," Caden chides after the servant disappears. "You knew I only meant that it wasn't fair that you got to enjoy yourself while the rest of us only pretend at it."

I shrug. "I took a chance that you'd be glad for one less ear on you tonight when there are already so many eyes."

His eyes warm on mine. "Dance with me."

The violins quaver an achingly slow waltz, a dance that requires a partner be held close. It's dangerous when I think about who my partner will be. My heart trembles a warning, but there's a singular advantage to the style. It's a dance that will allow me the chance to let Caden in on his father's scheme. I'll be able to whisper what I saw right into his ear.

The danger of getting close to him is still there, but who knows if I'll get the chance to talk to him any other time before Aleta and I make our escape?

His eyes soften, melting like slush in a rainfall. "I'm sorry. I didn't mean it as an obligation. I meant, *would* you dance with me, Bree?" He extends a hand, waiting for my answer.

Something gives way inside of me as I stare at his hand, callused from hunting and training exercises. I've fooled myself for this long, believing that by guarding my heart I'd somehow be *safe* from Caden. But despite his betrothal, despite who his father is, I can't deny how drawn I am to him. I can't deny that if things were different—

My heart aches. He deserves a real goodbye before I disappear. I spare a brief prayer that I and those I care about will get out of this alive and fix my hand in Caden's. My throat feels tight as I smile at him.

"Yes. I'll dance with you."

<hr>

We stumble a bit as we begin our waltz. I'm not accustomed to the slow dancing, much less having to follow another person's lead.

"Relax a bit. You're stiff as a board." Caden's lip

brushes my ear when he whispers into it. A thrill shoots through me at the sensation. "I know this waltz. It's a long one. If you don't stop concentrating quite so hard on trying to steer yourself, you're only going to step on my toes more."

I relinquish control of the dance lest I trip us both up and send us spilling across the floor. "Caden, I need—"

"That's a lovely color on you."

The compliment distracts me for a moment. The king ordered the gown, a midnight shade of blue that reminds me of the night sky. "Thank you. It's meant to indicate that I'm a Thrower, but I see plenty of people who aren't Elementals in the same shade."

We're interrupted by a smiling noblewoman, who puts a playful hand on Caden's shoulder. "Lady Breena, surely you don't intend to monopolize His Highness's last evening as a bachelor? I'm sure you don't mind if I steal a dance."

The waltz is still going, and Caden frowns at the woman's presumption.

"I do, actually," I say, vexed. "Perhaps you can dance with His Highness later."

The woman humphs and walks away. The disturbance is irritating but allows me to return to my original train of thought.

"Listen to me," I breathe into his ear. "And don't react." His hand clenches around mine. "Ow. You're reacting. Just...waltz, all right?"

He steers me mechanically through the motions, no

longer graceful but more like a poorly made puppet.

"I was in the rose garden behind the dungeons today," I continue. "On an errand for Aleta. And your father and Kat were there as well. They were planning—Caden, they're going to kill her. Aleta, I mean. Sometime after the wedding. The Great Makers only know when."

He sucks in a breath, a sharp intake of air. "My father intends for sole control of Nereidium," he surmises immediately.

"Yes. I haven't told her yet."

Caden pulls away to look at me incredulously, and I get defensive. "I've hardly had time. We've been surrounded by *your* people—"

"Don't confuse my father's people with my people. The terms aren't synonymous."

"Fine," I snap. "Your da's people then, if that makes you feel better." I take a deep breath to steady myself. Caden isn't where my anger truly lays. Arguing with each other will get us nowhere. I settle back into his chest.

"What are you going to do?"

We turn. The waltz nears its end, strings crescendoing and crashing against each other. "I wish I could tell you I had a solid plan, but that would be a lie. We'll break away from here when everyone is busy after the wedding, hopefully before anyone realizes we've gone."

"That's your plan then. You're leaving."

I pull back a little. A shutter's fallen over Caden's face, closing off any emotions he might reveal. "If you have another option, I'd love to hear it."

"I knew you'd be leaving, but..." He growls, frustrated. "We really shouldn't speak about this here. Just...wait. Is that all right? Will you do that for me?"

"I can't wait for you, Caden."

The cello draws out one last mournful note, low and sweet, and around us, dance partners separate, bowing low to each other.

Caden and I are nose to nose. I inhale deeply, imagining that I can smell him, fix it in my memory to carry away like a parcel. But that's the stuff of whimsy. I can tell myself that Caden is cedar and apples with the tang of steel and parchment, but it won't be his scent that I bring with me. It will be far more.

I step away, swish my skirts in an approximation of a curtsy. And this time, when the lady who tried to cut in earlier hustles for Caden, I let her have him.

I find a seat as the music picks up again. A cavorr, I think. I recognize the jolly rhythm. I wouldn't mind dancing one of those. It's a pretty common step, spinning round the room from partner to partner, legs kicking in a forward jig. I'd rather liked it on festival days.

"Would you like anything to eat, my lady?" a kitchen maid inquires.

"Yes, please." I sag in my seat, relieved to let my mind rest for just a moment. "Would you fetch me some of those olives and Nereid feta?"

"Certainly, my lady. Anything else?"

"Whatever isn't Egrian," I say grumpily. Never mind that I'm technically Egrian myself. I'm feeling a marked lack of patriotism these days. "Unless it's mead," I add. "I'd love a pint of Egrian mead about now."

The maid's lips fold over in a smile, and she's gone, returning nearly as quickly with a plate piled high with feta-stuffed black olives on a bed of leafy greens.

I dive in. "No wonder the king's willing to kill for the place," I say, mouth full. "I've never tasted anything as fine in Egria."

"I wouldn't go that far." I drop my fork to my plate with a small clatter. The king tilts his head when I turn and find him behind me. "You must not have tried my chef's stuffed figs. Now *those* are worth dying for."

"Your Grace—*Majesty*," I correct myself. For all of my bravado about defying him, the king sends a stampede of horses racing wildly across my chest. I feel like he can read my escape plans plain on my face. I fight not to show it. "I only meant—"

The king seats himself next to me. "I gathered what you meant, Lady Breena. And I further gather that you've finally learned the nature of your father's service to me before his betrayal."

I hesitate, then nod.

"And he's told you about Lady Katerine as well?"

Another nod. More than he knows. He's stopped having me report in after every visit with Da. Probably because he thinks his threat is enough to ensure that I'll find him if I have information. What he doesn't realize is that I've seen and heard more than he'd like. Grimly, I think of his plans for Aleta.

It feels like the king can read my knowledge in my bearing. Will it be revealed through my eyes? I meet his stare. Not to do so would be to cause unnecessary suspicion, no matter how difficult it may be.

My motions grow forced and the food grows tasteless the longer I look at him. The king's crown catches the light of the candelabra.

He doesn't deserve that crown.

Not content with an uncomfortable silence it seems, the king speaks. "Would you honor me with a dance, Lady Breena?"

The cavorr is over, but a tight smile stretches over my lips. I blink falsely at him and dab my mouth with a napkin. "How can I refuse, Your Majesty?"

It had been difficult to follow Caden's steps, but that's nothing compared to my second dance with the king. My awkwardness with Caden had more to do with the fact that I prefer to be in control. With the king, it comes from the knowledge that any semblance of control here is only an illusion.

"Perhaps I should have hired you a dancing tutor instead of a Throwing tutor," the king says when I trod upon his toes for the fourth time. He grimaces. It was an accident—but a happy one.

"I fear your treasury's entire holdings may not have

been enough to make me a passable dancer, no matter the tutor, sire," I say flatly.

Speaking of tutors… I don't like the idea of Larsden wandering the ballroom where I can't see him. I turn, seeking out his thin form in the crowd.

The king laughs loudly. "Tell me, do you look forward to the morrow, Lady Breena?"

My neck snaps back around to face him. "Of course." This much is true—I can scarcely wait to escape—but I add a lie atop of it for good measure. "It is indeed a grand occasion when two great lands are united."

"I doubt you've *seen* a civilized marriage before, have you?"

I swallow the ire, practically used to the digs at my peasant upbringing by now. They truly think I'm less than them because of it. I'll just scream into a pillow later.

"If you mean a noble one, then no, Your Majesty."

His smile is like a wolf's—hungry, with too many teeth. "My priest binds the two together with the blessings of the Mother and Father. It is called Ispri Blanchett. In the ancient tongue, it means 'Pure Spirit.'"

I can't even bring myself to feel surprised. He *would* choose to taint something like that and twist it for his own means. Pure, indeed.

He twists me around in a spin that brings me too close to his body. My stomach turns.

"Once the holy bond is forged, it cannot be broken. When the blood vow dries, the marriage is final and considered consummate."

Consummate. The hair on my neck rises with horror. "Surely you mean after they take to their marital bed." I struggle for a bored tone. He can't know how my breath hangs on the precipice of his answer.

He raises an eyebrow at me. "What does a young, unwed girl like you know of marital beds? I make no mistake."

My heart sinks. While my thoughts race, it's much easier to become the king's puppet as he steers me around the dance floor. I clap when the music ends. Bow to thank him for the dance and the unexpected blessing of information.

My head lost in a fog that has little to do with mead, I leave the Bonding ball, walking blindly down the stone halls. When I've walked until I am lost among dark and quiet corridors, I sink to the floor between two large columns and put my head in my hands.

I thought I'd have at least a half day more. That Aleta and I would flee when I could ostensibly be preparing her for her first night as a married woman. My hands shake. The marriage will be validated without that night. We'll have to leave sooner than I anticipated.

"Bree?"

I hear two stumbling steps in my direction and jerk my head up to see Caden. His eyes are bright as he watches me. Too bright. How much mead did he have after we danced at the banquet? I hadn't watched him after we'd separated.

I push myself to a standing position. "What are you doing here?"

"I thought you'd left." His eyes don't leave my form, and I flick my gaze away.

"I did leave," I say on a breath. "Just didn't get as far as I'd like."

He's silent, watching me. The air sticks in my lungs. Here's another similarity between father and son that I've managed to miss up until now: they both have eyes that see too much. I clear my throat.

"Your Highness—"

"Don't call me that," he interrupts. "It feels *wrong* from you. Call me Caden, call me Rick, but don't..." His expression twists into something pained. "I'm your friend. I don't want you to think of me as just...a *prince.*"

"Even in those brief moments in the dungeons—the ones before I knew who you were—I never thought Rick suited you properly." My smile warbles. Falls. "I suppose I was right, wasn't I?

The thought sobers him. "I wish you hadn't been. I wish that I could have been Rick for you. Just for a moment, I wish I could have been someone else."

"While you're busy wishing, could you also wish that my father hadn't been your father's assassin, that we'd never been discovered in our village, and that I wasn't an Elemental? Maybe then my life could be what it should've been."

"Bree—"

"Forget it." I strike what I've said with a wave of my

arm. "I need to stop dwelling. Things are what they are. They happened as they happened. There's no changing that. No changing who we are."

"Perhaps not. But we can still change what is to come."

That is a dangerous road to tread upon. Caden's eyes trace a deliberate path from my eyes to my lips.

Heart pounding, I change the subject. "The olives," I say, "were excellent tonight, weren't they?"

He sighs.

"I think I tasted rosemary in the cheese. We used to have a small bush behind the inn back home. Hardy herb. Can take the cold. Wonderful choice, I think. The kitchen chefs did an excellent job."

"Bree."

"Would you stop," I say, frustrated, "saying my name like that? I read far too many things into it."

He rocks back on his heels and changes tacks. "You have an eyelash on your nose," he says.

Irritated now for reasons I won't give a name to, I rub at it with the heel of my hand, and he shakes his head. "Still there. May I...?"

He swipes a gentle finger down the slope of my nose. Then, as if drawn back by a magnetic force, his hand returns to caress my face. When he rasps out "May I?" again, I know what he's asking.

I swallow hard. "I'm not sure—I don't want to be that sort of girl."

"What sort?" His hand moves to toy with the ends of

my hair. The other one brushes my hip. His eyes are steady on mine, gauging my reaction. Waiting for me to give him a real answer.

I steal my hair back from his fingers. "You *know* which sort," I say emphatically. "Whether your da arranged it or not, you're betrothed."

"But she and Adept Tregle—"

I shake my head. "If there's anything on Aleta's side, she hasn't admitted to it yet. And that doesn't matter." His silence is thick and sullen, but I continue. "If things were different... But they're not."

Caden's thumb slides the line of my jaw while he mulls over my words. "I think on it often, you know." He lets the statement hang in the air around us before explaining further. "What it would be like if you were *the* girl. My betrothed. I think on what it would be like if I could be someone else. Just for a moment."

I should move. I should *really* move. The scent of apples and cedar and mead engulfs me. When had he gotten so close? And have his eyes always had that rim of blue on the edge? I don't speak. I rather think my ragged breathing is doing that job for me.

He is *so* close. Just a whisper away.

"Bree. *Lady* Bree."

Makers bless, the way he says my name. Singsonging my title, each syllable rolled between his teeth like he wants to keep it on his tongue forever. I've never indulged in the vanity of the sound of my name before, but I close my eyes briefly, listening to the husky hum of his voice.

"You can't think that you could ever be that girl to me." He shakes his head and corrects himself. "No. You can't think that you could ever be simply a girl to me in any way."

He moves to close the gap between us.

My fingers cover my mouth a scant second before Caden's mouth can. His lips, warm on my hand, break the spell enough for me to take a step away. His eyes speak of his confusion. The gray is caught so between dark and light that I can't decide which they are, and he steps away.

"I thought we felt the same way."

And how stupid of me to have assumed that I could push my attraction to him aside, brushed like dirt under the proverbial rug. A humorless laugh escapes me.

"I think we do. But, Caden, if a lack of feelings were the only problem, then this would be far—"

Whether it's my confession or the mead that makes Caden bold enough to press the issue, I'll never know, but he slams into me like a tidal wave, his lips slanting over mine—warm, wet, insistent. I don't have the strength of will to deny myself twice.

Ether.

Am I truly a Thrower? I don't feel like one now. It isn't water but fire in my blood at Caden's touch. Flames race through me, burning me with their insistent need to be fed *more*. More of him, more of his lips.

My arms wind themselves around his neck as my toes

curl inside my shoes. His hands are in my hair, at my hips, caressing my cheeks. They're everywhere at once, but it's not enough. His mouth moves for a moment to my neck, and he breathes my name into my collarbone. I clutch his shoulders to pull him closer.

I let politics, war games, and history's mysteries fall away. I forget about being a Water Elemental to concentrate on the ebb and flow that is *Caden*.

His hands drift to my back, and I recline into them. He follows, his mouth chasing mine. My spine hits the stone of the hard wall, shoulder blades scraping against it.

It's that harsh sensation that brings me back to my senses, and I tear my mouth from his. Lifting a shaky hand to swollen lips, I swallow thickly. Caden's gray eyes are glazed as he blinks at the sudden loss of contact, reaching for me again.

And may the tides sweep me away, I want to go to him. But I grind my fingernails into the palms of my hands and use the pain to ground myself. I ignore my heated cheeks and the rushing of my heartbeat as I step to the side.

"This…isn't wise," I manage to get out.

"Wisdom is overrated," Caden says, reaching for my hand.

"*Caden.*" Exasperation and tension color my voice, and his hands fall to his sides as he hears it. "Someone could happen upon us at any moment."

As I speak the words, I realize the truth in them and look around, suddenly fearful that we've already been discovered. It isn't wise to let my guard down in the open like this.

"Closed quarters then. Your chambers. Mine."

"My chambers that I share with Aleta and that have a guard posted outside constantly? Be realistic," I say with a hand outstretched before me to ward him off. "We were foolish to let it go this far."

"Breena." Hurt echoes in his tone, and he steps back. "You don't mean that."

I turn away. I can't look back at him, can't see his expression entreating me to stay. I'm not sure I'll stand firm if I do. He's betrothed and the prince of the realm, and I am just me.

"Goodnight, Your Highness."

And good-bye.

Thirty-Six

I lean against the door to my chambers heavily. Have I made the right decision with Caden? What's one night, after all, in the grand scheme of things? I'd at least have the memory to hold onto in the future.

Unless the night changes things for me somehow and convinces me to stay, to subject myself to a future where Caden is married to Aleta, with a horde of tiny princesses and princelings milling about him. I picture a swarm of children with the lethal combination of Caden's gray eyes and Aleta's ability to squash someone with a look.

But even that's wrong. There will be no children— only the king at the helm of an empire spanning multiple nations and Aleta, cold and dead in the ground.

Right. *Best grasp hold of reality again, Mistress Perdit.*

Moving farther into the chambers, I find Aleta there already, framed in the window, staring up at the moon. It bathes her in a silvery light, and she closes her eyes as she tilts her chin toward it.

"I'm getting married tomorrow," she says without turning.

"At least you managed to evade the guard," I say, jerking my thumb toward the door. I still haven't quite caught my breath. "How did you manage that one?"

"They didn't see me slip out. I thought perhaps— maybe this time I'd be bold enough to use the tunnel for a real escape. Or to make good on my roses' promise. Yet here I sit."

I drop beside her and sit down. "Are you nervous?"

"About the ceremony?" She scoffs. "To be nervous, I'd have to be able to feel."

"You can't fool me that easily," I . say quietly. "You're not letting anyone win anything by admitting you have emotions, you know."

Aleta's shoulders slump, just slightly. She sighs. "Yes. I'm nervous. Marriage is so final. I envy the peasants in that. I'm not so foolish as to have some romantic notion of *love* in mind, but being able to make the decision for what might actually benefit *me*... It would be a nice switch."

It would be nicer, I know, if she *were* able to have some sort of romantic notion in mind. I think of the way that Caden looks at me. The way that Tregle looks at Aleta. Our leaving will be a blow to the Torcher. It's sure to be unexpected, but we need to go.

I look out the window at the capital. The lights of whatever festival had been taking place out in the city several weeks ago are gone. A few flickering candles glow dimly in some windows, but it's hard to see. Perfect cover.

We may truly be able to find ourselves lost there. At least until we can make a better plan, plot a more efficient route out of the city.

But first, I realize, I still need to tell Aleta of the atrocities that await her if she marries tomorrow.

"I need... There's something I must..." After several false starts, I manage to summon the words.

A degree paler, Aleta simply nods upon hearing the assassination plot.

"You don't seem surprised."

She shrugs. "The king has always hated me. He playacts well. I'm his doted-upon ward to any who ask, but I knew why he really kept me. He wants my land. My people." Her chin lifts. "He cannot have them."

"I thought the same. He wants whatever Da has, and he wants *me* as his weapon. He can't have us either."

"There's the tunnel," Aleta says. Her eyes are suddenly determined. "I *will* use it. I cannot hope to fight off so many guards with only my own Torching power, but I will go down fighting if I must. Better that my lands should officially transfer to my aunt than the king have them in his grasp."

"You won't be alone. Come on," I tug at Aleta's sleeve, suddenly breathless and wide awake.

What have *I been waiting for?* I think, suddenly impatient with myself. *Really. Now* is the time to go. The entire reason I'd intended to wait to flee until after the wedding was the belief that the rest of the palace would be occupied. I'd plotted based on the belief that the marriage would not be legitimized, unconsummated as it was. But I've learned differently and the nobility is occupied *now,* celebrating the impending marriage, albeit without the prince and princess.

And somehow, luck has it that both Aleta and I have slipped back to the rooms without drawing the gaze of a guard. Silently, I thank the Makers for the small blessing. I won't take it for granted.

Aleta removes herself from my hold. "What are you on about?" she asks irritably.

"Don't you see? Now's our chance to get *out* of here." I cross to the door in three strides, yanking it open.

Aleta pulls up short, a strange expression crossing her face. "You want to come with me?"

"What? Yes, of course. We've both got a better shot if we don't go it alone. But I need to get something first. Now, come *on.* "

I push the princess out into the dark corridor and hush her questions as we creep along the hall. My pulse beats a tattoo in my throat. If attendees of the ball leave early—if someone emerges from the corridor—

I hope I can manage to control at least a *little* water. Just enough to get them out of our way temporarily. I'd planned to pocket a waterskin somehow tomorrow, but it's a humid night, so if I have to, I can pull it from the atmosphere if someone surprises me.

I think.

I really hope we won't be surprised.

We leave the main castle and head for the building that houses the king's dungeon. The path that opens up before us is wrapped in shadows.

"*Breena,*" Aleta grunts. "Why are we on our way to the dungeons?"

"To get Da," I say slowly, confused. "I thought you realized."

Aleta's face darkens, her eyes narrowing to slits. "I did not. You surely did not believe that I would willingly ally myself with my parents' murderer?"

"I *believed* you'd have enough sense to ally yourself with whoever could get you away from the king," I say. A breeze whistles past my ears. I shiver. "We don't have time for this. Are you with me or aren't you?"

She hesitates for a fraction of a second. "With," she settles on. "But less than pleased about it."

"You can let yourself be pleased when we're free of this place."

She motions me forward. "Lead on then."

From our position crouched behind a bush, I can see that the guard at the front of the dungeon dozes fitfully. But getting *into* the dungeon won't be the problem.

I rise and walk up to him nonchalantly, chanting to myself all the while. *Placid like a lake. Placid like a lake. Placidplacidplacid.*

"Good eve, sir knight," I say loudly.

The guard starts awake, yanking his sword from his scabbard and leveling it at us.

With two fingers, Aleta pushes it aside. "Do you often make a habit of threatening the nobles of the realm?" she inquires icily, taking charge of the conversation. I let her. She's altogether more intimidating than I am. "The Lady Breena wishes to speak with her father."

The guard's expression sours. "The dirty Rider?"

"The *duke*," I correct him, sneering. I don't have to let anyone else insult Da. Or myself. At least, not anymore.

"Go on in then," he says, waving us inside.

I can hardly believe my good fortune. Ordinarily, the guard escorts me to Da's cell door himself. We'll gain a few precious minutes this way.

Aleta and I keep a decorous pace as we lift the skirts of our gowns to step down the steps and plunge into the dungeon. But once I think we're entirely clear of the guard, I race past the other cells, Aleta at my heels. The prisoners are quiet now, though a few whimper in their sleep. We slow, nearing the end of the corridor where

Da's cell is.

The stool I sat upon the last time I visited lays sideways, abandoned. A creak greets my ears.

"Da?" I call. A frisson of fear shoots through me as I dart to his unbarred cell door.

Only piles of filthy hay meet my eyes.

Da's cell is empty.

Thirty-Seven

My first impulse is, madly enough, to laugh.

Because really, it's *funny*. Here I am thinking that the Makers have bestowed some all-fired powerful *blessing* on me and Da. Least they could do after the muck-about they've turned my life into, right?

But I'm only a cosmic punchline.

Aleta shoves me toward the dungeon's exit. I push back, still laughing.

"What's your hurry?" I ask, feeling reckless. What's the point? Without Da, I've lost the war. Aleta and I will be the king's playthings forevermore.

Iron fingers grip my wrist, and my whooping chuckles trail off. My arm surges forward in Aleta's stern hold. The princess's eyes glow with the Torcher fire.

"It is far from over."

I let her lead me from the dungeon like a child, throwing a last look at Da's swinging door and the piles of hay, mussed from where he'd slept on it. I think again of the day I ran away from The Bridge and Duchess so long ago.

I'm running again, Da. But this time, I wanted you to come with me.

The guard waves us past with a careless hand. Once out of his line of vision, Aleta's stance shifts, and she hastens our pace through the gardens, dragging me in her wake. I'm sobering.

"Aleta? What if he's already dead?" Aleta's footsteps slow. "What if—what if the king pushed the deadline up because I didn't get him his information?"

Resolutely, she says, "Then there is nothing you can do for him. Grieve later."

We move swiftly, our breaths rattling the still air around us. Shadows reach for us, dark sentries standing guard around the palace.

"We must hurry. It won't be long before they're alerted to your father's escape. They're certain to think that we had something to do with it."

"We should have done." My heart is lead in my chest. "Guess saving his own skin mattered more to him."

Despite what I said to Aleta, I know Da's disappearance is not the king's doing. I saw the lock hanging from the cell bars. That wasn't a lock that had been opened with a key. Somehow, it had been forced open. Da left me behind.

I never would have thought it of him. Despite all of the lies, his secret past, the killings—even with those clouding my mind with doubt so I could scarcely *think* to puzzle out the mysteries of his history, I'd been so sure I *knew* him at his core.

"They'll try to tell you who you are, Breena Rose, but don't you listen."

I'd obeyed my father all these months as they'd called me a lady, an heiress, a Thrower, a duchess. I'd held myself separate from the designations of nobility or peasantry. I'm just *Bree*. I *know* who I am at the end of it all. But maybe I should have paid more attention to *him*. Maybe I should have listened when they tried to tell me who Ardin of Secan was.

"You're my daughter, and I swear to you I had good reason."

Where are his reasons now? All this time—*all this time*—I've held fast to that paternal bond. Trusted that when we left, it would be together. What kind of man leaves his daughter behind? My feet halt. Just as Da had said, it's all different now.

The fingers around my wrist loosen, and Aleta whirls me about. She grips my shoulders and bores her stare into me. "Do not. Don't you *dare*, Lady Breena Secan."

"It's Perdit," I mutter around a clogged throat.

"I don't give a toss in the coffers what you want to call yourself. Get a hold of yourself. Now."

"Maybe it would help if *you* didn't have such a hold on me," I spit.

Something like satisfaction slips over Aleta's features, and she releases me. How dare she look *happy* about this?

"If you haven't noticed my da just *left* me." It's a cry that cracks through the air. A bird flies startled from a tree above our heads. I poke Aleta in the arm, hissing. "You could look less pleased."

"I won't play at falsehoods and tell you that I'm sorry he's not with us. He cost me a family. That's not something I'll ever forgive."

"I—" My mouth closes. Am I actually going to defend him? Now? *Still?*

Aleta gives me a shove. "Grieve later. If *you* haven't noticed though, I'm still here. You've got the fire back in you. Good. We need a little fight in our blood tonight. Now, I *insist* that you move. We must make it to the tunnel if we're to have a chance. The man cost me a family. He won't cost me a friend, too."

My breath catches on a sob, and Aleta shoves me again. "Enough. Tonight we're *both* unbreakable."

As we slip between bushes, every pounding heartbeat is the tick of a clock. Every step, another few grains of sand in an hourglass. It's like watching a crop of thunderclouds move in—there's no escaping the storm, but no way of knowing when it will break.

It's quite different from how we left our rooms, me sure of my direction and spurring Aleta to follow me. Aleta leads the way now, blazing a trail.

At least Da will make it out alive. Probably. I can still be happy about that.

I put Da to the back of my mind. Aleta's right. If we're to make it through the night, much less make it out of the Egrian capital, we'll both need to be fully possessed of all of our senses.

The halls are miraculously sparse when we get back inside. When we arrive at our suite, the door is still vacant, the guard missing. Still at the ball? No, he's surely realized that his charges have left by now. Something isn't right. Putting a finger to my lips, I put my other hand out to stop Aleta, suspicions raised. Why would our guard still be absent? Unless…

I strain my ears against the door but can't hear anything inside save the whistling of the wind. We must have left the window—

No. Not the window. The distinct sound of shuffling feet reaches my ears, and my eyes widen. *Someone inside,* I mouth to Aleta.

Grimly, the princess raises her hand. A flame flickers to life in her palm. She nods.

We're as ready as we can be. I heave my shoulder at the door, and we burst inside.

The window is closed, but the living area is a mess. The settee is overturned, Aleta's rouge spattered against the wall. The washbasin is far from where it began the day, and its water soaks into the carpet.

But there isn't anyone in sight.

Aleta drops her hand, and her fire shimmers from existence.

I can't shake the feeling of unease. The wind I could have sworn I heard from the hall is still—erily so, like the calm before a storm.

"We need to go," I say, senses flaring.

By now, they've surely discovered that we aren't in our rooms, and soon the entire palace will be on the hunt for us. Someone has been here. There's a footprint where the washbasin spilled and—

I feel it. My eyes shoot to the darkened patch of rug. The water has different levels to it. I *feel* the shape of it, where it shifts and presses into the floor. I can sense where it's been disturbed, molding to a foot above it. There's more though. Water isn't just in the air around us or confined to that small space. What am I missing?

"I *have* been telling you," Aleta says, striding toward her door. "If there's anything you need, get it now."

"Wait," I say, suddenly realizing what it is that I've missed. It isn't just *one* footprint. "Aleta, someone—"

Her bedroom door glides open.

"—has been waiting for you to join the festivities." Kat grins.

The wet footprints led to Aleta's bedroom door. I close my eyes for a moment, chastising myself. *Stupid.* Kat has us right where she wants us.

Kat crosses her arms and taps her finger in the crook of her elbow. "You hadn't been intending to leave us so soon, had you?"

Aleta jumps back, fire flaring in her hand once more. Without hesitating, she flings the flames toward Kat's head.

The duchess laughs and bats them away, flames sailing through the air to alight upon the curtains. Once the flames have a taste of the velvet, they claw their way up it, consuming it like a rare dessert.

We can't waste time with this. It's just Kat. Just *one* person. If she's discovered our plans somehow, then time is all the more precious. Who knows what alarms she's sounded? Who she's told?

The puddle on the floor flips feebly when I wave my arm. I should have practiced more. It's just as Alys told me. Unfocused results are really no results at all.

I slip the knife that I'd hidden away from my sleeve. The time has come. Somehow, I'll have to get close enough to do this the old-fashioned way. I'd counted on fighting our way out but had prayed with all of my might that the Makers would spare us from Kat's abilities. I say a silent prayer now that I hope they'll listen to. *Get us out of here. Please.*

I charge Kat, but the duchess steps aside smoothly. I shoot forward and catch myself from crashing into the wall. I grit my teeth in frustration. My methods are untested. Certainly I've been in a fight before—bar brawls and scuffles with Kat where Kat has nearly always gotten the better of me.

Aleta squares her shoulders, and flames encircle her arm.

"How did you know?" I demand, trying to distract Kat long enough for Aleta to try another approach— hopefully one that has a bit more impact.

"That you'd be leaving?" Kat's eyes glint. She pauses, tutting and wagging a finger at Aleta, tossing a breeze at her. The princess's fire is snuffed out, and Aleta is knocked into the blazing curtain. I cry out as the flames engulf her like she's kindling. She doesn't stir.

"Stupid girl," Kat says carelessly. "She really should know better. I've been slipping my little wind whisperers into her room for *years.*" She chuckles, muttering, "'Unbreakable.' Pah. There is nothing about her I don't know."

The fire eats its way across the room, an appetite that cannot be sated. It flares bright over Aleta's discarded roses. I race to the window. I'll extinguish the blaze with the wind, like blowing out a candle.

But when I open the window, it only fans the flames higher.

Aleta is still, the fire cocooning her. I reach for her, intending to pull her from it, but the fire leaps out, burning over my skin, and I step away, uncertain. Perspiration cascades heavily over my face. The blow that Kat gave her rendered Aleta unconscious, but she's unharmed in the flames. It's true, what they say. It recognizes the Torcher princess as its brethren, leaving even her clothes unsinged.

Arms crossed patiently, Kat is content to watch. "Nor is there anything about *you* that I do not know," she comments.

"You know *nothing* about me," I bite out, turning back to her. One way or another, I'll finish this tonight.

"Of course I do." She runs her tongue over her teeth. "For instance, I know that Ardin's wife was barren."

"*What?*" That isn't true. Ma had been pregnant when she and Da had left the capital. She'd died birthing me somewhere along the way to Abeline. My eyebrows furrow. Hadn't she?

Kat leans against an enflamed pillar. The orange light gives her an eerie cast as the flickering flames waltz shadows over her features. Her eyes are eager on my face. "It's why she *left.*"

"My ma died birthing me," I say, suddenly unsure. I lick the sweat from my lips. The room is too hot, and my knife, which was an extension of my arm a moment ago, feels heavy and awkward in my clumsy fingers. "You're lying."

"Am I? Ask your father sometime, *Lady Breena.*" Kat snorts in disgust. "You aren't what you think you are. Filthy Nereid brat."

"Nereid?" Now I'm *sure* Kat is lying. Not that I could ask Da if I wanted to. He left. I push aside the complicated emotion. "I've lived in Egria my entire life."

"Wrong again!" She ticks the list off on her fingers one by one. "Wrong about your birthplace. Wrong about your birth *date.*"

My mind spirals. After my catastrophe of a Reveal, Kat had said something…

I haven't even reached my seventeenth year.

Haven't you?

"And," Kat concludes, "wrong about your birth parents."

"Do shut up, Katerine." A familiar voice breaks in loudly. "You always did have a tendency to talk too much."

I freeze. It can't be. *He left.*

But I turn, needing to see for myself. There's Da, standing proudly before me, silhouetted in the doorway.

He's undernourished. Pale. Dirty.

But he's there.

He toes the door shut so Kat can't call for assistance. He turns and rolls his eyes at me. "By the ether, Breena Rose, you're a hard girl to get a hold of. I've been searching all over the castle tonight."

"Da," I say, dumbfounded. Relief and confusion war within me. He's here. He hasn't left me.

"I might still be looking if I hadn't run into a certain prince and another Adept who were after the same thing I was."

Caden. And Tregle? What are they looking for me for?

"Wait for me," Caden had said.

Oh. They were going to get us out. Maybe the Makers are on my side after all if *they're* the only people Da ran into.

"I may not be in my prime, but keeping up with a Rider is no easy task. Wind rather speeds up my run, you know. Still, I expect they'll be along any moment now." He tilts his head. "Do we need to have a talk about the evils of men, Breena Rose?"

"I don't think now's the time," I croak. My head spins. It's too much. First I'm a tavern girl, then a duchess, then a Thrower and then...

Da...*isn't* my da?

Words stick in my throat. "Is that true? What she said?" I search his face. "I'm not your daughter?"

Hurt crosses his features, swims in the murky depths of his brown eyes. "Whatever else we both may be, I have *always* considered you my daughter."

"But by blood?" I insist. "Not by blood?"

Eternity is suspended on my heartbeats, and it takes too long for him to answer. He hesitates, then hangs his head and meets my eyes. "No."

"Then...who?"

Kat's whisper slithers between the fire's crackling. "I had wondered where the princess of Nereidium had gone to when I'd finished disposing of her parents."

My world drops from beneath my feet. "What?"

"Breena," Da pleads. "I will explain later. I'll tell you the whole story, leave nothing out. But tonight is the one chance we'll have to escape."

I ignore him. My breaths are coming in shorter as smoke clouds the room. The puddle of water lifts, hovering over the carpet to twirl midair.

"You brought the princess of Nereidium *here* to Egria," I say to Kat. Wildly, I point at Aleta's unconscious form. "That's her, lying there. Right. There."

"Enough," Kat said. "Do not feign ignorance. You're the first Thrower in Egria in sixteen years. You think it is a *coincidence* that the abilities ceased with the abduction of Nereidium's heir apparent? No. His Majesty suspected that Ardin had some knowledge on the subject. It's the only reason he kept him alive."

My thoughts coalesce. It's suddenly clear. "You knew," I breathe. "All of this time, you've *known*. That's why you kept *testing* me, why you kept *torturing* me. *I'm* the treasure the king seeks?"

"Of course I knew!" Kat snaps. Her features twist into a snarl. "I would not admit that I had failed His Majesty by failing to secure the babe. I found another, the same age, and brought her to court. It did not matter. I knew that one day we would take Nereidium for our own. The king doesn't need Throwers or a political tie for the throne. He has *me*. *I* will conquer all for him. And that is why I've decided to end this little game we're playing."

Lightning-quick, a shot of air knocks Da off his feet and across the room as Kat shoots toward me.

Not this time. I'm ready for it when Kat grips my shoulder and oxygen flees my body. The now-familiar burning fills my lungs as my body rebels, urgent for air. The Rider's expression is victorious, blue eyes crazed with glee.

But Katerine has forgotten. I don't need my Elemental abilities to fight back. With my free arm, I raise my hand, and the point of my blade presses an indentation into Kat's neck.

The countess stills, stiffening. Her chin lifts in invitation.

I press harder, raising a drop of blood. My vision darkens, dancing with spots. I can hear my own strangled attempts to breathe, but I meet Kat's eyes in a challenging stare. I could kill her. Stop her from stealing anyone else's life away again.

Air filters into me, and I gasp, breathing deeply, struggling to keep my frantic breaths even and my hand steady at her neck. From the corner of my eye, I see Da watching us warily, eyes flicking back and forth between us.

I barely have time to wonder why Kat's spared me when wind steals the knife from my hand.

And time defies itself. It moves slowly, but all too quick, an infinity wrapped in a moment. I watch as Kat's blood-red nails curl around the hilt of the knife, hear Da's shout of denial. He leaps, sprinting, the air at his back, increasing his speed until a cyclone propels him across the room, but I know he won't make it in time to stop her. I brace myself for it, to feel the blade slip through my skin and into my heart like it's nothing.

Da's nearly upon us. Kat smiles.

With a feral cry, she spins, plunging the knife into Da's throat instead.

The scream rips itself from my vocal cords as Da falls backward into a haze of flame.

"*Da! No!*"

Something in me fractures. I rush to catch him, but there's no wind at my back to aid my speed. He falls with a thud to the ground, choking, hands at the hilt of the knife.

I seize him under his shoulders and heave, dragging him to the center of the room, still free of flames. My hands flit over him, frantic, hesitant, *useless*.

"Da," I choke out. *Nonononono.* "What do I do?" I breathe heavily, rushed gasps that sound like whimpers.

"*Breena,*" he gurgles. Blood bubbles around the blade.

"Tell me what to do," I beg. "I'll do it, I swear. Anything."

"You can't do anything, *princess,*" Kat singsongs gleefully.

"Shut. *Up!*" I roar.

I bolt to my feet, and a river spirals in through the open window, crashing over the room and dousing the flames. Aleta coughs, but remains unconscious. The room smokes, steam rising into the air. I'm not sure if I've yanked the water from the clouds or summoned it from the ocean, and I don't care. It pools at my feet, waiting for instruction, and with almost no thought, I send it twining around Kat in a water twister. The Rider hovers in the liquid's embrace and laughs in my face.

"Why waste both of our times, little girl? We both know you don't have the fortitude to end my life." She grins her predator's grin, but this time *I* am the hunter and Kat is an animal that needs to be put down.

"Da was right," I say darkly. "You do talk too much."

My hand shoots out instinctively, and the water bends to my will. It floods Kat's mouth, and her eyes go wide, body bucking against the invasion. Air pushes against the water in Kat's lungs, but my anger is strong and I hold my water fast. Infinitesimally, the air gives, and Kat surrenders, closing her eyes as the water sweeps through her.

Her body crashes to the ground as I release my hold and fall to my knees, exhausted.

Da's breaths are labored now, his eyes bleary.

"*I'm sorry*. This is my fault. If I hadn't— if I'd been quicker—" If I just apologize, make him understand, he won't—"*Please don't leave me alone here*," I sob. "You're my da, no matter what anyone else says. And I forgive you for everything else. Just…don't go."

"I love you," he manages. He fumbles for my hand, and I grip it desperately.

"You say that like you're not going to see me in the morn." I say it jokingly but can hear how the tears clog my words.

"The Makers," he wheezes with a brave attempt at a smile, "are calling me home."

"*I'm* calling you home," I counter. "Wherever that is. *Please.*"

He sighs, closing his eyes.

"Da?" I shake him but stop at the jarring sight of the knife wobbling in his throat. I don't know how long I sit, crouched over him, counting his breaths, listening to the dripping furniture, the wind that now rushes through the open window, free of a Rider's hold. Gradually, his breaths grow shallower and shallower.

And then his chest is still.

But still I sit, staring at it, willing it to rise again. I'm hollow inside, drained of any ambition other than this. I have no real identity and the Makers have abandoned me and my father is dead.

Hands shake my shoulders, and I shrug them off blindly. "Get off."

They grasp me, lifting me bodily, and my water rises for another strike as I turn aching eyes to their owner and scream. "Get *off,* I said!"

Caden jumps back, hands raised, eyes wide.

When had he gotten here? Not caring, I dissolve into tears. My wave splashes down. "My da," I say feebly.

He shushes me, gathering me into his arms. "I know," he says into my hair. "I'm so sorry, Bree."

I cling to him like a lifeline, the only thing keeping me tethered to this world.

He pulls me back to arm's length and wipes my tears away with his thumbs.

"I wish you'd waited for me," he says—a little desperately, I think. "Adept Tregle and I had prepared for your liberation, but now my father knows that Ardin escaped the dungeon. Guards are likely on their way here now. If you and Aleta are to escape—" He stops, casting a glance over to the window, where, I see, Tregle has hoisted Aleta's unconscious form into his arms.

I've all but forgotten about her. I put a hand to my mouth in worry, scrambling to my feet. I can't lose someone else tonight. But Tregle nods to us both grimly, and I exhale with shaky relief. She's all right.

Caden also lets out a puff of air. "If you're to escape, it has to be now."

"There's a tunnel," I say, voice hoarse. "In Aleta's room. The wall behind the wardrobe." My gaze falls to Da—seeing his corpse at my feet is nearly my undoing. "Caden, I can't just *leave* him here like this. It's not right."

"All right," he says hurriedly. "You won't."

It happens quickly after that. Tregle sets Aleta down gently on the ground, and he and Caden move the wardrobe aside. I press the stones that Aleta had shown me to move the wall, and we slip inside. Dirt brushes over our feet.

Caden brings Da in and lays him at my feet. I swallow hard. If it weren't for the knife in his throat, I might think he's just in a deep sleep.

Caden follows my eyes and removes the knife without comment. "I know it's not enough," he says quietly. "But if you say your goodbyes to him here, I promise to find a way to bury him, with a proper marker and a prayer to ease his passing."

I nod wordlessly, looking away. He tries to hand the knife to me, but I shy away. It's tainted with Da's blood. I want nothing to do with it.

"Please." He presses it into my hand. "You may have need of it on your journey."

Unfortunately true. I take it.

Tregle cradles Aleta in his lap as he settles down and smooths back her hair.

We'll have to wait until she awakens to truly escape, but we're safe here in the tunnel. Kat's dead, and presumably all of her knowledge of Aleta's chambers has died with her.

"I wish I could go with you. But I have to stay. Try to keep my father in check." Caden presses a kiss to the inside of my wrist in farewell, eyes solemn and filled with regret. "I hope someday we'll meet again, Breena of Secan."

All I can see when I look at him right now is his father's eyes. My hand drops to my side, and he steps back, closing the tunnel's opening. Darkness devours my friends' faces. Tregle flicks his fingers to summon a flame.

"Put that out," I say dully. I've had enough fire to last me a lifetime. The darkness suits me right now.

It's a long while that we sit there, listening as the guards tear apart the room, yanking drawers from dressers. Aleta wakes some way through it, and Tregle claps a hand over her mouth to hush her questions, putting a finger to his lips and shaking his head. There's a harrowing moment when we stiffen as the wardrobe doors that protect our hiding space open, but we relax again when they move on.

I'm silent, damming up the emotions that have flooded from me this night. When all is still again, we'll leave the tunnel. Get to Nereidium. Make the Egrian king and all who are loyal to him pay for his crimes.

Sorrow drains from me, replaced with a boiling conviction.

They know that fire can burn.

But they've forgotten how water can scald.

Acknowledgements

It's never been possible that I'd view writing as a solitary endeavor and I count myself very lucky for that. I'm fortunate to have a slew of wonderful people in my corner, and this book wouldn't exist without them.

Lindsey Young and Alex Brown were my very first critique partners and readers. Their unfailing enthusiasm and support lifted me through my doubts, and they both had a knack for honing in on spots that simply didn't work. I owe them so much for that and for continuing to put up with my incessant (and increasingly less coherent) texts and chats.

Thank you to some of my other early readers. I doubt I would have made it past a first draft if Angel Cruz hadn't prodded me with just the right insightful question and Gillian Berry made the astute observation that I needed a little more menace and a little more Caden before I could call my draft final.

My family and friends supported me unquestioningly when I declared in college that my "plan" was to be a writer. I can't thank them enough for their support, but sorry, guys. I didn't write any of you into my novel like you requested.

Thanks is also owed to "the bevy:" Lindsey Young, Stephanie Moncada, and Katie Vincent. They've kept me sane through our all-caps and emoji-laden tweets, emails, and text messages…even if others might doubt our sanity if they were to read them.

I don't know that I could have made the leap to self-publish without Jamie Grey, who answered my questions kindly and with unflagging patience.

Thank you to the ladies of Inaccurate Realities for publishing an accompanying story to Threats of Sky and Sea. I love your magazine, and I loved writing Caden's short story.

I never could have done this without the U_M girls, simply because they are constant sources of laughter and inspiration. Who could have guessed that Sailor Moon would not only bring us together, but keep us together all these years later?

Thank you to Nathalia Suellen who designed a cover for Threats of Sky and Sea that's so beautiful it could make you weep. Thank you to Rebecca Weston for your copy edits and sharp eye. And thank you to Caitlin Greer for creating a beautiful book interior.

I owe a HUGE round of thanks to Team ToSaS, both the official *and* the unofficial members: Alex Brown, Molli Moran, Elodie Nowodazkij, Alexa Santiago, Christa Seeley, Melody Simpson, Aimee, Emilie, Gaby, Michelle, Nadia, Sara, and (once again) "The Bevy." You guys rock!

And then there's the YA book blogging, writing, and publishing community: you make me work to be a better writer every day.

I'm sure I've missed a person or two, but please know that if you ever had a hand in this book or in my writing, I am so grateful.

Finally, thank you, reader, for reading.

About the Author

Jennifer Ellision spent a great deal of her childhood staying up past her bedtime with a book and a flashlight. When she couldn't find the stories she wanted to read, she started writing them. She loves words, has a soft spot for fanfiction, and is a master of what she calls "The Fangirl Flail."

She lives in South Florida with her family, where she lives in fear of temperatures below 60 Fahrenheit. She makes her internet home at www.jenniferellision.com or you can find her on Twitter @JenEllision.

Made in the USA
San Bernardino, CA
23 May 2014